The War At Home

A Memoir~Novel

D0002254

Nora Eisenberg

Leapfrog Press
Wellfleet, Massachusetts

Published in 2002 in the United States by
The Leapfrog Press
P.O. Box 1495
95 Commercial Street
Wellfleet, MA 02667-1495, USA
www.leapfrogpress.com

Printed in Canada

Distributed in the United States by
Consortium Book Sales and Distribution
St. Paul, Minnesota 55114

First Edition

Although often drawn from memories, this is a book of fiction,
its characters and events created by imagination.

Library of Congress Cataloging-in-Publication Data

Eisenberg, Nora
   The war at home : a novel / by Nora Eisenberg.— 1ˢᵗ ed.
      p. cm.
   ISBN 0-9679520-4-2 (alk. paper)
      1.   World War, 1939–1945—Veterans—Fiction. 2. Bronx (New York,
N.Y.)—Fiction. 3. Brothers and sisters—Fiction. 4. Medication abuse—Fiction.
5. Communists—Fiction. I.
   Title.

PS3605.183 W37 2002
813'.54—dc21

                                                                  2001038081

               10 9 8 7 6 5 4 3 2 1

For my mother

"...mostly a true book with some stretchers...."
—*Huckleberry Finn*

1

Tippy

We were so lucky, we told ourselves, not having a *real* mother. We meant a mother like our friends had. Appearing day after day in girdles and hose, shirtwaists and sheaths to dust and mop, shop and cook. Inflicting night after night of liver and meatloaf, canned string beans and peaches at the kitchen table. We didn't have a kitchen table, or a kitchen, only a card table near the kitchenette that some super had slapped on the living room wall. But we were, we agreed, so lucky. For we had *her.*

"What are you in the mood for?" she'd ask us as afternoons waned. And once we'd decided, we'd run to 204th Street, our hands stuffed with bills and lists.

As she cheered us on from the high-riser, we'd prepare our favorite *inventions*: a can of pie cherries, a cup of milk, and a chicken for our pink-sauced "chicken flamingo"; or a box of bow ties with a can of black beans for "midnight macaroni"; or my favorite, an amalgam of all the little refrigerator leftovers—a wedge of cream cheese maybe, a stalk of broccoli, French fries salvaged from a White Castle outing—which we squished into a loaf and topped with our names in raisins, and called "tutti foodi." All proof that, though we were poorer than most in our working-class neighborhood, we were, under her sway, never meat-loafy regular kids with a regular mother, but special.

Sometimes, to give us more time to read or paint or make costumes for a play, she'd let us skip supper altogether and nibble our way through the night on Ritz crackers or pumpernickel rounds, which we'd pile with ham and cheese or, if money was tight, with chopped eggs and onions, which she called "fish-free caviar" and declared "very special."

As often as she could manage, we'd eat lunch out. When there was extra cash from her dance classes, we'd meet her at Bob's, our favorite luncheonette. Here, huddled in a red leatherette booth, we'd wolf down BLTs and fries, cheeseburgers, and malteds, watching out the window as the other kids marched dutifully home to peanut butter and jelly sandwiches and glasses of sad unflavored milk. If cash was low, if the weather allowed, we'd picnic in Mosholu, on leftovers and water from the fountain.

My brightest memories take place in that stretch of park across from our house—with its maple and dogwood, magnolia and lilac. Her weaving between the bushes and trees, with me or Nicky or both of us on her back.

We'd shout, "Down horsy," and she'd oblige, lowering us so that we could examine whatever had caught our fancy on the romp. Then "Up, horsy," we'd shout, and off she'd go again. That our mother's nickname was Tippy, after a wild horse by that name at the boarding school she'd attended, seemed particularly fitting those early years as we rode her around. From their benches, the other mothers would watch, amused, as our mother galloped, not yet the target of the gossip that later would haunt her. When she got winded, she'd light up a Camel and sit on the fence or join the women who regarded her still, in those early years, as a friendly elf.

Outdoors and indoors, my brother, Nick, and I did as we wished. Evenings, after creative cooking, or snacking and playing, we creatively cleaned. If our supper efforts produced a big batch of dishes and pots, we'd wash them in the bathtub, getting in with them for better grip and shine. Then, the dishes done, she'd fill the tub with Tide for our nightly bath, which we got to share with the day's dirty clothes. Leaning into the water, bubbles rising up from her hands, she looked like the girl in the White Rock Soda ad: beautiful and beneficent. Our very own goddess, of our small but special realm.

Not surprisingly, our little apartment was the hangout of choice for most of the building kids, eager as they were to escape the regulations and restrictions protecting their mother's mahogany living room and bedroom sets and wall-to-wall broadloom. If our father wasn't around, our two rooms transformed into a kids' clubhouse, where, with Tippy advising from the daybed, we made fudge and rock candy, wrestled and waltzed, produced talent shows, mock war crime trials, and tearful memorials for sparrows.

Once—I must have been five or six—I brought my girlfriends home for what promised to be the most extraordinary Tippy event yet. It was a spring weekend morning and we'd been out in the park, sitting under the giant magnolia, discussing women's bodies. My friends said they longed to see a woman's body but never had since their mothers dressed in the bathroom giving them at most quick peeks of longline brassieres, corsets and girdles. Tippy, I explained, thought the human body was beautiful and often ran around naked. I assured them she'd be only too happy to strip for them.

With no more said, the girls quickly formed a single line behind me, following me across the street, into our building's courtyard, and up the sweep of marble steps to behold her. For some "transgression," our father had been denouncing her the night before and well into the early morning, and when we arrived my mother was still sleeping, sprawled on the daybed in the living room. Knowing my mother was direct and candid, I'd planned on making my request direct and candid too. I'd prepared my words as we'd marched up the steps: Ma, please could you show them your titties and stuff. But I didn't have to say a thing.

For there she was for all to see: her small but well-shaped breasts facing the ceiling like alert eyes, her tiny waist and wide bony hips, her perfect dancer's legs, her buttocks, which as she conveniently rolled over, now jutted out like twin altar shelves, which I had to use all of my control not to kiss in reverence.

"She's gorgeous," someone whispered, and everyone nodded.

For a half hour or so, we all just sat there silent, like midget ladies in waiting, drinking in her dips and mounds, her little whistling snore, her rustling as she turned to our delight this way and that. Finally, she woke, and draping the white sheet around her and smiling her wide white smile, she said: "Oh, hi there, girls."

Then she asked me to get her Camels from the table and announced there was a batch of chocolate pudding in the icebox if anyone was interested.

And gathered around the bed eating the cold pudding, we watched the way her lips made a small perfect hole for the cigarette, and her nose blew perfect lines, and her eyes narrowed exotically against the smoke that rose up to the ceiling, which, one rainy winter day, with all of us helping, she'd painted the heavenly blue of a summer sky.

I remember looking at her, and praying to her. *Dear Mommy*, let it always be like this. Let him not come home. She was a goddess, an angel. Not those other things he said. For you never knew when he'd cut his roaming short and storm back in. *Dear Mommy*, I prayed, *dearest goddess-angel,* let him *never* come home.

But the next moment, I heard him. His key in the lock. His feet in the hall, marching. . . . Then he was there in the room.

Don't hit her, don't hit me. We'll be good, I thought to shout, but I couldn't speak.

His arm shot up. Where would it land? Who would he *get*? Down on the table it swooped, on the bowl of pudding—seizing it, hurling it, staining the sky-blue ceiling with a mean dark cloud. Then, without a word, he about-faced and marched out, disappearing as quickly as he'd appeared.

"Battle fatigue," my mother said when the door slammed and we all rushed into her arms. "Lucy's Daddy is . . . very . . . tired . . . from all the battle."

"He's tired but he jumps around all the time and shouts and stuff. . . ? That's funny. . . ," one of the girls said from under a pillow.

He'd been kind, and fun before the war, my mother said, as she'd said to me and Nicky a hundred times. With rest and understanding, the man she married was sure to come back.

"And then . . . guess what?" I said, improvising to distract from my fear and shame. "We're gonna . . . have a party . . . a welcome back party. And guess what. . . ? You're all invited!"

"Hey, we could make our famous fudge!" someone cried from under a blanket.

"And fill the fountain in the courtyard with our special punch!" I said. We'd raise our paper cups and say, No more battle fatigue or battles. And the whole building and half the Bronx would agree with our great idea.

"Yes," my mother said, holding me close. It was going to be a special time. A very special time. When the fatigue ended and the war, for us, was over for *real*.

2

Battle Fatigue

Everything those days was the war—and peace—the whole borough heady over the end of one and the start of the other. The Grand Concourse, the Bronx's main boulevard, was claimed in parade month after month, the war's survivors celebrating the war's sacrifices, civilians celebrating soldiers, everyone celebrating the end of battle, wrapping death and dread in a mantle of peace and hope. From the Fordham Road Recruitment kiosk and the Loew's Paradise, all the way down to the Bronx County Courthouse, soldiers and sailors and marines would march to wild cheers. If our father was in a good mood, he'd put on his uniform and, balancing Nicky and me on his shoulders like a couple of duffle bags, join the march. Eager to show off our sailor suits and handsome "un-fatigued" father, we'd shout, "We won!" to the crowds on the sidewalk. We wanted everyone to see his strong shoulders, his gleaming olive skin, bronzed from the years in North Africa and Southern Italy, his green eyes, his starched khaki uniform stretched tight against his powerful chest, the dazzling line-up of chevrons and medals.

On a good day, which is to say a day when our father managed to stay calm through the whole trek, he'd treat us to mustard-topped pretzels and *charlotte russes* from vendors in the park across from the Concourse Plaza Hotel, where the Yankees stayed when they were in town and where wealthy Bronxites held their weddings and charity balls. On a black wrought iron bench, we'd flank him and squeeze his hand as he pointed out perverts and lunatics, spoiled women, intelligent dogs, kids with character, asking him how he could tell for sure, and when we would know on our own. And then we'd say nothing, but study the sky together, loving how he smiled when he looked up, like he'd fought for that perfect blue in the war and brought it home for us.

But most days there were no parades, no pastries and pretzels, no beaming father bopping along with us in tow. The bad days his face became an iron mask, and he'd lift us up only to throw us to the floor. Then Nicky and I would panic, not for the pains he was inflicting, though these could be formidable, but for the torments that awaited us in the future: It was the fascists, our father said, who had destroyed half the world, killed half his friends, and robbed years from his young life. But watching his eyes go cold, his features harden as he prepared to attack us, we'd sometimes believe that this madman who rampaged before us had been responsible for the whole war. And if we didn't watch our step, maybe he'd start it up all over again.

The worst days, then, first thing in the morning, we'd check to see if his uniform was still hanging on the hook in the front hall, fearing the moment he'd put it on to fight again—slaughtering *us* this time around. Nicky, and me, and our mother.

"Poor Daddy," our mother would say. The war, the fatigue, the fatigue, the war. Poor us, we'd think, stuck in the same house with a mass murderer, who, on the days he was too miserable to shave and sprouted a dark moustache, we were sure was Adolph Hitler himself, escaped from his suicide bunker to our apartment.

Was she right? Had our father really gone off to war a sweet young man and come back the lunatic we knew? Eventually we learned that at fourteen he'd tried to join the Abraham Lincoln Brigade to fight Franco but, because of his age, was sent home with a pile of petitions to get signed; that the year before Pearl Harbor he enlisted in the army and almost died at the beachhead at Casablanca and again in the Naples hills. Back then all I knew was that by the time he returned home, he was still in battle, both physical and moral, and totally unfit for peace.

"Petit bourgeois brats," he'd scream as he charged after us, the closest enemy he had left. Drawing on the type of political rhetoric that may well have seen him through great battles, he'd yell how he'd defeated the Nazi monster only to be rewarded with us— "midget *lumpens*," "declassed debris of late-stage capitalism," "little bourgeois shits."

Our "offenses," had our poor father been blessed back then with any moments of calm and reflection, would have seemed pretty puny and probably funny. But shell-shocked into a state of steady agitation, he saw them as critical signs of a moral decay which could crumble civilization as we knew it, or could have known it in the better, fairer world he had almost died for. The toys or dolls we occasionally abandoned on the floor, or the table we occasionally put off setting told him we were moral enemies. And unwashed dishes, unmade beds, uncooked or undercooked meals confirmed that our mother was the major "lumpen instigator" of our "lumpen lowlife ways."

The truth was our mother was a distracted dancer with neither the organization nor inclination to clean or cook. Raised a poor girl with an absent father and a machine-operator mother, she'd been a brilliant student and had won scholarships to progressive boarding schools, where she'd discovered left politics and a passion and talent for dancing. Raised a poor boy, in a particularly vista-less working class home that worshiped tidiness, thrift, navy blue, and other markers of duty and order, our father fell in love with her for her free spirit, which he thought he could capture through marriage, but then condemned as so much "bourgeois self indulgence," vowing to rout it out.

He'd cry, "You're going to die," or "Now I'm going for the jugular." She'd say, "Calm down, Ralphie. Breathe deeply. Rest the fatigue. . . ."

"Don't kill her," Nicky and I would beg. "Please, Daddy, stop."

Sometimes, we'd get to him: the quake in our voice, or the light in her eye would remind him who we were, and he'd stop. But often he'd ignore us, grabbing her in a hold, taking her down to the floor, pinning her beneath him.

When we'd pry him off, he'd kick us, or knock our heads together, for butting into grown-up business. Then storm out, for hours, or days, sometimes weeks, or months.

"My wife doesn't respect me," he'd call, as he marched out the door. "An intolerable situation when a man's wife doesn't respect him. And turns the children against him."

We may have been the most frequent objects of my father's wrath, Nicky and my mother and I, but we were certainly not his only enemies. And when he wasn't fighting us at home, he was usually out battling strangers. Work with its inevitable indignities for a young man trained only in combat was particularly difficult for my father. At work, some "snit boss" before long would look at him the wrong way, take the wrong tone, ask for something at the wrong time, and our father would swing at him, then flee, happily forfeiting a week's wages for the sheer pleasure of inflicting injury and revenge.

At home, our father would proudly recount his battle, and Nicky and I would press for details. He'd beam, thinking that we too were pleased with his prowess, but actually we only wanted to make sure that he'd left his victim breathing. For what if one day he got carried away and crossed the line from fighter to killer? Then we'd be in even more trouble!

Our father claimed that his difficulty in holding a job resulted from his extreme morality. He *chose* not to participate in relations that were corrupting to both boss and worker. One night, after a particularly lengthy supper sermon on moral choice and work, my mother made the mistake of asking, "But can we really afford to be that 'choosy'?"

I remember being impressed that she'd said "we," thinking, That's smart . . . you just say "we" instead of "you" and you can't get in trouble. But my father thought differently and, slapping her in the face, ran out the door, leaving home for a couple of nights at his parents' house, to which he sometimes retreated when we failed to understand him.

Did he hit her harder that time? Slam the door louder? I remember we were more scared than usual by the thought of him out there on the loose, and when our mother fell asleep that night we walked up to the pay phone at the Irish bar up the street, where, beyond our mother's hearing, we called him at Grandma Bess's.

"We miss you, Daddy," we said, desperate to have him back to keep an eye on him. "Mommy says she's sorry she hurt your feelings."

"It's not a question of feelings. But of justice. Understand that, and I'll be a happy man."

"We really understand, Daddy," we said.

Bosses were not his only non-family targets. Neighbors also were suspect. And my father would lecture Nicky and me on which neighbors were good and which "stood for nothing." Perfectly nice parents of perfectly nice friends, he'd tell us, were "zip," "spineless nothings," "bourgeois drips." Which meant, I realized later on, that they didn't work in factories or in construction and didn't engage in physical fights. My father cast as major oppressors not only the occasional clothing factory manager in our largely working-class neighborhood, but all people who did not perform physical labor—even if they were poorly paid clerks, clothing salesmen, or bookkeepers.

My favorite building friend was a boy named Peter Liebowitz, whose parents had escaped Poland during the War. Peter was my age and my size but as blond as I was brunette, and we'd call ourselves Snow White and Rose Red and dress up together in his mother's gowns dragged across the globe and doomed to the back of a closet. Mrs. Liebowitz was a silent woman, crushed by the War into a life of continuous polishing. But Mr. Liebowitz was friskier, a blond-haired, apple-cheeked salesman of Selby and Red-Cross shoes. When Peter and I dressed up, he'd dig into his sample bag and always find something glittery for us to wear. How sweet he looked bowed at our feet; and how gentle his hands felt fitting us into a patent or silk or velvet pump. He'd been in the camps, I realized years later, but back then I knew only that when he was placing a shoe on me, his shirtsleeve would ride up and I'd see a number tattoo on his wrist. Taking this to be a shoe salesman's emblem, I'd wish then that my father was a shoe salesman too with such a calm discreet little tattoo, instead of his big eagle gawking out from his pulsing biceps, surrounded by the words: Democracy or Death.

But to my father, Peter was a "budding fag" and Mr. Liebowitz a "weak fool," not a true man. For true men did not waste their lives carrying sample bags in and out of cars. True men did something substantial with their hands. But sadly, those days, most of my father's work stopped shortly after it began, and his working man's hands were used mostly on our mother and us.

My father's uncles owned grocery stores on Boston Post Road, and from time to time boxes heaped with pot cheese and muenster cheese and sliced bologna and seeded rolls would appear at our door. A great aunt owned a knish store on Delancey Street and sometimes she'd send up trays of kasha and potato knishes. Besides the relatives' food, there were small cash contributions from Nan, my mother's mother, that helped us get through those days. She'd give up part of her week's salary as a machine operator in a dress factory, or borrow from her pension fund, if we were running low and rent was due. And then there was also my mother's work to help us stay afloat.

All through these years and for most of our childhood, our mother taught children to dance—and to hope. In stuffy basement studios, children became not only nimble prancers and twirlers but fairies and fish and zebras and stomping elephants and feathers and falling rain and glistening light. Some days I'd tag along to the Bronx Arts House, where my mother would put me in the class of girls my age with another teacher. Where, for an endless hour, some slave-driving Masha or Manya or Sonia or Sasha would glare and shout and weep at "oafish" "foolish" girls. Small wonder then that throughout the Bronx and Westchester, my mother's classes were famous. Delinquents were brought to them to be run around, calmed, and ultimately civilized, and it was not uncommon to find a young thug alongside more frilly ballet types, lying on the floor in a trance at the end of an hour with Tippy.

Her paraphernalia was considerable—scarves, hoops, tambourines, gongs—which she'd carry with her from studio to studio, community room to community room in big brown grocery boxes. Along with her, even when times were hard and she could scarcely afford even his reduced rates, was Arthur Bernstein, whom we called "Artie the Accompanist." A thin intense, Julliard-trained pianist, Artie played at the Martha Graham School most days, but traded in Graham prestige and dignity to schlep around three afternoons a week with my mother, with whom, I suspect now, he was madly in love.

What my mother's classes lacked in organization, they made up for in atmosphere. More often than not, she forgot *barre* work and floor work and would begin where most other classes ended—with across-the-floor runs and skips, which quickly became free-for-alls. Then, when the children were sufficiently hopped up, she'd send them to stand in the middle of the room, where the work, or play, would really take off. Here, the children would announce who or what they were, and my mother would ask how they knew. "Because a gorilla jumps like me," one would say, or "because a bear thumps like this." And then they'd dance as the beasts they'd found inside them. After this dance, my mother's beats became fainter and Artie's melodies lighter, and the children would slow down, emerging into their next reincarnation, gentler and gentler as the hour advanced, finally becoming the lightest and gentlest thing they could imagine being—a feather or moonbeam settling on the floor as the lesson ended.

What dreams of her own she must have brought to those sessions. Watching the kids jumping around, I suspect, called up her own struggle with wild beasts and crazy spirits, and quieting them, as the music quieted, must have made her wish she could subdue our father's ferocity once and for all. At the end of an afternoon of classes, riding beside sweet Arthur, the melodies and rhythms playing inside her still, the memory of long pauses and rests soothing her tired body and mind, didn't she ever want to make it last—the peace and quiet she had captured lying on the floor with dreaming children? Didn't she ever want to turn to Artie, who had a sweet boyish face and the adoring brown eyes of a spaniel, and say, Take me away, Artie, to some quiet place? I imagine her riding home from classes in Yonkers and Mamaroneck, guiding Artie's old Studebaker to the side of Central Avenue, to some hideaway lounge or motel, to let the peace last beyond a final chord.

Sometimes, when our father really looked wild, Nick and I wondered if our mother might not entrance him as she did the children. One awful morning as he raged on, we handed her the tom-tom. She burst out laughing, studying the drum, as if she might give it a shot. But before she could knock out a single beat, our father grabbed the tom-tom from her hands and threw it against the wall, cracking it in two.

And once again we scattered, lest we be lifted and cracked ourselves, and tossed in the giant heap of cracked and broken things—bowls and plates and drums and toys and dolls and chairs and tables—that our life was so quickly becoming.

3

The Haunted House

We lived at the east end of Mosholu Parkway, a wide ribbon of planted parkland running the couple of miles between and Bronx and Van Cortlandt Park with their planted gardens, meadows, and woods, which old park guide books insisted were remains of the ancient "virgin forest." In spring we looked from our windows out onto Mosholu's forsythia, magnolia, lilac and dogwood; in fall onto crimson maples and oaks. Each day, no matter the weather, Nick and I would spend hours on Mosholu's benches and fields, or the gardens and woods of Bronx Park. In winter, we'd ice skate well into the night on the pine-encircled Twin Lakes, holding flashlights and torches to light our way. In summer, we'd swim in the Bronx River, soothed by the rush of the water falls, scared and thrilled by other sounds, which we told each other came from the wild animals in the woods around us, or animals escaping from the nearby Bronx Zoo.

Once I was old enough to go to school, most afternoons I'd do my homework in the glass Conservatory of the Botanical Gardens, a heavenly Edwardian greenhouse. For someone with my peaceful, timid nature, this was the perfect spot. With my books in my lap, and the lush rubber trees, palms, and orchids above me, I'd sit hugged by the humid air, tickled by the gorgeous scents, feeling worlds away from the dangers of home and forest. The daring Nick, meanwhile, three years older and a hundred times bolder, in most any weather, would be out there in the thick of it, roaming the woods in search of arrowheads and trouble. How I loved sitting in my glass enclosure, savoring the rare solitude, yet certain too that I was connected and protected: Nick was always nearby and soon enough he'd be coming back to get me.

Our first apartment was actually in the back, but what a wondrous back. Behind our building were the remnants of the VanDam orchard, the southern tip of the old VanDam estate, which fifty years earlier had stretched north to the point where, eventually, the northernmost IND subway station was built. In the nineteen twenties and thirties when our grandparents on both sides migrated to the Bronx seeking blue skies and fresh air, there were still working farms dotting the borough. By the time I was born, just after the war, there were still scattered remains, an occasional clapboard house with a quarter acre of trees wedged between five and six story apartment buildings and brick row houses or—if you traveled far enough north and east, toward the Long Island Sound—stretches of grasslands with roaming goats, stragglers from a bygone era. But by the early 1950s almost none of this was left, and so it was all the more wondrous that our daily perch on the fire escape afforded a view of a big old gray wooden farm house, a cluster of lilac bushes, a half dozen fruit trees, and old Mr. VanDam, the last scion of Dutch settlers.

How glorious he seemed, enthroned on his red Indian brand motorcycle, traveling back and forth between his law office on Fordham Road and, as we liked to think, us. Every day, we'd set ourselves up on the fire escape with paper and crayons and wait for a daily reunion with our favorite neighbor. This never occurred face to face, but with us looking down from our "balcony" and him looking up from his "orchard." For had we climbed down to him, we would have landed first on the alley separating our apartment building from his property, and we would have had to walk around the garbage cans lined up against the red brick wall that was the back of our building. From where we sat on the fire escape, though, the alley was out of view and we could see only the trees and old house—a more romantic setting for our daily dialogue, our romantic respite from the clanging realities of our domestic life. Lord VanDam, I called our neighbor, and his dark wooden house and scrappy yard, VanDam's Manor.

As soon as we heard the motorcycle, we'd begin lowering a small laundry basket filled with drawings and scrawls of greeting; and Mr. VanDam, dismounting, would accept our gifts and bow, quickly filling the basket with reciprocal treats—whatever fruit was out, or lilacs, or, if it was winter, packs of Chiclets and Charms. I'd always let Nicky hoist up our basket, not only because he was stronger, but because I wanted to be free to watch our neighbor as he stood, tall and lean in his garden, his arms rising as the basket rose, in a sympathetic and graceful gesture worthy of an opera star.

For a change, tough Nick indulged me in my fancy fantasies. Generally impatient with my cravings for gentility, he was right there with me. For if the old house was not a manor house but a battered bungalow to my brother, it still provided him with hope— of endurance if not elegance. And the old man was, as much to my brother as to me, the hero of those early years. As we'd await Mr. VanDam's arrival, I'd start up some hodge-podge of what I thought courtly speech, "*Methinks me heareth himeth. Hark, our lordeth cometh down the block.*" And Nick, dropping his tough guy talk, the "dis" and "dat" he liked so much, would join in: "*Oh, yeseth. Himeth. For sureth. Our best friendeth.*" Without a shred of irony. Then, leaning over the fire escape, we'd both wave wildly as if rippling a patch of air might magically move him to us.

Neighborhood kids were seriously impressed by our connection to VanDam. To them, the unelectrified house was "the haunted house" and Mr. VanDam, despite his respectable suit and apparent courtesy, was the "Spook." Even the toughest kids would scramble away from his motorcycle as it charged up the street, believing that the smiling, balding man could inflict great harm. Only Nicky and I, expert in reading character and detecting real danger because of our father, were unafraid. So, though we were poorer than most in a poor neighborhood, and though our father screamed louder than most in our often rowdy building, we became admired by neighborhood kids for what they thought our special relations with a dangerous neighbor.

If we were out on the street playing stickball, punchball, or ring-o-leevio, and VanDam zoomed up the Parkway or the side street, the kids would scatter. He'd call out our names and toss us packs of candy, or stop and tousle our hair and ask after our mother, or perch us on the back of the Indian and tour us around the Parkway. After which, children who routinely declared us mortal enemies for killing their Lord, Jesus Christ, would ask to switch to our team, or offer to buy us egg creams and snacks at the candy store up the street.

"Hey, they could talk to ghosts!" the kids would shout when VanDam was gone. "Did ya see 'em talk to the Spook?"

Then Nicky, with me nodding in agreement, would lecture them on their ignorance. There was no such thing as ghosts or ghouls. While Mr. VanDam's house was unelectrified, inside it was cozy and regular. We knew, Nick lied, from all the times we'd had supper over there.

The Halloween when I was six and Nick was nine, the neighborhood kids suddenly came up with the idea of trick-or-treating at VanDam's. In earlier years, though we'd roamed in packs, unescorted through the dark streets, no one had ever considered approaching the dark house. This year they decided we would—or rather Nick and I would. When I think back, I see, of course, that this was a kind of test of both us and VanDam. How brave were we really, Nicky and I? How bad was VanDam? How connected were we with him? And what was the nature of that connection—magic, witchcraft, bullshit? Neighborhood reputations can have short street lives, and I think our peers were tired of respecting and feeding us.

For Nick there was nothing to the challenge. Mr. VanDam *was* an old friend and my brother would visit his old friend, get lots of candy and toss it at the feet of these fools. Nicky was truly brave— he was beginning to meet even our father's fury with his own fierce looks and words. "You've got the wrong enemy, Daddy," he'd say.

26

"Find the right enemy, buddy, and I'm with you, by your side, ready to die."

For me, though, the situation was much more complicated. Being a much more timid child than Nick, my reputation for bravery was based strictly on my association with him. True, with the kids watching, I managed to catch Mr. VanDam's candies with some aplomb, but their stories about the old man were getting to me. Why *was* his house so dark? What *did* it mean that his office was on Fordham Road? And how did that relate to his almost total baldness? His refined speech, fancy suits, and age told me he wasn't a member of the infamous Fordham Baldies gang, but was he somehow connected with them? Maybe he was the gang lawyer responsible for getting them out on bail and on the street, where they could do the terrible things they did. But I didn't dare tell my secret fears to anyone, not even my generally sympathetic mother. Loyalty was a central family virtue, and just as I was bound to love my father, who was battle-fatigued not evil, I was bound to love our old neighbor, electricity or not.

That Halloween a larger than usual gang of trick-or-treaters assembled, as friends brought friends from a block or two away to see the real haunted house, the "Spook" in his habitat, and Nicky and me for who we really were, whatever that ended up being. The night would tell.

I wore a sheet and went as Casper, the friendly ghost. Panicked ghost was more like it. I shadowed Nick, who led the crowd, dying to hold his hand for comfort. But because this was a gesture outlawed—except for teenage lovers—in this quasi-tough neighborhood, I had to settle for the fringes of his Indian costume, gathering whatever strength I could from that.

By the time we reached VanDam's the crowd was holding back, leaving Nick and me to approach the house alone. The oldest in the group was ten, but they all leaned on cars like teenagers, their faces twisted with what could pass for contempt. Even then I knew it was fear that kept them at the curb, for I was feeling terror rise in me and could sense it, almost smell it, floating from them.

Nick took the steps two-by-two, pulling me with him.

He knocked, and Mr. VanDam appeared at the door in a paisley silk robe. In one hand he had a candle, in the other an opened can of Chef Boyardee spaghetti.

He smiled and said, "Hello, children, you've caught me in the middle of dinner."

"Sorry," several kids shouted from the curb, their voices quivering. Some crossed the street to watch from a safer distance.

"We'll come back another time," I whispered.

"No, I'm glad you came," Mr. VanDam said, opening the door wider for us to enter, which we did, there being little choice.

As I felt my way into the darkness, holding fast still to Nicky's fringes, I thought about all the things the kids said about VanDam. That he had killed his brother and buried him in the house. That his father had killed his mother and fed her to the family dog. That Mr. Van-Dam kept the house dark so no one could find the bones.

Out of a sense of politeness, or humor—I'll never know which—Mr. VanDam left his front door open and the kids on both sides of the street watched, as best they could, our little holiday tableau.

We sat down on a settee in the front hall, feigning familiarity with the dark dusty house.

"Haven't changed a thing," Nick shouted, so the kids could hear. "Still the cozy old place."

Mr. VanDam played his part perfectly. He patted our heads, like an uncle. He gave us Charms and I sucked a handful of them hard to re-supply my mouth with saliva and my body with the energy to endure sitting there. For, despite what my brother said and probably believed, nothing about the place seemed cozy. Kerosene sconces flickered on the wall. Even my brother's familiar face seemed odd in this uncertain light.

Mr. VanDam brought out some popcorn, which Nicky stuffed into his mouth as he chit-chatted with Mr. VanDam about the weather, school, our mother, whom Mr. VanDam sent his best to. Finally we stood and Mr. VanDam shook my brother's hand and kissed my cheek, handing me a shopping bag of apples.

"Now, my dears, you've been to the haunted house," he said.

"We don't call it that. *They* do," Nick said, pointing out the door.

Of course my brother was explaining out of kindness and righteousness, reassuring our old neighbor of our enduring regard and loyalty, accusing our peers. But that minute, I heard it entirely differently. It sounded like my brother's voice when he'd argue with our father not to hit, and I decided he was pleading for our lives and began to scream: "Don't kill us. Please. We'll be good."

I still remember the sound of my cry—a weak, whining siren—as I felt my head get light and my body get heavy. I remember seeing the can in Mr. VanDam's hands and knowing with certainty that it was not filled with spaghetti but with worms just as I knew that the apples that were falling from my arms were poisoned. I remember seeing Mr. VanDam's candle-lit face as I sank, his nostrils lined with fire, looking like my father's furious nostrils just before he'd grab us. For the endless second before I passed out, I was sure my father was there—in the room. Hiding, getting ready to pounce. To murder us for real.

When I came to, my mother's face was above mine and she was stroking my hair. To get in the spirit of Halloween, my mother would usually come up with some costume from a thrift store bin. But I forgot this as I sat up and studied her tiara and wedding dress, the fake diamonds dancing on her jet hair, the satin shimmering down her frail frame.

"Have we gone to heaven, Mama?" I said, for she looked like an angel. "Did he get us?"

"Shhh," she said, pulling me to her.

Did people feel this warm when dead in heaven? I wondered.

I began to ask her but she said, "Shhh" again. "Don't worry, Lucy. We're *here*."

Here. I looked around and saw we were at VanDam's, and suddenly all the danger seemed gone. The place suddenly *did* seem cozy, like Lassie's old house. I leaned my head on my mother's chest and felt peaceful—as I often did back then when I touched her.

Poor Mr. VanDam was saying, "I really should get electricity in here once and for all. But the place is too big and frankly I'm think-ing of moving to the apartment above the office. I promise, dear Lucy, next Halloween I'll have lights for you or be gone." Then to my mother, he said, "I'm so sorry. I'm so sorry you had to come out tonight. You look awfully tired, dear."

I looked up at my mother's face. It did look tired, and lined with worry. Our father was tearing around day and night, and our mother was pacing and smoking to get her through the nights. I began sob-bing because I hadn't noticed before how really ravaged my beauti-ful mother had become and because, now that I'd noticed, I didn't know what I could possibly do about it.

My mother dabbed my wet cheeks with the train of her dress. "It's okay, Lucy," she said. "It's a nice old place. Sweet . . . and quiet." She smiled up at Mr. VanDam appreciatively, then back down at me. "But you're not used to the dark and it frightened you children."

I wanted to tell her. It wasn't the dark, but the light . . . in his nose. It looked like Daddy's nose. It's Daddy who scares me. He's going to kill someone one of these days. But I knew she'd say my father was just "fatigued" and we all had to stick together. And be-sides, Mr. VanDam was still standing there and I knew I shouldn't talk about family outside the family. So I said nothing and just nestled into her again.

"Frightened us children? I'm not frightened. Just her," Nicky said. "Jesus Christ, this one's always scared of something."

Outside the crowd of kids had swelled as the drama heightened with me going down and my mother moving in on the scene. I held my mother's hand as we left VanDam's. My brother dawdled for one defiant moment with Mr. VanDam, shook his hand ostentatiously, and followed us out, keeping his distance from me and my defeat.

"We heard he ate you," Mary Foster, a cross-eyed member of a large hooligan family, said.

"Shut up," my brother said, "He's our friend."

"Lucy had a tummy ache," my mother said. "Too much candy."

"We heard he poisoned her and then cut her up."

"Yeah, and then glued her back together with glue from his human glue pot," my brother said. "You morons."

I started feeling woozy again and leaned on my mother.

"Enough," she said, turning to Nicky.

"Yeah, not another word from you cretins, or else. . . ," my brother said.

We never went to VanDam's again. A few months later he moved to the apartment above his office on Fordham Road. The next year, Mr. VanDam died and left my mother his mother's lace collection as well as his bedroom set. They were carved rosewood pieces with black marble tops, which I could never look at without wanting to cry—for both their dark beauty and my terrible disloyal fear of my old friend that Halloween night. And also for other lingering terrors that wouldn't go away.

Maybe our father *had* been in the house that night. He must have seen us feverishly mixing VanDam's fruits into pear mush, applesauce, lopsided plum pies, and lowering them to our neighbor with best wishes from our mother as she read and smoked on the daybed. He must have suspected we were up to something. And weren't we? Scouting out his replacement? With enough crazy concoctions bestowed on the old man in our young mother's name, didn't we hope he'd open his orchard and his arms to us forever? Replace *him* forever?

For months after Mr. VanDam died, the thought besieged me that our father, in a jealous rage, had killed Mr. VanDam and the only way I could dispel this miserable idea was to climb out on the fire escape, where I'd sit for hours, pretending Mr. VanDam was still alive, that the scar in the ground below wasn't there, that they hadn't bulldozed his house and orchard to make way for a parking lot. I'd pretend Nicky was sitting beside me and it was early spring and we were looking down at the tent of treetops, the fragile pear blossoms fluttering below us like snow.

4

Snack Fair

Between my seventh and eighth year, our lives started shining with promise. Seeing he could work for no one, our father went to work for himself, and suddenly we stopped being poor. Suddenly there was money for clothes: for me, knee socks that stayed up, perky felt skirts with pom-pom poodles and clowns, bright white saddle shoes; for Nick, Levis and thick corduroy slacks and crisp button down shirts for shame-free appearances at school assemblies, that is if the proud Nick ever suffered anything like shame back then. That year we both got lessons—real lessons, not just tag-along Miss Tippy stuff. I took ballet, whose formality I was craving as an antidote to the chaos and unpredictability of our home. Nick got to take guitar lessons and began singing, not surprisingly, given his absorption of the family ethos and pathos, folk songs of all people especially traditional Black blues. All in all as a family, we got the first break we'd known since my father came back from the war, and watching our mother kiss our father goodbye in the morning, adjusting his collar, our father kiss our mother back, patting her hair, it seemed peace had come at long last.

We moved from the two small rooms to a spacious five-room apartment the next block up on Mosholu Parkway. And we "decorated," or at least started to, in our own odd way. To most other families coming up in our Bronx world, decorating meant going to

Ethan Allan or W.J. Sloane's on Fifth Avenue for matching mahogany or fruitwood pieces, the warm tones of which a store decorator would accent or play against with drapes, upholstery, and deep broad-loom. For us, it meant my father renting a machine and scraping our floors, covering them with coat after coat of shellac, till my mother declared them "dance-floor bright." It meant we kept our few old oak and pine pieces, and the rosewood bedroom set, of course, from the old apartment. But now we got to pick out *new* old stuff at the Salvation Army store on 149th Street and Park Avenue. And most importantly, our decorating involved the sudden appearance, for the first time in our lives, of our mother's father, my Grandpa Jess.

Who cared if other families had fancy broadloom, we had our glamorous grandfather! A cultured Muscovite, he spent his nights at the Metropolitan Opera and his days in rich people's houses, painting their walls and ceilings, it was said, like a "real painter" not a "house painter." As word somehow reached him that our father was working and we were decorating, he appeared, a canvas bag of brushes in his hand and a Galoise in his mouth, to lend us his skills and style.

How joyous our introduction to Grandpa Jess, and our mother's reunion with her father! Following her lead, we brushed his beauti-ful white hair with our hands and settled on his lap—as if we'd known him forever. He told us he'd galloped over from the Con-course on his golden horse, "Brandy," who waited for him down-stairs in the park. "Brandy, Brandy," we called, opening the window wide to look. She was invisible by day, he explained. "A magic horse?" we squealed, and he put his finger to his lips for the secret to stay ours alone. And then he got to work

Every day—all fall, all winter—just before we left for school, he'd appear. In the spring, halfway through his stint, our home ceased looking like a Bronx apartment and more like the *dacha* of a Russian nobleman—or at least the bungalow for his bastard child. And our mother, Jess's bastard, coming into room after room, after her father had done his magic, would twirl and prance and clap her hands.

My grandfather never tried to hide the fact that Tippy was his child. Indeed, I think now he was proud of her and her beauty and grace, proud even of her illegitimacy—with the added unconventionality and daring it bestowed on *him*. But until he appeared to redo our apartment, in all the years after Grandpa Jesse had left our Nan pregnant and impoverished, he had found few occasions to show his affection for the pretty child who became our pretty mother. For despite his freethinking and Bolshevism, my grandfather suffered from a case of common snobbery. Over the years, as our mother was growing up, he might appear at one of her dance recitals, or swimming meets, or figure skating competitions, or galas at boarding school. But for the more mundane sides of her existence, he had little use. "He doesn't like details," our mother told us, again and again, as her father worked in our rooms, trying to explain, to herself and us, his disappearance during the first years of our lives, and all those years when she was growing up. And we'd smile with appreciation for our new grandpa who lived above the details of food or clothing or shelter or school. We understood, without saying, that her marriage to a ragged G.I. connected to a family of grocers and knish makers and *shtetl* cooks would seem dreary to a man with an invisible golden horse. But now my father was suddenly successful at work—and interesting work at that—so Tippy and her home suddenly appealed to him. And in our new apartment, our grandpa seemed hell-bent on demonstrating his distinct and dazzling love—and we on receiving it.

My grandfather's specialty as a painter was "graining" and his tromp l'oeil rosewood and marble were in some of the more elegant lobbies and homes around the city. What fun to watch Grandpa Jess cover landlord pea green and beige with magical swirls so that we and we alone in our building—and indeed in the entire Bronx we believed—would have an alabaster foyer, an oak kitchen, a rosewood living room, and teak and cherry bedrooms, which, fake or not, promised to be grand. Indeed, as wood and stone appeared from our grand-father's wizard hands, we felt sure we were the closest thing to royalty in our whole neighborhood. And that it was *us*, so ragged and precarious so recently, thrilled us and filled us with immense cheer and hope.

For my mother, the year must have been the time she'd been waiting for all of her thirty some odd years, filled as it was with her father's love. As Jess worked—if she wasn't out teaching or shopping or doing family errands—she'd bring him Turkish coffee and snacks and *Gauloises*. Sometimes she'd strut before him in an outfit we'd never seen before, announcing, "my graduation dress, Papa," or "my wedding suit," or the "dress from when I got a little fat after Nicky. . . ." "Look, Papa!" And our grandfather would look and call her *krasavitsa*—Russian for beauty—and toss her kisses, as she preened, calling, "*Brava, brava, bella krasavitsa.*"

And that our father was suddenly loving too must have doubled her joy. How he beamed each night as he entered the apartment, finding not only his loving wife and children but the added bonus of another true "working" man with gnarled hands and a tired back. Nicky and I were at our best too that year, adoring her still, and only too pleased to polish anything she hauled in from the second-hand store—marble tops, brass handles, inlaid planters—to decorate our new rooms. Even my father's family found room in their hearts for our mother, suddenly suspending their contempt for her bastard status, and bestowing on her new respect, founded, I suspect, on her father's sudden presence.

My Grandma Bess was a stingy woman. One of the few times Nicky and I went to her house, we found a closet stuffed with nothing but brown grocery store bags and bakery box string. Among the things she wanted to hold onto were her sons. But since my father's brother, my Uncle Pinky, had escaped her, first to war, then to alcohol, getting my father back became a full-time mission. He didn't belong with my mother; my father came from "good stock" while my mother was "a *mamzeh*" (bastard) and her mother a "*kurveh*" (whore). For degrading her son and the entire family, Grandma Bess despised my mother and bid my Grandpa Abe to hate her too. Grandpa Abe was a weak-willed man who did what his wife said, "getting the car," "getting a bite," "taking it easy," "making it snappy," as told. Now as the walls took shape and we began to look substantial, Grandma Bess ignored the carpet-less floors and told Grandpa

Abe to do the same. Each week they'd appear with big brown bags filled with family "riches"—old candy dishes and platters and music boxes and fox and beaver stoles, which for years Grandma had hidden in closets away from our mother's eyes. If Jess, who had no small reputation as a "downtown fancy painter" and who lived on a very fine block just one building in from the Grand Concourse, was acknowledging her, they felt it was proper for them to do the same. And that year, my father's parents ceased to be the shadowy figures they'd been, coming with bundles and smiles to our pretty new house.

The synchronicity of happy events seemed magical—like the good end of a scary fairy tale—as our father found work he not only tolerated but loved, we found a new grandfather, my mother and her father reunited, and our "mean grandparents" became nice. Even our Nanny seemed happy that year. Though she'd been only a little over fifty when I was born, she'd always seemed stooped and ancient, Jess's rejection and treachery withering her prematurely. Young freethinkers, they'd made a child in freedom, our mother always explained to us with Tippy candor. They'd planned a life together, thought up names together for the child they'd made together—Free Thought, May the First, New World—and then suddenly he left. She was all alone to have her, name her, raise her. The shock reverberated through the years in Nan's countless sad sighs. And telling us, Tippy would sigh, and Nicky and I would catch it like a yawn, lamenting too our Nan's sad life. What joy then, that one day as he swirled the back hallway into a deep dark cherry, Jess should suddenly put down his brush and cry out, "Lily, if you only knew the nights I've cried myself to sleep with regret. I've loved you most!" Nan, who was sitting on my bed braiding my hair, put down *her* brush, and said with the only bitterness I'd ever heard in her voice, "Should I cry for your sorrow, sir?" But then she beamed like a girl. And Nan too joined the happy chorus wandering in our new bright rooms.

Our father's transformation, then, was just one among many in our family that year. But, of course, to Nicky and me, it was the most astonishing and important. It was based on his sudden success in a little business called Snack Fair, which wholesaled snacks to grocery stores throughout the Bronx and Manhattan. Olives, halavah, chitterlings, sausage, pig's feet, salami, grape leaves, and dried herring were among my father's specialties. And he stored these in an East Harlem warehouse, a cool dark cavern, where Nick and I would poke around as often as we could, half believing we'd find a genie or two in some barrel or vat—so exotic did it all seem to us, and so full of promise.

How Snack Fair started I can only imagine. My father's old army buddy, Tony DiPalma, had a deli on Pleasant Avenue in East Harlem, where my father sometimes hid out when he had no work and was too tired to fight. Did he dream up his business talking with Tony? Unemployed and frustrated, did he look in Tony's dark eyes and feel understood, his edginess melting in the pools of good will? Maybe they ate while they talked—some salami and bread, like they had back in Naples. And maybe my father thought, I love Tony, love his food, and he loves me and mine . . . so why all the crazy differences and divisions in this world? Italian salami, Jewish salami. We all should share. And then, Snack Fair?

Certainly that was the basic idea behind Snack Fair. And to make the idea a reality my father offered "people's packaging"—a plain little cellophane baggie with a single sturdy staple—which allowed him to sell his treats at a very low price. And cheap prices meant that stores as far north as Gun Hill Road and as far south as Canal Street would buy up his stock. The financial benefits of all this were reassuring, I'm sure, to my father, who wanted to make a living as much as the next man. But first and foremost, I think, Snack Fair was a political undertaking—expressing the vision my father had marched for in his youth, and gone to war for in young manhood. With its international goodies in the see-through bags, Snack Fair would allow all people equal taste opportunities and so expand the terms of their existence. What he imagined was a kind of international commingling of flavors—Jewish pastrami in Black groceries alongside pigs' feet; chitterlings beside prosciutto in Italian delis; chicherones besides pistachios in Greek and Arab groceries; and so on—leading to a similar commingling of people. Under the aegis of Snack Fair, the different people of the city would snack on each other's treats until they learned tolerance and love as he had. Calm, my father was capable of sweet dreams and grand, if impossible, plans.

For Nicky and me, Snack Fair seemed nothing less than the beginning of a great new world. And riding besides our father in the station wagon, smelling the nuts and herring and chocolate, we felt heady with joy. How proud we were of him and his wagon, of the slogan he'd painted on the wooden wagon door—SNACK FAIR—FLAVOR TREATS FOR ALL. How important he seemed, like a circus master or a Chamber of Commerce hotshot, bestowing his goodies and good will. And he was kind suddenly, under the banner of Snack Fair, content and indulgent, never slapping our hands when we reached greedily for chocolate jells and Slim Jims and cold cans of sweet tamarind juice. Nor with his new generosity did he mind if I gave treats to neighborhood kids, which I did routinely in order to repair my reputation, destroyed that fateful Halloween. "From my father's concern," I'd say handing out candies and nuts—thinking "concern" worked better than "business"—making me sound important yet kind, like him and Snack Fair.

Our mother, hating to cook and eager to have our father happily occupied, was, of course, a fierce Snack Fair supporter. Indeed, from the first days of its existence they saw eye to eye on everything, which was not at all surprising, I realize now. For Snack Fair yoked his grocer background, too solid and grounded for either of them, with her whimsy in a form that to his mind was an improvement on both, having as it did "both substance and vision," as he liked to say. No wonder then that her evening calls to him to bring home "a nice little Polish ham and one of those cute Arabic bean tins" were met with the most sincere enthusiasm, instead of the former charges of self-indulgence and decadence.

All in all, life that first year of Snack Fair felt like what our father told us life under socialism would be, with plenty of food and sharing and good spirit and hard happy work. Afternoons, Nick and I went to the warehouse to stuff baggies. Saturdays, we made the rounds in the wagon. Evenings, we worked on the new apartment in the glow of love radiating from our parents and grandparents, and the new relatives we'd hardly known before. For my father's cousins appeared too at our house, hugely overweight women, whose solidity, cheerfulness, suede t-straps, and blue cat's eye glasses Nicky and I admired along with their apparent comfort with their bulk. Sitting at our table, filling their black tent dresses, none ever showed the slightest self-consciousness as she wolfed down herring sandwiches and chocolates. They'd organize fascinating flavor tests comparing the sourness of different pickles or the saltiness of different olives. Olives were their favorite Snack Fair snacks and Nicky and I secretly renamed our new cousins according to olive grades—Miss Large, Miss Colossal, and Miss Jumbo instead of Minnie and Marsha and Flo. And my father's aunts and the grocer uncles came too, praising our walls, our food, our mother's beauty—now that they'd been allowed a close look with the lifting of my Grandma Bess's ban. All in all, that year in our bustling apartment with our parents, our grandparents, our cousins, our aunts and uncles, life seemed aglow with good will and connection. Whether we were closer to socialism or feudalism as we squeezed around our kitchen table, I couldn't say. Just that we were happy and secure at last. That the war had ended for us too. *

After a while, though, it became clear that people like what they know, and after Snack Fair's initial leaps ahead, fueled by the appeal of novelty, the business began to limp. Now my father discovered his only loyal customers were Tony and a few Jewish storekeepers who liked him because he was "a nice Jewish guy"—just the kind of provincialism Snack Fair tried to counter—and a few Puerto Rican and Black shop owners who never forgot the credit he granted them, repaying by buying their own ethnic specialties from him instead of from a compatriot. And soon the business began straining our newly emerging finances, and our father reverted to his old screams and slams. Now when our mother held her nose, as she always had, when she rode in the wagon, which doubled as the family car and smelled of dried herring, he no longer laughed. Instead, he'd shout that she should go back to boarding school if she was so fancy—she was certainly useless in real life. And if she would dare to say that *he* should try taking care of two kids and the house and work, he would settle the matter by slapping her across the face, and tell her to get out of the car and go make a meal, which in the first spell of Snack Fair's success they'd agreed they didn't believe in.

At first Nick and I didn't know that Snack Fair was going under and took evidence of failure as a sign of success. Shortly before my father went bankrupt, having no more cash or credit to pay for the warehouse or merchandise, he started bringing the stock home. Before this we'd been indulged at home only with small packages and tins.

I still can see the ten pound hams lined up in our foyer, the big wheels of Swiss cheese and cheddar sitting on the couch, the barrel of pickles perched in our bathtub. I can still feel the thrill I felt coming in on all of it beside Nick. The two of us crying, "We're rich, we're rich."

But then the next month, when there was no place to walk, the truth became apparent. And as we poked in barrels and boxes, we knew we'd find no genies, but only the most immediate and fleeting solace. As Snack Fair failed, Nicky and I, anxiously devouring nuts and chocolates day and night, grew from skinny to chubby, as if cushioning ourselves for the crash that was coming.

"You're nothing but fat losers," my father screamed one day, discovering us in the bathroom finishing off a box of Dutch fudge, squeezing our bellies till we swore we'd be good.

In short, after a year of bliss, we ended up in worse shape than ever, with a higher rent and a father, from his recent disappointment, more desperate and furious than before.

As Snack Fair went under, Grandpa Jess—sensing that fairly common poverty and chaos was about to replace his daily Snack Fair diet of smoked kippers and oysters and a passable if not thoroughly inspired bohemianism—suddenly disappeared, his graining only half done. And my other grandparents, taking his cue, decided my

mother was a bastard after all and not worthy of their indulgence, re-
treating to their apartment on the other side of the Bronx with the
troops of cousins and uncles and aunts. Only our Nan remained
true, but then she'd always been around with her loyal love and sad
sighs, which now returned in full measure.

For Nicky and me, the saddest part was seeing our mother sitting
in her bedroom, where her father's work had come to a halt. This
would be the best room, he'd promised, with green marble trim and
cherry panels, whose falseness no eye could ever detect. Now we'd
watch as she sat on her new and first double bed studying her
father's first applications of stain—which far from looking like
cherrywood, looked to our eyes like smears of brownish blood or
reddish shit. And watching her sigh, Nicky and I would sigh too,
struggling to suppress our tears.

At night, we went back to figuring out a future for our father.
Sucking on the last of the sesame candies or the coffee Hopjes, we'd
rack our brains. Salesman, deliveryman, store manager? Nothing, of
course, seemed right. Just imagining him out in the world again,
having to say "Yes sir" and "No sir," having to smile and cater and
accept, filled us with renewed terror.

Day after day we'd watch our mother knot our father's tie in a
Hollywood wife gesture, and our father take off to scour the city,
looking for a job. But as he roamed around finding nothing, his fury
grew and our larder shrunk.

My mother upped her teaching hours but for this she won few
points. Bereft of income and dignity, our father clung desperately to
his domestic "rights," and if supper was not on the table when she
came back from work, lugging bongos and gongs, he'd throw things
all around.

And the sweet peace we had known, in no time at all, was
pounded into the dust of memory.

5

Jew Coward

It's hard to say how much worse our father really was after Snack Fair. He surely seemed worse than ever, his outbursts, if not new, shocking contrasts to the good cheer of the past year, and supplemented by a new sorrow that was perhaps scarier than anything yet. Watching him sit at the kitchen table drinking a cup of coffee in silence, without a book, a radio, even a modest shout, we didn't know what to think, never having seen our father sad or still before.

How long would he sit there? we wondered. Should we let him be or try to cheer him up? As we watched him gaze into the waters of his wretchedness—recalling the rides in the Snack Fair wagon, him popping snacks in our mouths like a mother bird—we longed to bring him back. But pecking his cheek or rubbing his arm won us only his baffled stare. And the only contact was the old beatings that inevitably followed the creepy calm.

In short, our father's still silences only compounded our sense of danger. Everything could change in a moment, from calm to crazy. My walk those days looked like a spastic's tango. Above and behind me I'd check again and again, to detect ambush, suddenly tiptoeing and twirling, to avoid the mines that might be planted anywhere. Every moment, however calm it might appear, became suspect as violence, or my anticipation of it, spread like infection from home to our relatively peaceful Fifties neighborhood, across the city, out across to the other side of the globe. By now, I had my own case of "battle fatigue," no doubt. Some days I understood that the war raging in our house had made me jumpy, causing me to imagine peril where there was none; but other days, everything outside seemed truly precarious. On those days, I viewed our home not as the main cause of my anxieties and fears but as kind of boot camp, training me for all the battles facing me in the outside world. And as my father stared and brooded, slapped and screamed, I'd sometimes convince myself it was because he cared so much about us. And some days, when my dread was so thick that it was hard to breathe, I'd feel only gratitude to him, for preparing me for all the battles awaiting me. Or at least trying.

St. Xavier's, the neighborhood Catholic school, dismissed its students a half-hour before our public school. This allowed the St. Xavier boys to position themselves outside our school to attack us with pea shooters, sticks, rocks, and threats of murder by their cousins or cousins' cousins—members of brave Irish and Italian gangs who liked to kill "Christ-killing Jews." There were two major gangs in the Bronx those days—the Fordham Baldies and the Golden Guineas. The Baldies, it was rumored, scalped you and killed you, or, if you were lucky, just scalped you, while the Guineas painted victims in gold paint "so the skin couldn't breathe."

"Are you a Jew coward?" the boys would ask as they attacked us with flying split peas and spit.

"Meet me at Twin Lakes at midnight and I'll show you my Jew dick and piss in your face," brave Nicky would shout, spitting back, jabbing, kicking.

Passing them, I'd whimper and run. *I* was who the boys wanted. I was a Jew *and* a major coward. My performance at Mr. VanDam's had made that apparent to every kid in the neighborhood. Even my own brother was ashamed of his chicken sister. After that night he'd walk yards ahead of me down the street. It was only a matter of time before the St. Xavier boys got me or told their Baldie or Guinea cousins to come for me.

I was most afraid of the Baldies. They were rumored to be bald—shaving their own heads to show you your future—and I went to bed each night afraid they'd climb through the fire escape window as I slept and claim my scalp. Not that the Guineas didn't scare me, but I felt I had outsmarted them by sleeping in socks so that even if they climbed in and painted me, I could "breathe" through my soles. At night I'd lie in bed, one hand on my head, the other roaming my skin, half stock-clerk taking inventory of my endangered body parts, half supplicant praying for a little more time with them.

To protect my scalp, I began sleeping in a kerchief. But my mother wouldn't allow it. Despite her natural playfulness, my mother had an equally innate knack—probably sharpened by years of living with my father—for anticipating situations that could be physically dangerous, allowing her to see even from blocks away holes in construction site fences that children could fall through to their death, or potholes that old people could trip in, breaking their back. Discovering me sleeping in my scarf, she told me that it could tighten as I slept and strangle me. This had happened, she explained, to Isadora Duncan, one of her idols. But when I then tried to sleep in a plastic shower cap, she said that it could slip on my face and smother me. But she did allow me to lock all our windows at night and to string small silver bells across our fire escape as an alarm, which she then helped me camouflage with cheerful red bows.

My father tried to help too. A tragic truth about my father was that when he wasn't busy suffering his own torments or creating ours, he could be amazingly sensitive, reaching out in sympathies that were as potent as they were infrequent and fleeting. Seeing me in my desperate get-ups, he became his Snack Fair best and tried to reassure me that no one would come to get me. Having belonged to gangs on the Lower East Side, he said, he knew how they worked, then and now. The idea was gang versus gang, not gang versus little girl in bed. But as touching as I found his wish to comfort me, I found his reassurances less convincing than the St. Xavier boys' descriptions and threats.

I'm not just another little girl, I wanted to tell to my father. I'm a

Jew coward girl. The kind they like to *get*. But I said nothing, not wanting to agitate him by seeming unappreciative.

It didn't help that one night I found my father in the hallway, crying. He looked frightened, not angry or brooding on his way to anger, so I walked up close to him and asked him what was wrong. "Mean boss?" I ventured, for he'd just started a new job painting cars.

My father shook his head—that wasn't it. He'd been remembering that as a boy he had pierced another's boy's eyeball with a fountain pen. And remembering, he couldn't sleep.

"Was he mean?" I asked, suppressing a gag.

My father shook his head. "He was very nice. And I did that to that very nice boy with my Waterman's pen, just like that."

"You were young," I said, to try to normalize things and comfort him and me, hearing, of course, even at that young age of eight, the failure of my remark.

My father just stood there dragging on his Lucky Strike. "A nice kid with nice blue-gray eyes. Imagine," he kept saying.

And I closed my eyes and imagined the Baldies taking *my* eyes before they took my scalp. If that had happened to a nice kid, surely it would happen to a Jew coward.

After that, there was nothing anyone could say to comfort me, and bedtime became a dreadful ordeal in which I'd enact frantic strategies, protecting various parts of me with caps, socks, sneakers. Sun glasses.

Finally, the only thing that could distract me from my terror of the gangs was a new threat from a new enemy, this one on the other side of the world.

In anticipation of an air attack from the Russians, the New York public schools initiated a daily "take cover" drill. "Take cover, class," teachers all over the city would say, speaking lines from a mandated city-wide script, and students from the Bronx to Staten Island would dive beneath oak desks, contorted and silent.

What terrifying moments for all of us, bent in half, protected only by a wooden board from the red bricks which, along with flame and radiation, were sure to tumble in on us when the bombs dropped. For me, though, the drills were doubly terrifying and completely confusing: I was scared of the Russians; but I was also scared of my family's wrath if they found out I was scared of the Russians. For both my parents, anarchists temperamentally and too disorganized to be Party members, were nonetheless, ideologically, communist sympathizers who did not believe for a second that the Russians were coming in any shape or form, by bomb or boot. They directed me not to believe the "garbage" taught in school about the Soviet Union.

At home, I believed what my parents told me to believe. And wishing to please my father and make him calm, I'd say things like, "Gee, all they really want is peace, those Russians." And sometimes, if he wasn't too distracted or furious, he'd pat my head. At school, though, Russian peril felt palpable and, as the teacher began her command, I'd be the first to dive beneath the little desk. And there, watching kids kiss the crucifixes and medals and stars of David and *mezuzahs* that hung around their necks, I'd pray with them. I'd bow my head and say things like, Please, God, kill the Russians and keep us safe. And then, oddly, I'd feel the greatest calm I'd known in my nine years. Crouched in the dark room, in the dark beneath the desk, I'd escape my odd family and become like all the other kids. I'd hear my breath synchronize with theirs in small scared sips of air, and a wondrous peace would claim me. I belonged.

Then I'd panic. Don't kill me, Daddy, I'd think. And, paralyzed with anxiety, I'd stay down as the class rose, seeing his angry face. Or Nicky's, purple with rage, or turned away because he couldn't bear to look at a traitor.

Countless bonds, unspoken and unseverable, united my brother and me those years. But a small wedge was intruding between us as Nick's own fierceness grew. In part Nick's enhanced boldness took the form of defying our father—or anyone else threatening him or me physically—with boxer's stances and explosive "pow" sounds suggesting what was in store for them if they didn't back off. In part it took the form of *following* our father, whose political rhetoric he found compelling. As eager as Nick was to fight him on the domestic front, that's how eager he was to join our father in battle against our political enemies, wherever they might be. Nick, then, adopting the party and family line, did not care what the "deadbeats in the class" thought about him and would not participate in the take-cover drills which "distorted the reality of the Soviet Union and diminished the dangers of the A bomb and radiation," as he liked to put it in speeches before the bathroom mirror. That I participated, and so eagerly at that, won me his contempt and wrath. I was a sellout who left him alone in a one-boy campaign.

Years later, organizing his juvenile delinquent friends in the neighborhood and his intellectual friends in his high school, my brother led a city-wide boycott that stopped bomb drills once and for all. But at Public School 52, he was a lone rebel, constantly sent to detention—an oak swivel chair outside of the principal's office, on which he would turn round and round, occasionally extending his legs into the hallway as if to stretch, but really to trip the well-behaved monitors streaming between classroom and office. I was a devoted and responsible school monitor, but it was torture for me to perform my duties after a drill, dreading both Nick's kicks and curses, and the ridicule of classmates for being the sister of the school Commie.

"Did you hide, you goody-goody collaborating shithead?" Nicky would call to me as I passed, pretending I didn't know him.

One day, I walked too close to Nick, allowing him to grab my arm. As I tried to pull myself free, he said, "You know, eventually you're going to realize what a friend we all have in the Soviet Union and what a little moron you are."

I wanted to say, You're the moron, getting yourself into trouble. But I didn't want to be seen speaking with him. And besides, only half of me believed he was wrong to do what he had done. Half of me was proud of his rebellion. So I said nothing.

"You're a pathetic little people-pleasing moron," he said. "A coward to cowards."

I bowed my head—ashamed of his screaming, my sniveling. Afraid that someone could hear.

The principal must have been listening on the other side of her office door. For suddenly the door flew open and she was standing over my brother, bearing down at him with a wooden pointer in her hand.

"Apologize," she said.

"Absolutely not," Nick snickered.

"I said *apologize*. At once. Or you'll see who's a coward."

"And I said *absolutely not*. I say it to you and I say it to your . . . weapon." He began laughing, pointing at her pointer.

"That's it," she said, lifting the pointer high and hitting him on the shoulder. "You deserve that and more. . . . For your general attitude and un-American actions."

Nick said, "You know, violence is often the mark of the desperate. I pity you."

I can still see her red face, her heaving bosom, her hand shaking toward her neckline to find a tissue to mop her brow.

"Lucy, you'd better tell him to say he's sorry," she said, turning to me.

"Nicky," I whispered obediently, "Tell Mrs. O'Shea you didn't mean what you said." She was sweating hard now—was she getting ready to hit again? "Please, Nicky," I begged.

My brother stared ahead silently, dramatically rubbing his shoulder.

"And tell him to tell you he's sorry too," she said. "You're a nice child and don't deserve him. He's a ruffian and a Red!"

"Nicky, please," I said. "Just apologize to her. Not to me." I whispered, "Or else I'm afraid she'll hit you again."

"I hit no one," she said. "You never saw me hit a soul."

She looked at me, with nervous little blinks, as if to say, I know I can count on you—you're not like him. I looked away to Nick. But he wouldn't look at me.

I studied his brown smooth skin, his eyes narrowed in disgust and defiance. He looked like the Indian on the nickel, and he kept staring ahead, as if he didn't know me. How it hurt me, the stab of his judgment and rejection.

Suddenly I heard myself saying, "You did so hit him!"

"I hit no one," Mrs. O'Shea shouted.

"You hit him," I shouted back, surprised by the boom of my voice. "You hit my brother. You did, you did."

Throwing my arms around Nick's neck, I began to cry, "Did she hurt you? Did she hurt you, Cocoa?" How good it felt to call him by the special affectionate name, in honor of the color of his skin, which we brought out for the tender family moments we still sometimes managed. How good it felt to hear him say, "Watch the shoulder, Missy." *Missy*, my own family name, short for Miss Mouse, whose fearful scampering and squeaking and twitching now seemed worlds away.

The next moment we were flying down the hall, and then— though it was a full half-hour till dismissal—down the steps to the street.

Out on the street, Nick raced ahead of me in his usual fashion. The St. Xavier's boys were already posted at the corner. They smirked as Nick passed, but you could feel in their silence, their fear and admiration.

As I approached, they asked *me* the usual—was I a Jew coward who wanted to die? I began my usual whimper and scamper, but then stopped. I remembered how I'd stood up to O'Shea. No whimpering, no twitching, no fainting! I coached myself.

"You're punks," I said. "Meet me at the lake at midnight and. . . ." I tried to remember the brave words my brother always used that made them so afraid. "Meet me at the lake and . . . I'll pee on you," I said.

Back and forth they rocked in laughter, "Yeah, you and who else, little Jew coward?"

Who else? Nick was halfway down the block. I felt pee welling up. I wasn't going to pee on them, but all over myself. I was trembling and twitching. In a second I'd be soaking for all to see.

Then Nicky was there beside me. "And me . . . her brother," he said.

And then he made good on his threat, peeing on them in big brave arcs that gathered the afternoon light and filled me with pride and hope.

"Yeah," I said. "Watch out! We're together."

And walking beside him, feeling his hunting knife in his jeans jacket pocket pressing my side, catching the bounce of his developing delinquent walk, I felt safe and brave—for the last time in a long time—as we made our way back home.

6

Liberty

By now we were used to almost anything from our father—violence, silent indifference, periodic absence—but except for a few bouts of tears when *her* father had disappeared, our mother had stayed dependable and steady, carrying us through the worst of it. But now *she* had begun to sink.

Which, in retrospect, is not surprising. After the long spell of post-Snack Fair inactivity, our father returned as energized as a grizzly in spring, now devoting a good deal of his largely unemployed time to threats of leaving "for good." And then one night, finding an excuse in an overcooked spaghetti dinner, he flipped over the platter, tipped over the table and, packing a bag as we all cried, walked out the door—leaving us, if not for good, for long enough to change our lives forever.

True, by now we were accustomed to his disappearances after one of his rampages, his escapes to his mother's pristine apartment where he'd cry about his disgusting life with us, and Grandma Bess, cooking his favorite treats, would cry back from the kitchen how a mistake was a mistake but enough was enough and he should come home. But this was different. For now he'd left, lured not by his mother's rugelah and reassurances, but by the call of Liberty.

Liberty, Liberty. A whole terrible summer and fall, our parents seemed not to sleep, and at night we'd hear them whispering about

Liberty. Liberty, Liberty Liberty, day and night it was Liberty, so that our home often seemed less a Bronx apartment in the mid-twentieth century than Constitution Hall in Philadelphia in 1776. Our father would say, "Liberty," he wanted "Liberty." And our mother, breaking into low terrible cries we'd never heard from her before, would say, "But what about us? You have us . . . why do you need *her*?"

Liberty's real name was Libby Glickstein. Sometime in early adulthood, as she told it, she realized the "sovereignty" of her "be-ing," and changed Libby to Liberty. Because she'd lived for many years with a colorful Cockney named Tommy O'Hare, she was called by most, Liberty O. Nick and I, wrapping yet another hurt in yet another joke, called her to ourselves, Oh Liberty. And our mother, covering defeat with rage, called her to anyone who would listen, "The cow-titted, home-wrecking whore."

Breast size was only one of countless points of contrast between Oh Liberty and our mother. Unlike our mother, our father's new love liked to cook, specializing—to please our father, who missed Italy and the war—in red-sauced creations she'd throw together, licking her lips to show the intensity of her creative labor, wringing her apron in what we came to understand as her cheesy imitation of an Italian peasant.

Other differences between Liberty and our mother included the fact that our mother spoke for fun in a variety of accents, her favor-ite and most frequent being a raspy, Bronxy, Donald Duck kind of voice, while Liberty, though Brooklyn-bred, preferred an English accent, which only occasionally dipped into serious old-neighbor-hood dentalizing. Our mother was an artist, a dancer, who in her more accommodating moments hoped to develop the organiza-tional and typing skills to become a receptionist and so impress and keep our father, while Liberty was a cracker-jack executive secretary who planned eventually on trimming down and taking some acting classes, claiming she had the voice and, with weight off, the profile, too, of Claire Bloom. And then there was the fact that our mother had us, while Liberty had no children, though from time to time she'd announce, her voice dipping into deep Dame Judith Anderson-like tones meant to reassure us, I guess, that soon we'd be hers.

One immediate result—to us a benefit—of our father running away to Liberty, was that he took with him his record collection of Puccini operas, which we had come to hate. Often it was a Puccini aria that would kindle my father's warm-ups in self-pity, which, in turn, would ignite his fiercest anger. Down at Liberty's Bank Street apartment, Puccini would scratch away again on the phonograph, but our father now would simply smile appreciatively as Liberty bustled about. And we'd smile too, glad that we had to listen to this wailing only once a week, then sneer discreetly at our father sitting so quiet and calm in his new found civility.

Eventually, her sauce done, Liberty would light candles in the small spotless kitchen, and Nick and I, hungry but feeling traitorous for being there, would wolf down Liberty's food, then discreetly spit some out in our hands for quick deposits under our chairs. How we'd ache then to return to our mother's meals of cheese and crackers or chips and dip—and even our father's angry glares as we all sat together around our old kitchen table.

Of course, we never told our mother about our days with Liberty. The first few visits, returning home stuffed with a nauseating mixture of food, sorrow, and guilt, we told our mother we'd been to the movies—which is where we'd really wanted to go in the first place—and acted out for her some movie we'd read about in the paper but had been unable to convince our father to take us to. Our mother, once the most appreciative audience for our theatrics, would stare at us as we bounced around the room, her eyes narrowed in distrust at every word and gesture we made, making us feel worse than we had before starting the charade. And so finally, unable to convince our father not to take us to her, we'd return from a day with Liberty and simply confess: "He took us *there*." And then reassure: "But we *hate* her and we *love* you." Which made all three of us cry with an immense sense of pain and relief.

"I'm prettier," our mother would say. "Much," we would agree, stroking her bouncing black curls. "And smarter," we would offer, "and funnier and nicer." How much we loved her then: for forgiving us even in her needy frailness; for her natural superiorities, which she surely now doubted, but tried to cling to with her sad little brags; for all the ways she was different from that officious martinet who had the nerve to go by the name Liberty and threaten to replace our mother.

Why our father liked this Liberty was, to us, a total enigma. Her food was as terrible as it was plentiful. True, she flattered and listened, without signs of boredom, to his records; to his stories of war; to his diatribes about the burdens of marriage and fatherhood; to his frustrations about not being able to take advantage of the G.I. bill because of us while millions of "dummies" could and did; to his dreams of being a writer. And, true, recently we had begun to cover our ears when our father's operas shrieked about human yearning, and our mother had started laughing in his face when he shouted about a "young man's dreams." But for years our mother had indulged his tormented soul and urged us to do the same—only partly from terror, and mostly, I suspect now, from feeling the depth of his frustrations, which, after all, were much like our own.

How Liberty became our father's instead of Tommy's was unclear too. Our mother, while Nick and I tried not to listen, offered that fateful year several versions of adulterous plot and dialogue. In one, Oh Liberty, when Tommy O goes down to the store to get some ale, turns to our father and says: "You're a lonely misunderstood man, Ralphie," and puts her hand in her blouse. Our mother tells us that our father has never really liked big breasts—and, indeed, of all her body parts favors her little titties, which he calls little plummies— but that he is, despite his tyrannical ways, a weak, insecure man and a sucker for a fat cow. In another version, our father's kid brother, Uncle Pinky, a legendarily handsome young alcoholic, who is Tommy O's best friend and drinking buddy, gets tired of fending off fat Liberty, who likes to squeeze alongside him when he passes out on Tommy's couch, and tells her: "Go fuck my big brother. He's overwhelmed by the burdens of family life and would welcome the distraction of even a big-titted slob like you."

Then our mother would tire from her heated narrations, and take to bed. "You know, children, I do believe I'm going to die," she'd whisper. And she'd cry, and we'd stroke her small darling head, hoping that with a little sleep she'd wake up her old self again.

Some days she was so absent—so different from the mother we had known—that it felt as if she had died. And grieving privately, Nicky and I would wander in silence through our lives, too ashamed to confide our loss to others, and too confused and scared, at first, to discuss it with each other. If we said nothing, maybe nothing was really wrong, and besides, it was hard to say what *was* wrong. For just as it seemed we'd never see our old mother again, she'd skip back again for a frolicsome day or two. Though less and less as the year, and his absence, wore on.

At ten, of course, I couldn't have said that it was severe depression, or overwhelming anxiety, or debilitating panic that transformed our mother beyond recognition. But I did know with a dreadful certainty that shortly before he left she had stopped eating, had gone from thin to haggard, losing the energy for anything much except worrying. Before that time, she'd had plenty to worry about—where our money would come from, how many classes she could teach in a week and still oversee us, whether our father would stop screaming and hitting, when the "fatigue" would leave for good and he'd return to the old self that she still claimed to remember and love. But that year, I think, was the first time she questioned whether she could go on. Suddenly everything in her life seemed uncertain. How she would manage teaching in studios all over the Bronx and Westchester when she was suddenly afraid to walk down an open street or get in a closed car. How she'd survive when she was sure that most foods would get stuck in her throat and choke her. I can still see her staring at something I or a kind neighbor had made for her to eat, with a look of both fear and contempt on her face. My heretofore grateful and cheerful mother, now looking up in horror and anger as if to say, You really don't get it, do you? Eat that, and I die!

That year I was in the fifth grade, and I started staying home from school to take care of her. Till then, except for the fall when I was six, I'd never missed a day. I loved school and, despite the incident with O'Shea, I still loved it—the order, the simple rules, the even-tempered teachers with their neat bulletin boards, chore charts, and clean handkerchiefs tucked into their bosoms. But as much as I loved school, that year I began to feel pulled from it, back to my home, where my mother needed me.

I'd be sitting in school engrossed in the kind of tedious lessons I'd always loved, something I could memorize and be good at—the kinds of helpers in a community, the types of bees in a hive—when I'd feel my mind suddenly drawn from the room to my mother.

I remember distinctly the day I decided my mother needed me more than I needed school. It was a day that had started off wonderfully. I'd just written on the board in my perfect penmanship and in alphabetical order the states in the Midwest. I remember the teacher praised me, and I returned to my seat beaming. But then she said, "We call the Midwest the breadbasket because it feeds the country." And when she said that, my mother's scared skinny face popped into my mind, and I thought, But the breadbasket does not feed my mother! No one feeds my mother! And here I am when I should be home finding her food that she can swallow!

My guilt suddenly overwhelmed me and I started writhing in my chair and crying, saying my stomach was hurting. The teacher sent me down to the office, where the school clerk called home.

"What's with your stomach?" my mother said when she came to get me. I could see genuine concern breaking through her new self-absorption, but I didn't want her anxious about me on top of all her other anxieties, so I said nothing and just rubbed her hand to let her know, bellyache or not, I was there for her.

When we got downstairs I told her the truth. That I'd left because I was worried about her and her not eating.

Her eyes got wide and worried again, and she said, "You need to go to school, Lucy."

"I will," I said. "Just not all the time."

Waiting for her in the school office, I'd come up with a plan. I'd go to school two days, stay home two, and split the last, going to school in the morning and taking care of my mother in the afternoon. I was a veteran attendance monitor and knew that attendance was based on morning presence—the truant officers weren't called in unless you were out more than half the time, which, with my plan, I wouldn't be.

"Really, Ma, don't worry," I said. "I have it worked out. Besides, I'm smart," I said. "I'm never going to fall behind. I'll still do fine."

My mother's deep hazel eyes, those days, sometimes looked yellow, sometimes green, sometimes devilish, sometimes wise. I watched my mother's eyes change color and expression as she struggled to be a mother, then collapsed into a child, found gratitude and concern for me, then detachment as her own dread claimed her again.

"I guess you will," she said. "It's not as if we're not a family of readers and thinkers." She laughed a nervous little laugh.

"Yeah, I'll read. I'll think," I said. "At home."

With these words, we created a kind of contract, I guess, an agreement that it was okay with both of us for me to start spending days at home looking after her.

On the walk home I held my mother's hand and told her I was sure she could perk up and start eating again. All she needed was a little TLC, which I would provide, and the right food, which I could make or buy.

We passed the Horn and Hardhart take-out store on 204th Street. I guided my mother to soft foods—creamed spinach, clam chowder, macaroni and cheese. "Less Work for Mother," was the retail store's motto. I thought, How perfect, imagining, as I eyed the soft selections, how my mother's tired teeth and tongue and throat and stomach would have less work to do now that I'd found these new smooth foods.

But my mother shook her head. "Too substantial and textured," she said, whispering her odd new concerns.

Finally I made her buy tapioca pudding, but she just played with it when we got home, saying the tapioca balls were larger than she'd expected and looked like they might cause trouble on the way down. I picked out the balls and pushed the rest of the pudding in front of her for her to finish.

Feeling the pressure of my anxious watch, I guess, she said, "I'm trying." But she still wouldn't touch her plate.

I said, "I know, Ma. It's just that you're so fussy."

"I really can't help it," she said. "I think it's a condition, darling."

"A condition?"

"You know, like a disease," she whispered.

"That's silly," I said. But I went into the kitchen to cry, covering my noises by turning on the faucet. I studied the discarded tapioca balls that were gathering at the drain. They looked like a bunch of eyeballs. Of course my mother couldn't eat them. I felt them looking up at me accusingly, as if to say, We see you, you're useless. And that's why your mother has that condition.

My mother must have heard me crying. She came in and put her arms around me.

"Everything's going to be all right," she said, and I settled against her chest and let her words stroke my worried mind.

But then suddenly she lifted my head and studied me. And I studied her back, her eyes flickering from a little shame to a lot of need. Then she bent her head and laid it on *my* chest—and nuzzled against me. And for one long frightening moment—though I was only ten with a flat bony chest—I thought she would try to suckle. But she just rested on me, saying again, "Everything's going to be all right. . . . Right, Lucy? Right, Lucy?" And I stroked her head and told her everything was going to be all right.

7

Poison

Our working-class neighborhood—composed equally of Irish, Italians, and Jews—had its share of drunks. Some neighborhood fathers pretty much lived at McCorley's, the local bar, a bottle of Rheingold fused to their fists and the smell of pee glued to their staggering bodies. But when our mother started staggering, she still smelled sweet and there were no telltale bottles, and so it was months before we discovered what was happening.

The revelation came one day when Nicky and I had stayed home from school. I'd convinced Nicky to skip school and stay home with me to fix up the apartment—another strategy for cheering Tippy and winning her back—and together we ventured into her room for a thorough clean-up. With our mother asleep on the couch, we became aggressive in our efforts; and crawling on the floor to attack the fortress of newspapers and magazines, dirty clothes and dirty dishes surrounding her bed, we discovered a Bob's luncheonette malted glass filled with a murky liquid. Lifting it, we sniffed, but smelled nothing familiar. Not her usual old coffee, old tea, old juice. Indeed, we realized, it could be nothing old at all for Bob had just given her the giant glass for her birthday. Curious, we dipped our fingers in to taste. But nothing could have prepared us for that putrid bitterness. And rags in hand, we sat there trembling

"Poison," we both whispered. "Poison."

Last time we looked she was still napping. But maybe that wasn't napping we'd seen, but a person slipping into a coma, Nicky said. From poison. Then saying no more, we stood to race to her side.

But before we could reach *her*, she had reached *us*, lurching into the bedroom, shouting, "Don't touch that!"

Her urgency only convinced that we were right—the glass contained poison. And our mother, hearing our cries as she entered her coma, had been roused by the powerful pulls of maternal love, dragging herself from the brink to save us from the potion she'd already sipped.

It had been weeks since our mother had tousled our hair or pinched our cheeks or imitated a neighbor for fun or told us she loved us. Touched by her caring, and relieved that the poison had not killed her, we reached up to embrace her. But she pushed us away and lunged at the glass, which now sat on the night table.

We began crying, totally confused.

Then she began doing something with her lips, twitching them around, and for a moment I reasoned that the poison crisis had brought her to some kind of religious feeling and that she was now praying some sort of thankful prayer. That we'd saved her from the poison, that she'd saved us. But then I realized she was licking her lips with craving, as if a real Bob's malted were awaiting her.

"We thought it was poison," I said, bursting into tears again.

"Such sillies," she said. "Just medicine. Now give it to Mommy."

We usually called our mother "Ma," referring to her as "Mommy" to each other or our father, and to her directly only at special moments—"Happy birthday, Mommy," "We love you, Mommy," and so on. My mother signed notes "Mommy," but referring to herself as "Mommy," like so many other mothers did—"Don't dirty Mommy's floors" or "Come to Mommy"—was a corny convention she had spared us. But now, these past few months, she had been trying it out, as if to convince both us and her that she was just like everyone else. A regular mother, a "real Mommy," not a helpless heap.

Suddenly she was charging at Nicky, who'd seized the glass.

"Please, Mommy," I cried. If I called her that, would she return, my old darling mother who would never simper and slobber and call *herself* Mommy? "Mommy, Mommy, please," I said urgently now, "Let Nicky keep the medicine."

My mother shook her head. "Give," she said to Nicky. "Give Mommy that right now."

"No," Nick said. "How do we know it's not poison?"

"It's not poison! Would Mommy take poison and leave her little sillies whom she loves so, even if she's a little on the nervous or low side?"

"I don't know," I said.

"Well, *know*," she said. "I'm just not that sort of person."

"We were really scared, Ma. We thought it was poison," Nick said again.

"Well it's not. How many times do I have to tell you dummies?"

"Then what is it?" I said, suddenly knowing, as she continued to grab at the glass in Nicky's hand, that it was some sort of drug.

"I told you, nothing. Just some silly medicine. That's the last of it anyway, kids. Now that I see how much my children love me, I feel a hundred percent better. And besides there's no more medicine left."

"No more medicine *ever*," Nick said. "We want you to promise."

I said, "Yeah, Mom. I think the medicine is what's making you so tired and funny. No more, please."

"Okay," our mother said. "Just this one last dose. It's dangerous not to take the whole prescription, you know. Like antibiotics. You can't fool around with this stuff."

"Really, no more," I said. "You've had enough."

"One last smidgen," she said. And then taking a slug from the glass, which she'd pulled from Nick's hand, she fell back. And there on the hills of her bed, in the mounds of newspapers and books and clothing, she passed out, smiling like a happy hiker resting at a tough pass through the mountains.

As our mother slept, Nicky and I felt a new alarm go off inside us. What were these medicines anyway? Gingerly, so as not to wake her, we excavated the mound of papers around her bed, hoping to find those instruction sheets they sometimes give out with prescriptions which would explain what we were up against. But the only paper we could find were newspapers and a few wrappers from Three Musketeers candy, the mushy bars being one of her new food staples. Digging beneath her bed, though, in the deep dark cavern amid dust balls and stray shoes and coffee cups, we found a squad of small plastic bottles.

"Dexedrine, Seconal, Dexedrine, Seconol, Seconal, Dexedrine, Dexedrine, Dexedrine. . . ." Nicky read the labels aloud, some twenty bottles in all, some empty, some half filled. What was all this?

Our Nan had a cousin, whom we called Uncle Mort, who was a doctor in New Haven. We hardly saw or knew this Uncle Mort—a "selfish spoiled bachelor," according to our father who only visited when he felt like going to Roseland and, needing a good dance partner to show off, dragged our mother along. Selfish or not, uncle or not, we needed to understand what was going on now, and felt too awkward and ashamed calling Dr. Schaeffer, our local doctor.

Still, even with Uncle Mort, we tried to hide our predicament. Nicky took charge and dialed, and then, getting jittery, handed me the phone.

A gruff voice came on the line, saying, "Dr. Hochstein here."

I said, "Dr. Hochstein?"

"Call him Uncle Mort, you phony," Nicky said. "What's the big deal that he's a doctor. I'm not going to lie down and kiss his feet." Nick was marching around the room now, trying to distract himself from our particular crisis and his sudden lack of nerve with universal defiance.

I covered the phone with my hand. "Shush," I said.

"Hello, hello," Uncle Mort was saying.

"Hello," I said, clearing my throat. "This is Lucy. Your niece."

"Cousin's daughter's daughter," Nicky prompted. "Jesus."

"Oh, Lucy. How's Mom? I've been meaning to call," Uncle Mort said. "Last time I took her dancing, I was worried about that girl. I said to myself, 'Mort, Tippy's not Tippy.' Nothing wrong, I hope."

"Oh, nothing," I said. Everything was fine. I was calling, I said, because Nicky and I had found a bunch of pill bottles in the park and wondered what we should do with them. They looked dangerous. And there was a lady on the bench who looked weird, and I was afraid she'd taken them.

"What sort of pills? How weird?"

I told him the names of the pills, and how the lady had bottles of them and staggered around shouting, then lay down and looked dead. Though she was definitely not dead. We'd gone up close to her and asked her if she was okay and she'd said, "Yeah." But we were still a little worried.

"Damn her!" he said.

By then we both knew we were talking about Tippy.

"Damn her! I gave her one prescription for the amphetamines when she was very down when that son of a bitch first took off. And one for the barbiturates when she couldn't sleep the last time I was in town. But that was months ago. Where the hell did she get the rest? Tell me, honey, is she flying?"

I didn't know what he meant by "flying," but I found myself saying, "I guess so. Not right now, though. Right now she looks like she sort of . . . crashed."

"Damn it, she's mixing them. On the street, they call them goofballs, when you mix uppers and downers like that. Listen to me now. You take all those pills and you throw them out. You hear me? I love that girl. You tell her that her Uncle Mort loves her and wants her never to take another pill again. You tell her that from me, honey. She should stop taking them and then soon I'll come down and we'll go dancing. I'm busy for the next month or so but I'll be down one of these days. Jesus, she's some gorgeous dancer, that girl."

"Thank you, Uncle Mort," I said, hanging up.

"What did he say?" Nicky said.

"Goof-balls," I said.

And we both stood there, shaking again. For there were rumors circulating around the neighborhood that the Fordham Baldies took goof-balls before they went on a rampage. But our mother?

Quickly, we put all the bottles in garbage bags, and with the pills out of sight, we felt better, and smiled at each other as we walked to the front door to go down to the basement garbage room. Whatever it was, there'd be no more of it now. Uncle Mort had said so. And she had too. *No more medicine.*

But as we reached the door, she came running towards us, some junkie radar evidently having roused her. And she grabbed the bags from our hands and dug through them, throwing bottles all over the floor screaming that she would kill us if the pills weren't there.

Then finding the bottles, she suddenly calmed down. "Mommy got nervous because she needs to take the full course."

As she took inventory of her stock, we tried to wrestle the bottles back. But her grip was iron and we gave up. We thought to call Uncle Mort, but were too embarrassed to bother him again. And besides, we knew she'd never forgive us if she found out we'd told anyone.

"Mommy just takes a little," she said, "and dissolves it in plenty of water to flush her system and keep her healthy."

I was only ten, so innocently, foolishly, I tried to counter her drug madness with logic designed to convince and shame. "You don't care if you're healthy. If you did you wouldn't take this. And you only dissolve it because you're afraid you'll choke on it, not to be healthy." And I began crying, remembering back a couple of months when our only problem was her not eating, not swallowing, feeling fury and guilt war in my stomach. Had she eaten the food I made her, had I made her better foods, she wouldn't be swigging her liquid goofballs now, and we'd all be okay.

"Mommy has her vulnerabilities like all human beings," she said, spewing banalities that only a few months before she would have mocked with great gusto. "But that doesn't mean you have to get angry with Mommy and hurt her feelings."

"Stop this Mommy garbage," Nicky said. "Just cut the Mommy garbage. And the medicine garbage. . . . We know what it is now and it's making you crazy. And it's getting Lucy real upset," Nicky said, blinking back his own tears.

"Mommy will stop," she said, sipping demurely. "As soon as this is finished," she said pointing to the handful of half empty bottles she had retrieved. "Mommy plans to turn over a new leaf. . . . Really she does. I mean . . . really I do, I do, I do. I promise a terrific new leaf." Then she stumbled to the couch, curled up into a ball, and quickly passed out for the rest of the day and night.

New leaf. Regularly, in the months that followed, she'd make this pledge to us, only to withdraw it weeks or sometimes even just days or minutes later, the new leaf not turned but tossed like so much else around us. What flotsam and jetsam we'd have to navigate those days—the contents of closets, drawers, button jars, flower pots, which, flying on her "medicine," she'd hurl about our apartment. Fueled with drugs, she began to undertake major campaigns of domestic reorganization, designed, she assured us, again and again, to improve our lives beyond measure.

A whole winter and spring, while our father was down at Liberty's, we watched as she sipped her concoctions and rocketed into activity. At least in the early days, twin notions warred in our minds. That our mother's projects on the drugs were mad, wrecking our lives. And then that other thought, which surprised us as it took hold, that our mother's projects were mad, but in some crazy way, if she could accomplish them, might lead to better times.

Might *not* clean closets mean a fresh start, with or without him? Might *not* house plants, removed from pots in which their roots were being crushed, and replanted with room to spread and grow, usher in no less than life on whole new terms? With horror and wonder, we'd even help our mother in her campaigns, feeling at once the senselessness of her activity and some flutter of hope that it would bring her, and us, peace at last. In those early days when she and we were fresh to her addiction, we were more gullible and more inclined to believe that "A little reorganization will do the trick," or that "It would be a big relief to know that the plants are doing well." In the past our Tippy had been able to transform thugs into fairies, rusty fire escapes into glittering balconies. Might she not be able to pull off some magic again?

But at the end of a binge, yarn collections that had been pulled out of the closet for a good sorting now tangled together hopelessly. Touch typing books gathered from the local library for a crash course in skills she thought would enhance her attractiveness to our father, or independence from him, or both, lay on the floor untouched under piles of clothing she'd torn from the closets to go through once and for all. More often than not, during a binge, the plants died for lack of sufficient soil or overly zealous pill-head snipping or just simple dehydration. For inevitably, midway through a week of drugs, our mother would lose the ability to focus, and her initial efforts at human or botanical salvation would come to a standstill. She'd rant, write vicious letters and, now and then, at a real peak of a high, kick and bite us and bang our heads against the wall. All in all, at the end of a binge, our apartment looked like a bomb site and Nicky and I like ragged survivors. Our mother looked dead, passed out somewhere, and more than once we'd put a mirror under her nose to check that she was breathing.

After a while, the preamble to the binge became as scary as the binge itself or its aftermath. Desperate for an excuse to take lots of drugs and already sipping small quantities, she'd distort our every gesture, however solicitous, into a sign of our disloyalty and disregard. A low voice meant to soothe was thus seen as proof of our smug judgment; a high voice of alarm as outrage and anger; a casual hand on the hips, undermining impatience; a hand on the mouth, smirking contempt. Her system rippling with uppers, she went on and on with her exegesis—our raised brows, furrowed brows, narrow stares, blank stares, all signifying how disgusting we were, how disgusting we thought her, and all in all, how necessary it was for her to take heaps of drugs.

"Ma, you're not going to start are you? Ma, is everything all right?" we'd call to her then, knowing in our hearts she had started already and everything was not all right and would not be for several days, perhaps weeks.

By then we knew the signs. In addition to the wild criticism, there were the dry lips, which she'd lick like a cat; the awkward movements as jerky as a robot's, which would replace her natural grace; the shopping bags lined up in the foyer, which, no matter the season, we were instructed to carry quickly to the Botanical Gardens and fill up with earth before it was too late for the roots of our plants, which, like her, were in profound danger.

Actually, in some ways the beginnings of binges were the most frightening stage of the whole ordeal, for she stood there between two worlds, not quite loaded but not quite sober, half human, half monster, it seemed; and we stood grasping at this slippery stone-eyed sphinx, unable to pull her back to our realm. To do so would have involved us in search and destroy missions for her drug stashes, which would have been impossible to accomplish, given her ingenuity, and involve us in physical fights we couldn't win, strengthened as she was with her speed.

At her most desperate, I think, my mother stole prescription pads from doctors' desks. But for the most part she got her drugs without prescriptions from local druggists she worked into submission with a warm-up act that readied them for the bigger show. The four drug stores up and down 204th Street, our shopping street, ranged in style from classic pre-war pharmacy—drugs plus perfume—to more modern enterprises, half pharmacy, half something else—chocolatier, housewares store, toy and stationery shop. What a terrible moment coming home from school to a living room cluttered with boxes of scented stationary, fudge and truffles, travel irons, perfume and talcum powder, Monopoly and Chinese checkers sets. Or even worse, to be dragged into a drug store on our way home from school where, cruising the counters, she would ooh and ah over crap we now had closets full of at home and which, I knew, we could not afford in any terms. After purchasing her selections, she would whisper her wild requests to the druggist. Having just made the biggest sale of the week, he could only nod, his eyes lowered. A gesture which my own developing powers of interpretation told me meant contempt and revulsion.

At home, she'd explain she had no intentions of taking pills, explained that in fact she had no problem with pills. Her problem, she'd say, was people understanding her. If we understood her, she wouldn't have to take any pills, or maybe just one or two to lift her spirits a bit. One or two and she'd have it under control and, come to think of it, accomplish something productive at the same time. She couldn't be a dance teacher forever. How about a little typing and shorthand? She knew we wanted to bring friends home like we used to. How about a little redecorating? A little project would do her good. A little pill or two would help her with the project. And if we were good kids and didn't bug her while she still had it under control, everything would work out.

Inevitably, though, we bugged her. A gesture or sentence or look would push her too far, she said.

And then she was off.

8

Spring Break

Nicky and I never lacked for friends. We were both pursued—I for my accommodating ways, and Nick for his energy and dare. But that spring, after the ordeal of the past few months, we didn't feel fit for the company of most of our friends, whose lives seemed to mock ours with their normalcy. My friends tended to be small, smart Jewish girls with substantial collections of sweater sets and organized mothers who planned their daughters' lives sensibly, including cheerful holiday activities and outings. A couple of these friends were in Florida for Easter break; the ones who were around had plans to go clothes shopping, or to eat lunch in Chinatown, or ice skate at the rink in Riverdale. They called for me to join them. But we had no money and, besides, I didn't want to leave my brother alone. For even Nick's more working-class, tough-boy friends had Easter dinners and Easter suits, a couple of days in Philadelphia or Washington, a grandma up from Scranton for the holidays. So we ended up hanging out at our home away from home—Bronx Park and the Botanical Gardens.

It was one of those bitter Aprils that feel more like February, but still we took off for the woods. We'd ice skate and look for arrowheads, Nick suggested. But the Twin Lakes, we discovered, were starting to thaw, and the paths in the woods were muddy and slicked with loosening ice so it was hard for us to walk very far comfortably.

Since the Conservatory, and not the woods, was my realm, I wasn't particularly troubled. But for Nick, eager to lift his spirits with treks along the ponds and river, the conditions were disheartening.

I was not unhappy in the hothouse reading and drawing the holiday lilies they'd planted all around; Nicky though, trying his luck in the woods again and again, would return cold and wet and restless. Finally one of his boot soles wore down to a wide hole and the freezing forest floor and wet riverbank became impossible, and Nick joined me for good in the greenhouse. But stuck indoors, Nicky was like a monkey loose in a palace, ignoring the "no running" signs, racing and crashing into trees and glass. We had to find something to keep him busy and out of trouble. It occurred to me that we should try to volunteer here in the Gardens. We'd had months of experience helping our mother repot her plants, so how could they not want us! And except for a fleeting feeling of guilt for our constant theft of soil from this place that had given us so many days of joy, I felt suddenly full of hope.

"Volunteer?" Nicky said, "That's for rich sissies. They'll make us serve tea or something."

Luckily some workmen were digging up bulbs along the borders of the hall. Crouched down against the glass, catching the light and heat, they gave off waves of physical contentedness. And I could see Nicky warming to their strong, dark bodies. My brother was strong and dark and so was our father, and every cell in his young body felt intense camaraderie with other strong dark bodies, wherever they were. Nick's room was a temple of worship to his strong dark heroes, one wall plastered with the photographs of Indian chiefs, the other with pictures of Black blues guitarists, all looking out at him, their black eyes charging him, I'm sure he thought, to keep up the struggle on whatever front. Politics. Music. Hand to hand combat in the woods, if it came to that.

"Maybe we'll get to plant in the earth," he said.

"Why not?" I said.

"But I'm not serving at any of the ladies teas. And I'm not doing any fruity flower arrangements."

72

I nodded, and we took off.

The Education and Volunteer Office, I knew from a week-long rose garden program I'd done the summer before with my friend Teeny, was at the north end of the Gardens in the museum and administration building. How I loved this building with its dark mahogany paneling, formal drawing rooms where they *did* serve tea from time to time, and cheerful laboratories up on the second floor. But most of all, I loved the auditorium, where most any hour you could see a film on the life cycle of some plant or other narrated by a deep knowing voice, which more than once had sounded to me like the voice of God.

That day as we passed the auditorium to get to the Education Office, we saw that a film was showing about the life of water lilies. We stood at the door, lured by the splash of color and the deep resounding tones of the narrator. It was a beautifully filmed study which speeded up the flowers' glorious unfolding. I'd seen it before and loved it. But that day, standing at the door, watching the quick bloom, I couldn't help but imagine equally quick deaths, and I felt a terrible stab of sadness about life passing, and pulled Nicky's jacket for us to be off and doing something.

Miss DiFrancesco was in charge of the Volunteer Services at the Gardens, and I knew her from the summer. She was a thin, pale woman of about thirty, pre-Raphaelite I'd say now, but back then I thought nun-like—pale and unadorned except for thin wire-rimmed glasses perched on a fine bony nose. Her sisters were nuns, my friend Teeny said she'd heard, but Miss DiFrancesco's love of science had made her bypass the convent for college, graduate school, and the Bronx Botanical Gardens. I'd been fascinated by the story— the earnest, dutiful sisters; the quiet, sober woman—an appealing contrast to my own family, the recklessness and the bombast.

Miss DiFrancesco was working at her desk when we arrived. She remembered my name. She remembered my weeding skills. She said she hoped I was coming to help out again.

I said, yes, and so was my brother, introducing Nicky, who shook

73

her hand too heartily, I thought, embarrassing me. The movie and her smile evidently had warmed him to our project.

"Not enough young people think about helping"

I said, "We didn't want to make vacation plans. We wanted to devote our vacation time to helping others. And flowers," blushing as I spoke.

Nicky said, "I like to work with my hands. I'm very strong."

And again I felt embarrassed. He was sounding like our father on a "working man" riff. Here in my rarified gardens.

"I can see you're strong, Nick," she said. "Let's see those hands."

Nicky held out his hands, which were beautiful and big, and she said, "How about some digging and a little building?"

And my brother beamed.

Could she see we were poor? Did it show in Nick's nervous hands? My needy eyes? Had she spotted the broken boot? She said, "There's a lunch and dinner stipend for Easter volunteers because we're really short on help right now and particularly grateful."

Charity or not, we took it. Every day from nine to five, we were there. In the morning I'd help Miss DiFrancesco in the office and water the vegetables she was growing as part of her plant nutrition research. Afternoons, I'd join Nicky planting over at the Conservatory.

The first afternoon when I went to the palm room to meet him, I couldn't find him. For one scary moment, I was sure he'd gotten bored again and had climbed one of the trees. But looking up, I couldn't see him, just a canopy of leaves and bunches of green bananas, panes of glass, and gray sky. He'd probably run off without finishing the first day, ruining everything.

Then I saw him kneeling at the side of the room by a bay of lilies. He was with one of the men we'd seen digging the day before. Down in the earth, dirty and happy.

"Lucy," Nick called.

"Get a spade, Lucy," the man said. "I'm Jack. Come, Lucy, we'll all work together."

At the end of the day, it was hard to leave, and trekking home up

Spider Hill—the sloping stretch of meadow connecting Bronx Park with Mosholu—we braced ourselves for our mother, who seemed all the more frightening a prospect after our happy day. But she was out cold when we got home and, having already eaten supper in the museum cafeteria and feeling tired from the day's work, we fell asleep, happy, if weary, from our labors.

The next day was equally wonderful. Miss DiFrancesco praised everything I did: how well I stacked paper, how well I labeled folders. Jack said we were born workers. He said we had the work ethic. Lots of kids didn't. There were lots of brats out there. Lots of kids who took everything for granted and never did a thing for anyone. We were different. And we had the hands to show it.

We listened to him go on, looking at our hands, looking at his hands, finally looking at each other. I knew we were thinking the same thing. Daddy. How we missed him. His speeches. About brats, about hands. How we missed his hands. Not the hitting hands, but the cooking hands, the hands that fixed a thousand things, made a million gestures, that his brutality had knocked out of our memory, and now a winter and spring alone with our poor mother was making us remember, or imagine we did.

I saw Nicky distract himself from thought in hurried digging with Jack, but I couldn't shake the thought of our father from my mind, and I sat in the dirt, remembering back to when he first left. How we'd felt hopeful and almost happy with him gone. How we'd made supper, lured our mother from her room and into the kitchen with promises of a smooth swallowable meal, washed dishes, done homework and gone to sleep in a quiet house. When our mother cried, we'd said, "But you two hate each other. Now it's better." And she would shake her head and tell us that one day we'd understand about mushy mixed-up feelings. Now, looking at Nicky and Jack— whose hair was a black-blue like our father's—I thought I did.

Walking home that night, I asked Nicky if he thought our father was ever coming back.

He shrugged.

"I didn't figure it would turn out like this," I said.

And Nicky said, "Yeah. When we told her this was better, we meant peace and quiet. Right? But not this. Right?"

When he was nervous, Nicky would say, "right?" I nodded several times, to calm him and reassure him that I too had not figured on absolutely no Sunday breakfasts with eggs, sausage, potatoes and pancakes, no stories about the infantry, no coaching in boxing as the Friday night fights played on the TV, no joyous make-up scenes after fights, no gooey reunions with jelly donuts when he'd return contrite from a couple of days of "R and R" at Grandma Bess's apartment.

That night up in our apartment, our mother began the evening rewiring some lamps, and then abandoned that for repotting, furious with us for being useless and self-centered in not bringing home fresh dirt from the Gardens when she had asked for it and we'd known how choked the roots were feeling.

"What do you want?" Nicky screamed. "You want dirt, you got dirt!" He kicked at the heaps of debris—electrical wires and papers and clothing from the week's projects—that she was too strung out and wiped out to take down to the garbage room. "Heaps of dirt, heaps of shit . . . here." He screamed and kicked.

And our mother said, "For that you're in trouble," and slapped his face.

"She misses him. Right?" Nick said to me, biting his knuckles so he wouldn't slap her back. "And she thinks we miss him, so she's being both mother and father. Thanks, Mom," he said.

"Shut up, you fresh boy," she said, staggering to her room. "Or else I'll slap your face. I promise I will this time," she called, evidently having forgotten her recent wallop.

"Now there's a novel idea. Right?" Nicky said, sitting on his fists.

That night decided things. The craziness had gone too far. We wanted him back; we wanted her back. We'd managed to get jobs, we'd manage to get our family together again. But it meant playing our cards right.

The next day was our last day at the Gardens and we said

goodbye to Miss DiFrancesco and Jack. I felt like we were kids in a fairy tale, setting out from one set of parents, traveling in the forest to another. And walking down the Conservatory's wide path with its stretch of towering oaks, I prayed that our tale end happily on the other side of the woods. At the phone booth near the railroad station, we called our father at Liberty's and told him we needed to talk to him about a thing or two.

In his rare peaceful moments, our father was a talented analyst of human character. And the next day, a Saturday, away from the chaos of home, in relatively civilized calm, we tried to appeal to that side of him. The cold had suddenly broken and as we walked beside him around the Village streets, we didn't say we missed him, or tell him about our mother and the drugs, afraid the truth would scare him off. But in everything we said, we set out to win him back.

Nick began. "We're not saying Liberty's not a nice person, Dad. But did you ever notice how she always tells you how nice she is? Did you ever notice how she always says, 'I'm the kind of person who can't abide cruelty.' Or, 'I'm the kind of human being who cannot tolerate stupidity'?"

And then I said, "But you know what, Dad? She's the one who's cruel and stupid."

And then we told him how she had said she was going to be our mother, and looked into our eyes with phony compassion, told him how it was mean and moronic for her to say what she said, how it had hurt us and scared us.

"Jesus. You poor kids," he said, taking it well.

But it was getting late, he said. He put us on the subway home.

The next day, Sunday, we called him early. He'd stayed cool yesterday; maybe he'd really listen to us today. We asked him to meet us as soon as he could and he agreed.

Block after block, walking beside him, we explored Liberty's character. Did he notice that she could be "a real bore"? I tried. My father stayed calm. "And a phony," Nick said. Then we went into details: the phony accent, the phony niceness, the real crudeness and meanness. "Once she told me I was a bad dishwasher," I said. "And she's not," Nick cried. "And once she told Nick he should chew with his mouth closed, but he wasn't chewing," I explained, "just spitting out her disgusting noodles."

Our father walked beside us, silent. Now and then he said, "Poor kids." Nothing more. Finally, frustrated, we both began to cry.

"She's got a lot of nerve. . . . Who does she think she is? I mean she's not our mother!" I blubbered

"Don't *I* know," he said. "She's not your mother at all. . . ."

And then his face got all twisted, and for a moment I thought I'd gone too far and ruined everything and he was going to hit me. But he started laughing.

"The woman's a total dud. And I'm more than a fool to have been taken in by a few stupid sauces. God save me from the *balebustas* of this world."

Then he grabbed our hands and kissed them and his voice got low and sad. "I'm so sorry, kids," he said.

We felt his nose begin to run in our hands and we realized he was crying, and our hearts jumped with joy. We kissed him hard to show we loved him still and, if he came back, would never hold a grudge.

"I want to come home," he said. "Jesus Christ, kids, I really want to come home."

In anticipation of his return, we scrubbed and polished till the apartment shined. When he appeared at the door the next week, we announced that our mother had cleaned to welcome him back.

"Did not," she called from her room. "My cleaning days are over. If the man wants clean, he can go back to lard-legs Liberty. Or his whore mother."

I remember grabbing my father's hand and saying, "She doesn't mean it. Please don't go."

"I'll never leave again," he said.

"A likely story," my mother called from her room. "Give the weakling time and see what ensues."

"You're being mean," I called to her.

"Yeah," Nicky echoed. "He's trying."

And again we took his hand. By now our memories of his excesses were fading, and compared to our actively maniacal mother sequestered down the hall, he seemed reasonable, his past transgressions forgiven.

"I'm your father and husband and I love you," he said.

"A beautiful sentiment and beautifully phrased," my mother called. "Now excuse me while I vomit."

I can still remember how we watched our father to see if his face was tensing, his arms clenching, getting ready to attack. But he was doubled up with laughter.

"She's still so adorable," he said, rubbing tears from his eyes.

"Oh, shut your hole, prickless wonder," she called, "before I shut it for you!"

9

Our Idas

All spring, after his return, we delighted in our powers—our rhetoric, which had swayed him; our character, which had won him. And
we delighted in *his* powers—his powerful love for us and her. But by
summer things had grown worse than ever. His being back seemed
only a daily reminder to her that he'd been gone, that after all she'd
put up with *he'd* abandoned *her*. Every day she was higher than the
day before, and his "I love you" and "I'm so sorry" talk quickly dried
up, replaced by pledges to kill her by morning. The war was on
again, but wilder than ever before.

"Kill me now," she'd cry—in place of her old "Calm down,
Ralphie. . . . Breathe. . . . Rest the fatigue. . . ." Emboldened by drugs,
she'd break a vase or jar, wave a shard in the air, call, "Kill me now,
oh big soldier hero man. . . . Let's see you try."

Soon Nicky and I tried to monitor their every word and movement. For without our intervention, our tearful calls for crucial
truces, one or both of them would soon be dead. Summer to fall,
fall to winter, day after day, we posted ourselves at the edge of their
battlefield.

In time, as their new, enhanced war raged on and on, we got
jaded. It often seemed a show put on for us. And more than once
we wondered if, without us there to watch, it would have ceased to
run. As our exhaustion and resentment grew, we let their fights go

on longer, pulled them apart later, even slept through some putative "close calls." But at the beginning of its run, the year he came back from Liberty—and the next couple of blurry years at the center of our childhoods—we were a little chorus at the side of the stage, chronicling their deeds, crying for peace.

Like most actors with a little success, our parents became contemptuous of their public. Once he drove her to a nearby hospital with a renowned psychiatric service to "dry her out and fix her up." Nick and I sat alone at the kitchen table, relieved and scared, loving our mother, yet having come to fear her as much as we'd feared him.

We heard him at the door, back from the hospital. Then we saw him stride toward the kitchen.

We stood to greet him, our lone guardian now. We raised our arms to cry on him. And then *she* walked in.

"Fooled you," they both screamed, jumping up and down and laughing wildly, like quiz show winners. "Got you!"

I still remember that moment—catching my tears, releasing my laughter, as commanded.

"I didn't fit in, to say the least," my mother said, blowing happy tears from her nose, distracted from her sorrow by the car ride and drama.

"Serious stuff over there," my father said. "Majorly serious illness."

And then they competed for the stage, describing and imitating the people who'd talked to devils, sung into coffee cups, laughed with loved ones who hung in the air.

"Real nuts," they agreed, clasped in each other's arms. "Bona fide crazies."

Their reunions those days were as flashy as their battles. Vowing to turn over a "new leaf"—a term and concept they both came to like equally—they'd pump each other's hand like a vaudeville team. Sometimes a handshake was followed by "contracts" which we were asked to sign as witnesses of their intentions for the new era. To make good on their promises, they'd hold "planning meetings," where Nick and I were invited to say how we might accomplish goals. Then we all hugged. For a couple of days or weeks, we rejoiced in peace.

How heady those celebrations! Our parents would hail our virtues as a family, which included superior beauty, humor, intelligence, emotional sensitivity, taste buds, musical pitch, and physical grace. All families have their myths that make them feel special, but chaotic, crazy families hold to their myths as if life depended on them. In their brief peaceful respites, our parents would salute each other like heroes, praising each other's eyes, strong chins, overall bone structures, while doing imitations of weak-eyed and weak-chinned slobs in the neighborhood. They'd include Nicky and me in their praises, for even if we weren't as lean as they were—worrying over the years had made us put on weight—the potential beneath our chub was apparent, they claimed. Good bones meant a lot in life—as did good musculature and good eyes and chins. They meant character and values and depth and decency. Without them you were lost, which our family was not. And our family had humor! The day after a big fight, if he hadn't left, they'd make a joke of their near bloodbath, mimicking each other's lunges or plunges, or moving on to something else they now found equally amusing: our terror, a neighbor's angry shout to be quiet, the neighbor's stupid voice or walk or mother-in-law. Inviting us to join the fun.

Then it would start up again. With or without blood. With or without cops. More and more of the same.

What got us through those times? Our father was still a "working stiff" those years, which meant in and out of work and fights. Our mother still taught dance, but stayed home as many days as she showed up. There was Nan, of course, to help us through. Many days, through and after the Liberty years, she'd come by after work, bringing the best meats and the freshest vegetables. If she was down, our mother wouldn't notice; if she was high, she'd scream. What's *that*? she'd shout at Nan's platters—into which Nan, never having learned to cook, had steamed all her sad sweet love. A gray lamb chop? You think I can swallow a fat gray lamb chop? You'll kill me! Go away, stupid old lady!

But besides Nan, there were neighbors, whose kindness we really did depend on, if not financially, in countless other ways. The three apartments we lived in each had a special neighbor. In our first building, before our mother went under, we'd had a neighbor named Ida, a jolly domestic talent who tried to supplement our mother's odd daily fare and teach her to cook. When we moved across the street to the next building down the Parkway, we were miserable about leaving Ida. But then in our new building there was another neighbor also miraculously named Ida, and in our next apartment in the next building too, another Ida, each new Ida as ardent as the last about fixing our family with food. How crazy this coincidence of roly-poly Idas. Back then, though, we took our Idas' omnipresence for granted, using Ida between us to mean "helpful lady neighbor," which Nick convinced me was its original meaning in Yiddish.

All three of our Idas, though American born, often abandoned English for a rapid animated Yiddish as they coached our mother on techniques for keeping a home and a man. Somehow we understood, though our mother, judging from the bored, bewildered look on her face as each Ida went on and on, seemed to make out little of the language she'd learned at her mother's knee. Poor Idas. How their eyes glistened with hope for this pretty young girl, whom each was sure, given proper guidance, could be transformed into a bona fide *balebusta* who would keep our father happy and calm. Till that happy time they offered their own casseroles, soups, and healthful fruit-based desserts. Though few religious notions have ever claimed me, looking back I can't help but see our Idas as heaven sent. How else explain this wondrous trinity?

The first Ida's husband was a bandleader who went by the name of Bobo Martin instead of his real name, Bernard Morgenbesser, attempting to pass as much as he could for a Cuban or Italian or, as he liked to say, *Cubalian*. He had a pencil-thin Latin lover moustache, white skin, dyed hair the color of eggplant, and sad black Jewish eyes. He would schlep amplifiers up and down the stairs cursing in Yiddish; but because he was desperate for gigs, and saw everyone as a potential "buyer," he'd break into pigeon Spanish or Italian for most any neighbor, dropping his equipment and raising one arm in the air, hugging his belly with the other as if making ready to rumba.

Some nights he'd take his son, Jerry, his daughter, Ellie, and Nicky and me with him to help carry and set up ostensibly, but I think now actually to give Ida some time after her day of cooking and baking, to clean up and refuel—and our mother some time to relax after her ordeals with our father. We'd go to ballrooms in the Bronx and Queens mostly, fluorescent-lit catering halls where we'd hang out in the lobby nibbling meatballs and Hawaiian chicken off of tiny plates. Sometimes we'd find an empty office and practice dancing together to the tunes of the Bobo Martin "orchestra." Ellie and Jerry were much older than us and gave us lots of tips about the mambo and tango. That they tolerated us, so young and so heartily adopted by their mother and father, speaks to great generosity of character I realized later on, but at the time I took their goodness for granted. At home, I'd expect them to save us cookies and, at the halls, to let us come up on the stage to sing alongside them at the mike once the party had wound down.

Jerry, who was five years older than Nicky, played the clarinet and wrote and sang his own songs. His favorite was "Miami Beach Schlepper," based on his unrequited love for the daughter of the hotel owner for whom Bobo worked Christmases. Jerry would blow a few sad lines of melody, then sing his sad song. "I watch you in the water and I long to be your porter. On your chaise you lie and I want to dust your thigh. Each day at your table, I want to deliver to you a cable. I pull out your chair, but you don't know me from anywhere. I'm just your Miami Beach Schlepper. . . ." Then he'd do a slow dignified box step, embrace himself and bow, whispering, "I'll never forget you, Wanda."

Ellie, who was a teenager when we met her, sang Eddie Fisher songs. Most often she sang "Oh my Papa," making herself cry. Bobo used to come up to the mike and kiss her when she finished, turning to the band—which was packing up—and saying, "Is this a daughter, or what?"

Nicky and I had standing invitations to sing our own solos. Nick usually sang, "Joe Hill" or "The Banks are Made of Marble." And Bobo, whom my mother had explained was "apolitical as the kitchen floor but as good-hearted as they come," would always turn to the band and say, "Nick here's a regular little Red. Let's have a hand for little Nikolai."

I was too shy to sing a solo, but joined in on the quartet we usually did just before we left the hall. Our favorite number was "If I Knew You Were Coming I'd a Baked a Cake," which we sang in four-part harmony, blending so beautifully, we thought, that we'd get all tingly. "How d'ya do, how d'ya do, how d'ya do," is how the song ends. But Ellie, Jerry, and even Nicky agreed on a new arrangement so that a fourth "How d'ya do" was added, which I sang, smiling out at the busboys clearing tables, my voice tremulous with possibility.

The second Ida lived with her family in the apartment just below our apartment. Ida's younger daughter, Nancy, a skinny little laughing thing they'd nicknamed Teeny, was my age, and her son, Billy, was Nick's age. As soon as we moved in, the families joined forces—at least the mothers and children—and our two apartments, when fathers weren't around, became a "poor man's" duplex as the mothers liked to say. Our front doors usually open, we'd run in and out of each other's house; sometimes we'd climb up or down to each other on the fire escape. And then there was the joy of the garbage dumbwaiter—on which Teeny and I would send back and forth scribbled messages and jokes, homework, and sweaters we wanted to swap for the next day. Adults used the dumbwaiter socially too, and many days I'd come home from school to find my mother stationed in the kitchen at the dumbwaiter door, chatting with Ida Klein. I can still see my mother sitting there on the step stool, facing the dark well, listening to Ida whose voice boomed into our kitchen with urgent messages like: "I'm telling you, Tip, there's always time to throw a chicken and some vegetables into a large pot."

Ida Klein was my first real coach in domestic life, and I'd love to watch her make applesauce in her food mill, protect her porcelain kitchen sink from scratches with a well placed wash cloth, throw in those extra onions that meant the difference, she insisted, between a real or half-hearted pot roast. As my mother grew more distracted, Ida turned to me as I turned to her. "Your mama's tired, Lucy," she'd say. "You help her out." And she'd start her instruction.

I'd follow Ida around asking questions, like how do you know when a baked apple is truly baked, and how can you be sure you've gotten all the suds off the floor. Some of these were sincere and important to me—my mother, of course, would choke on food that wasn't soft—but other questions I asked Ida just to feel close to her and to make her feel important, so she'd be on my side if and when I really needed her. When Ida Klein would explain to me her firm belief in the vinegar after-wash for kitchen floors, and demonstrate its application, I'd nod enthusiastically even though my heart was yearning for more tips on food preparation. From the floor, where she was crawling to scrub, she'd call up and say, "Teeny doesn't pay attention. So who's going to be in better shape for life later on? I'm betting on Lucy, Teeny." Which would make Teeny produce a little whinny of a laugh and gallop from the kitchen, where I'd remain with Ida, rinsing the rag for her as needed.

The third Ida came into our lives a little later, when to escape the swirls of stain Grandpa Jesse had left us with years before, my mother moved us to an almost identical apartment across the court, with bright white walls and no memories of abandonment and betrayal. My mother, while in the middle of a drug binge, from time to time had initiated projects to cover her father's fake wood, but her heart wasn't in it and, after a dab or two of primer, she'd give up in tears and fury. In time, moving seemed the only solution, and one fall a couple of years after Liberty, when my father was away again, she packed us up and, box by box, we made our way to our third Bronx apartment—and our third Ida.

This final Ida, a widow with grown children, spent her days collecting used clothing for the local synagogue's monthly rummage sale. "The shmata chairman," my father called her when he came back. And though we adored this Ida, we'd end up laughing, wanting to encourage his involvement, however condescending, in local life and keep him from running away yet again to Greenwich Village, where, our laughter tried to remind him, there might be no shmata chairmen, but neither were there appreciative children.

To her face, however, we called the third Ida "Tanta Ida," as she requested, respecting this busy woman enormously for her frisky altruism which had her washing, ironing, and folding all rummage contributions, as well as cooking when her hectic sisterhood schedule allowed. Big pots of soup were her specialty, which she'd leave at our door; and Nick and I would reciprocate by picking up old clothes from top-floor walk-ups as far north as the Yonkers line. Our mother, by this time, was floating off much of the time and the final Ida had to settle for our mother's thanks in the form of vacant smiles and smoky kisses blown distractedly across the hallway. Indeed as she deteriorated and withdrew more and more, our mother grew less appreciative of our kindly neighbors, and more jealous, although in a rather half-hearted, preoccupied way.

"You lousy kids don't need me anyway. You got your Idas. Always have and always will," she'd say. "Thank God for that, I guess."

By now the first Ida had moved to Mount Vernon, and the second was preoccupied with Teeny's concentration problems and, I suspect now, a little hurt by our mother's rarer and rarer gestures of gratitude.

"Of course, we need you," we'd both say, meaning our old mother, not the lunatic staring us down, chanting, "Yeah, yeah," as she wandered back to her room, leaving us largely to each other's care and the attentions of the final Ida.

10

Pohogo

Summers, those years, also brought us relief. Somehow, despite whatever else was going on—a new girlfriend on the side for him, the old phobias front and center for her, a winter and spring of the usual bouts and binges—we managed for the two months of summer to escape the worst of our lives.

If in those bad times our parents started to seem like a set of weird twins—if not identical, then still similar enough in their odd energies and habits to make life apart for any length of time seem strange—in summer some purer, more authentic selves appeared. Our father became the bachelor he had wanted to be since he'd come back from the war, and we happily abandoned him to the city. Our mother became something like the old Tippy, taking us to a lake community about an hour from home where, in the northern-most reaches of Westchester county, Nicky and I stored up enough days and nights of joy to carry us through the rest of the year.

It was Alice, an old school friend of my mother's, who brought us to Pohogo. Visiting our apartment one day, watching my mother jump around, she offered her a job as dance teacher at the Pohogo Colony Day Camp, which she ran. She described the colony—the people, the music and fun, the vast lake—with such energy and en-thusiasm that before she walked out the door Nicky and I were hunting for our bathing suits, ready to dive into a new life.

I still remember our first visit to Pohogo. The winding lanes, the riotous gardens, the lake which, shimmering in the summer light, reached far beyond our view promising unseen, unimaginable pleasure. But most of all I remember the friendly, charming people, as quirky as our parents but, to our delight, nowhere as crazy. It was a beastly hot day, that first day we came to inspect Pohogo Colony, but the folks at Pohogo managed to turn it into a delight.

What happened was that our dog, Rosie, like all dogs, was banned from the Pohogo beach and Nicky and I had to take turns checking on her in our car in the blistering parking lot, bringing her Dixie cups of water. The woman from the beach committee manning the gate must have felt sorry for us scurrying back and forth. On our fifth or so check, she said: "I got an idea. Let's make this Dog Day." And after chatting with a few other locals on the beach, she made it official. And that afternoon, not only Rosie but dogs from all around Pohogo Colony—as word spread—were brought to the beach to loaf and swim. Though dogs were never allowed to swim in the lake again, when I think of Pohogo, I always see dogs swimming and sunning, Rosie lying beside us on the diving raft sporting our mother's black sunglasses and red bandana, and feel the thrill of that pure, unexpected joy.

Over the years our mother had regaled us with stories of her boarding schools filled with barns and gardens and swimming holes, and students and teachers who stayed up late at night translating French poems and Russian stories, falling asleep on haystacks. Pohogo, that first June day, made me think of those places. Seeing our mother's tired face glow with youth as she watched our dog paddle beside us in the glistening lake, I thought, This was *our* New Jefferson, *our* Summer Valley, remembering the names of all those schools and the possibility they had promised her, feeling full of my own fresh hopes as I splashed about.

But returning to the city from this visit, I was riddled with anxiety. I knew I had to have Pohogo in my life, but I knew our father would be against our going just as he had been against our keeping Rosie, who had just recently wandered into our lives. His post-Liberty

mellow was totally gone by now, and he was back to declaiming his
beliefs again. Everything we liked was bourgeois: music lessons,
dance classes, making fudge and brownies. Even the dog, when she
appeared a month earlier, had been declared "middle-class," which
meant, as with all his other prejudiced judgments, that *he* never had
one when he was growing up. So, we shouldn't.

Teeny's father had found the stray mutt out on the street, on his
way home from work. The dog was all fur and bones with black
markings around its eyes giving it the sad weary look of a coal
miner, and Nicky and I claimed her in a flash. We were already familiar with our father's anti dog-as-house-pet stance, but we
thought the dog's special raggedness might qualify her as a proletar-
ian pet and win her to our father's heart. No such luck. Taking one
look at the scraggly white and black hound, our father had
screamed, "It's me or the bitch."

"That's easy," our mother had shouted, carrying the pup off to
her bed to hang out and watch television beside her.

Our father stayed, but he still complained bitterly about the dog,
which we named after Nan's sister, who, Nan said, had the sweetest
eyes in the world before she died in an oven. And coming back from
our visit to the lake, we were afraid he'd fight us fiercely on Pohogo,
since he'd lost to us on Rosie.

We were right. When we began begging to be allowed to spend
the summer there, we heard: "*I* never went to the country. *I* was perfectly happy playing in the hydrants on the Lower East Side." We
heard we were "*petit bourgeois* brats." And then we heard: "It's either
me or Pohogo."

For days he repeated his challenge. Finally, one day as he
screamed on and on about the corruption of resort areas, our
mother, by now fighting frustration with drugs, staggered from her
room and shouted, "Deprive my children of country air and fun just
to indulge a posturing Pitt Street gutter snipe? Nossirree, buster. Absolutely, positively, nossiree."

"Have it your way!" he said. "Just know I don't approve."

Usually, when our mother started taking drugs I wanted to smack her, but that day, watching her victory, I hugged her in appreciation. For this time, her drug scheme had actually worked—a "little smidgen" had allowed her to accomplish her project. Pohogo we would go!

How happy I felt watching our mother stagger defiantly from the room and busy herself "packing," which meant she emptied the contents of closets and bureaus on the floor. And then Nicky and I, while she finally slept, poked through the debris to gather the shorts and jeans and bathing suits we'd be needing for the summer.

What joy! High on the spirit of the place, our mother took no drugs at Lake Pohogo. During the day, the children of Pohogo went to Alice's Pohogo Colony Day Camp, where our mother was the "dance specialist." The drama specialist was Sally Randolph, a blacklisted Hollywood actress whose husband, Lance was a blacklisted scriptwriter, who, when he wasn't back in their cabin pounding out screenplays under a pseudonym to keep them going, served as the Pohogo Colony Day Camp "script specialist." Our "music specialist" was Duane, a blacklisted composer who tried to play his movie themes for us instead of leading us in song. Luckily though, his teenage son, Andy, rumored to be Pete Seeger's godson and traumatized, it seemed, from the Hollywood purge, followed his father around with a guitar in his arms and the words to yet another folk song on his lips.

Like countless other colonies within twenty miles of it, Pohogo Colony had been founded in the thirties to fulfill a social vision, and its constitution dedicated the colony to advancing "a fresh start for mankind in the fresh air." But Pohogo was the most playful of the local colonies—a fact we gleaned that first day from the dog swim— and the most artistic with its Hollywood and non-Hollywood residents alike eager to foster the fresh start for humanity with spirited extravaganzas produced by the "guest artists."

Our first year at Pohogo Lance wrote a play about the men who build tunnels. Duane wrote songs for it. Nicky, who was thirteen, with dark velvet eyes and a deep melting voice, got to play the leader of a work crew who guides the other men out of a frighten-

92

ing cave-in up to the top of the earth.

With piercing accusation as the residents of the lake looked on in the summer night, Nicky sang: "*Why must we die in the bowels of the world? Don't we need air like the rich? / Why must my child live a father-less life? Why keep me trapped in this ditch?*" And then a low lament, "*Why, oh why, oh why, oh why?*" which all of us other trapped workers joined in on, our voices rising to such heights that the earth cracked opened and we climbed out and joined our wives and children—the audience—for a joyous party.

Our mother was a favorite here, as she'd been in the Bronx in the early days. Back home recently, though, as our circumstances and she became weirder and weirder, she'd lost her special standing as neighborhood elf, and the rare times she emerged to participate in neighborhood life, she contorted herself into the shape of those around her, even taking up Mah Jong to win some normal status for her and us. Which never happened. But here at Pohogo, she was in her element and as natural and happy and loved as she'd been in her finest Miss Tippy days.

Still, to our father Pohogo was "fancy" and "phony" and, in his sporadic weekend visits, he'd accuse her of thinking she was entitled to this life because of her "fancy shmancy" "phony baloney" child-hood in boarding schools. The fact that Pohogo wasn't luxurious at all, that we lived in a two-room cabin and that our mother worked at camp six days a week to keep us there didn't dispel his class accu-sations. And the fact that the rest of the "specialists," despite their Hollywood days, were almost as down and out as we were, didn't count for much to him either. But we didn't really care. At Pohogo we were largely spared his rumblings. He visited only three or four times each summer, largely boycotting our cabin as if it were an ostentatious Newport mansion, leaving us in peace.

For three summers, Nicky and I knew friendships we'd never known before. Like us, our Pohogo friends were outcasts, especially the new arrivals from Hollywood. In the winter, like us, they went to public schools, hiding the truth about their families—the lack of work, the politics, for one or two the threat of jail. So what if our secret included in addition to our parents' politics and our financial hardships, beatings and drugs and abandonment? And so what if we didn't tell our Pohogo friends the exact details of our lives? When one of them would cry, recounting her last look at her pool before the family had to get in the car to drive east, or about having to sell jewels for grocery money, Nicky and I nodded in sympathy. Our pain had been different, but here at Pohogo, we were all in it to-gether, our Hollywood friends and us.

The third year, though, everything changed.

It had become routine for our father to be gone when we got back in September, using his summer freedom to find a new girl-friend. But, in truth, when we returned from summers and found the apartment empty, our mother, calmed by Pohogo, seemed to ac-cept it, even finding some of her old post-War pity for our father. "Daddy needs a vacation, I guess," she'd say. "A *fall* camp? For *fa-thers*?" I asked the first time. Until I understood: He'd left us again. But, like her, I was still too happy from the lake to care much, and frankly, like her, relieved by the reprieve from his lunacy.

But that third summer our father came to like Pohogo, and to spend time there. And his sudden presence in her magical retreat robbed her of the escape she so sorely needed and the opportunity for that fresh start in life she thought she had found for us at last.

Camp Pohogo was big on camp-outs, and Nicky and I became expert at starting fires and campfire cooking. Of course, our outdoor skills were only an extension of our indoor domestic skills and forced self-sufficiency, a fact that I didn't want anyone to know, re-flecting as it did on our family. I tried to hide my skills outside of the family, but Nicky showed them off for all to see every chance he got, winning "best outdoor camper" award, year after year. I remem-ber one of his acceptance speeches, Nick standing in front of a fire of his making, saying, "You never know when you'll have to live outside. Every person should learn outdoors skills in case." How ashamed I was as my brother beamed before the whole camp.

Anyway, everywhere you looked back then, Nicky was starting a campfire and cooking. Back at our cabin, he'd often show off his expanding repertoire to our relaxed and appreciative mother, grilling and boiling and even baking over the coals. And one day, when our father was up, Nicky made a surprise supper out at the little stone pit we'd built near the path to the woods. It was rabbit, which Nick had killed in the field with his bow and arrow, and though neither my mother nor I could manage to eat any part of the animal stretched out on the grate, crucified and scorched, my father and Nicky wolfed the creature down.

"I thank you, son," my father said, with unexpected solemnity. "I ate a lot of rabbit during the war. I take this meal as a sign of your recognition of what I suffered as a soldier. I thank you man to man."

My mother and I were eating our roasted potatoes but we looked across the little card table to each other. And then I tried to catch Nicky's eye too to laugh a little at the big pompous spiel. But Nicky was standing up, shaking our father's hand as if he'd gotten another cook-out award. And then he had his head on my father's shoulder and, for a moment, it was hard to tell where one ended and the other one began. What about me? I thought. *I'd* set the table, picked the dandelion greens, scrubbed the potatoes. So what if I don't kill things. Don't I count?

Just then we heard a rustle in the woods. Dammit, more rabbit, I thought as Nicky lifted his bow. But it was an old, tall and skinny, pug-nosed man in a white straw hat and chinos. He extended his hand and said, "Will Woolsey. I smelled your rabbit."

"*Big* Will Woolsey?" my father said.

"Some call me that," the old man said, blushing.

"From the Wobblies?"

Big Will nodded and sat down on the chair my father offered. "We hobos ate our fair share of rabbit."

And Nick pulled up a chair, and said, "*I'm* planning on being a hobo."

"You don't plan on it. It just happens to you. Hard times," the man said.

95

"I think I want to be one anyway. For a while. It teaches you stuff so you can take care of yourself. I mean . . . if you ever have to."

I wanted to join in and say, We've planned on running away if we have to. Just the two of us.

For once or twice that winter, walking the streets late at night, depleted from refereeing round after round of a fight, we'd thought about not going back. Would it come to that? we'd wondered to each other, reassuring ourselves, scaring ourselves with the thought of a life beyond our parents and our home.

But it was a secret and, besides, nobody would have listened to anything I said. Big Will ate the rabbit, his eyes on the young *brave* who had caught it and skinned it and cooked it. Our father was looking between Nick and Big Will, explaining how the old man had been the bravest labor leader in the west, how he broke heads and built unions, how he'd been a Wobbly leader and a communist. Again, my father was standing like an awards master.

I wanted to say, I know about labor. I did a report on the International Ladies Garment Workers Union that got an Excellent plus. I interviewed Nan for it.

But they wouldn't have listened. Nan was never a hobo. She just rented rooms in other people's apartments, cooked her food on regular stoves when it was convenient for other people to have her in their kitchen, and hunched over a sewing machine every day, till her back was bent for good.

"My Nan is *almost* a hobo," I tried. I meant the uncertainty of her existence, coming to America alone, having Tippy alone, sleeping alone in her narrow boarder's bed.

"Lucy's crazy," Nicky said. "Nan's sweet, but she's no hobo. And no labor leader. Maybe a hard-working rank-and-filer, I'll grant her that."

What sort of talk was this? I was used to my brother's rhetoric. Speeches in the schoolyard, one last year in a school assembly on just and unjust wars in human history. But now we were home, among ourselves. Why was he making a speech? And talking that way about Nan!

Then all three of the men were standing, arm in arm, saying something I couldn't hear.

My mother and I wandered back to the cabin and I made some tea on the stove. We played a game of Scrabble and my mother let me win.

"No one meant to hurt your feelings, you know," she said.

"I know," I said.

"Your father's found a friend," she said.

Real man. With real man's hands, I thought. I said only, "Don't worry, you have me," thinking, Whom do I have?

"That's maybe all that matters, Luce. I got you."

"You have Nicky too," I said. "He's just practicing being a big shot."

"Practice makes perfect," she laughed.

"He acts tough. But inside . . . I know how he is," I said, calling up in my mind his dark sad eyes to convince me of my words.

My mother began rubbing my back. "Don't you get tough on me too, Luce. I couldn't bear that."

"I won't, Mom," I said. And for a long moment, I wanted to be always sitting with my mother, the way we used to when I was little and she was okay. I wanted just to stay beside her, talking, looking out at the field and the flowers, counting the colors, thinking about the colors of eyes, how my Nan's were changing from brown to milky blue from the years, how I'd save my money to buy her something special from the lake store. A Mexican comb—mother of pearl to match her eyes. I'd tell her it was from me alone, and not from Nicky. Though I'd never tell her the mean things he'd said or that he was an asshole show-off.

"Look at them," she laughed. "Tough guys."

And watching them talk down by the woods, gesturing like spastics, I wondered if you could learn toughness, like campfire skills. Jesus, how I suddenly wanted even just a little of that, feeling her fingers digging in my spine, seeing a hint of yellow in the maple at the edge of the field, knowing she would fly away from me on her drugs again as soon as summer broke.

97

Nicky, I thought, closing my eyes. Come here. I need you on my side. Come here, Nicky.

And when I opened my eyes, Nick was walking up the porch steps, calling, "Thank you, son, thank you, son," with a mock John Wayne accent.

I was supposed to understand that he was sorry and laugh at his shtick to show I forgave him. But I couldn't.

Had he forsaken only me, out there at the pit, I think I would have forgiven him right away, or at least pretended I had. But I couldn't forget how he'd talked about Nan.

"Don't do that again," I said. "Okay?"

I expected him to say, What? What did I do? Fighting me with stubborn obtuseness.

But he said nothing, except, "Okay. Sorry. Really sorry." Then with a John Wayne accent again: "I must a been drunk. It won't happen again, Ma'am. Really."

And then I laughed.

"Miss, I mean . . . I mean really. I'm really sorry . . . Missy."

I was twelve and Nicky was fifteen, and that was our last year. For once our father found Big Will, he was around all the time, sitting with the old man at the end of the field, hearing about old strikes and struggles, mimicking the Hollywood phonies, my mother's friends. Happy, hooting at the edge of the woods, our father was here to stay.

That last summer, he showed up at some of our evening productions, sometimes with Big Will at his side. One, a musical we made up from scenes from Tom Sawyer and Huckleberry Finn, featured us kids in lots of different roles including several Toms and several Hucks to give everyone a chance. Nick played the final Huck, delivering a resounding speech of love for Jim and hatred for all prejudice, culminating in the song we wrote with Duane: "*I'm just a poor boy, but I got eyes to see. / On the raft of life, I'll ride with Jim, until we both are free!*" Lying on my belly in a wagon that I wheeled with my hands, I played the raft, and Nicky and the boy playing Jim, sitting on my back, rode me down the river. At the end, all the children came out to become waves in the river of life, gentle and cooperative, helping the heroes to freedom and happiness. My mother's wave choreography was inspired, with coordinated somersaults and flips, and then the stillest calm—the old Miss Tippy at her best, bringing peace to the hearts of children.

The audience went wild. And as we took our bows, I scanned the crowd, eager to see my father's face, which I was sure would be lit with appreciation. The play may have distorted Twain, but surely it "stood for something." But our father was nowhere to be found.

Later, walking onto the beach from the bandstand, where our productions took place, we saw two figures out on the diving raft. Even in the dark, we could make out our father's skinny body, Big Will's long lanky frame, their arms flailing in narration of their respective dramas.

"Daddy," we called, beckoning him to us.

But he just waved back, staying out there.

"They're naked," my mother said. "Let them be. I don't want him coming back till everyone's gone. With his miserable little rat's ass wagging in everyone's face."

But we knew it wasn't that. Skinny-dipping was not uncommon at Pohogo, and our mother was a natural nudist. It was simply that she didn't want him back on shore, showing his contempt for her effort, for all our efforts, critiquing all of Pohogo with the enhanced energy and authority he'd gained from his new friend and comrade.

Back home, later, standing on the porch, wrapped only in a towel, he announced it was "a sweet production" but it lacked depth.

"When exactly did you swim away?" our mother asked.

"When Lucy was getting painted."

"God damn it, that was the first scene," my mother said.

In scene one, I was the fence who was supposed to get white-washed by a girl named Margie playing the first Tom.

"Did you see my fence dance?" I asked.

My father shrugged, only a little embarrassed.

"She was great," Nicky said. "You shouldn't have left, Dad."

I'd stood there rigid on the stage, so Tom would paint me clean and white, and erase all my marks and woe. Then when he neglects me, I dance around him, reminding him of his duties.

Now I stood rigid again. To remind *him*.

"Look at her," my mother said. "And your son. He sang his heart out, you asshole. Look at your children."

But he wouldn't. Defiantly, he stared ahead, his face tensing, looking like he would swing any minute.

"Get out," she said.

"I'll leave in the morning."

"Now," she said.

And nodding, he lifted his arm and we all flinched. But he just swept the table of the plates and glasses left over from dinner.

"This place is a disgrace," he said. "You're a fucking slob."

"Right, and I like it that way. Now get out."

"I feel better," she said when he'd left. But you could see she didn't. All night she stayed up watching the field he'd walked across—on his way to Big Will's, we suspected.

"He'll be back," we said, waiting up with her, trying to reassure her as we had years before when he'd gone to Liberty, the falls before when he'd escaped for his last licks of summer love.

"I don't want him back. He's bad for all of us."

And then we all started crying because it all seemed such a hopeless mess, even here at Pohogo, where we'd thought we were safe.

By morning she was licking her lips and we realized she'd started taking her pills.

At noon, our father appeared, and she allowed herself to be put to bed to sleep it off. You could tell he felt sorry, even picking up the broken dishes from the floor, which he hardly ever did. But it was too late—at least for us and Pohogo. As we swam laps together that afternoon, Nicky and I both knew this would be our last summer at the lake.

At around six the sun would send pinkish rays onto the raft, and Nicky and I loved to lie out there, feeling bathed in magic.

That afternoon when we finished our laps and climbed up on the raft, I half expected the glowing light would be gone. But it was there, as radiant as ever. Which made it doubly hard to accept that it would all soon be gone.

"You think we'll come back next year?" I asked Nick.

He shrugged. "What do I look like, a gypsy?"

He did, his skin a dark chocolate from a summer of sun, his eyes sad and flickering with light.

"You were a good Huck," I said. "Really, Cocoa."

He was biting his lips, trying not to cry.

"You were a good fence, Missy," he said.

Even now, at twelve and fifteen, when one of us looked like they were going to cry, the other would often burst into sympathetic tears. But now I just smiled. Because for one magical moment, as the light danced on us and the worn wooden planks, I thought, Hold still and you'll be clean and fresh. With no marks. With no memories.

"Hold still," I whispered to Nick.

And then the saddest thing happened. Nicky obeyed. And actually seeing this big hulk of a fifteen year old lying there on the raft, waiting for salvation, like one of the children in our mother's classes, I lost it. And I jumped into the water, so Nicky wouldn't see me crying and start bawling himself.

About the middle of August, about a week after their big fight, my mother got it into her head to organize the biggest Pohogo Gala ever—an end-of-summer square dance. She'd been feeling bad and sleeping little, and I guess she thought dancing would get her going. One day, coming home from day camp, we were surprised to find her home before us and on the phone. At Pohogo she hardly talked on the phone and always stayed late at camp to drive us home. Back in the city, though, we were used to our mother's "inspirational" phone calls, which lasted hours as the amphetamines would race her to highs and the highs would have her talking and planning with vigor and detail to whomever was on the other end. That summer day we came home from camp to find her lying on her bed talking to Alice, explaining she had left camp early to plan a fabulous end-of-summer fling for all of Pohogo.

We made high signs to her to cut it, but she was blind to our entreaties. Off the phone, she said she was tired of our undermining her. A little gala would do us all good. She loved square dancing—we loved square dancing. She'd let us be her assistants. We should have the faith in her that she had in us, and on and on. Hadn't she kicked our father out of the cabin on account of us, and so on.

A week passed. Our mother went to camp, missed some days, took some drugs, slept, told Alice she was fighting a flu but would be fine for the dance. Publicity went out for the Pohogo Scholarship Say-Goodbye-to-Summer Fling. Nightly, Nicky and I would beg her to cancel, but she wouldn't hear of it. By the time the dance came, she'd have it "under control," she promised.

Before the dance our mother made a few trips into the city, ostensibly to get some records she needed for the big night. But of course we knew it was to see her local druggists. For up at Pohogo, she'd always been clean and had no sway with local pharmacies. The day before the dance, our front porch was stacked with chocolates and a variety of body creams and sachets, and Nicky and I, knowing what was coming, begged her again, and again she reassured us that it would all be okay.

The night before the dance, predictably, our mother didn't sleep, but stayed up organizing her square and folk dance records so she'd be in good shape for the next night. Midway through the night, of course, she abandoned this plan and began working on hooking up an illegal telephone extension, one of her favorite binge pastimes, but totally unnecessary in the two room cabin. By morning, the phone wasn't working and the floor was covered with dismantled phones and trails of red and black wire. Still, she claimed, things were under control. By noon, licking her lips furiously, she went back to the records.

Nicky and I pleaded, but she was deaf and defiant. She'd volunteered us as dance decorators and, eager to get rid of us now, she insisted we leave for the dance. For some reason I'll never understand—fear, awe, magical reasoning, madness—we obeyed.

For three hours we climbed on ladders with our Pohogo friends, who knew nothing about our predicament, twirling crepe paper across the vast room, losing ourselves in the activity. As a final touch, my friend Margie made a banner: Tippy's Say-Goodbye-to-Summer Fling, and, our hearts sinking as the hour advanced, we obeyed Alice and helped to hang it from the rafters of the rec hall.

Up on the ladder, I felt dizzy. Looking across to Nick, who was on his own ladder, I thought, We are apart from everyone else in the room, everyone else in the world, stuck here forever. I thought, Jump. Let's just jump now. Be done with our torment for good.

Below us Alice was saying, "This is going to be quite a night. Tippy can really call them." And I thought, You moron. You know nothing. Tippy can call shit, imagining how our mother was probably passed out somewhere in the cabin or in the woods. Jump, I thought again. Then suddenly the room began to glitter with little white Christmas lights that someone had brought in and I thought, Maybe she'll come. Maybe she'll pull it off after all.

By seven, we'd transformed the plain cinder block room, which had been a school cafeteria to begin with, into a kindly barn with big gingham bows and twinkling stars and twirling ropes, and looking around at all the wonderful fakery we'd managed, I took heart again. For the night and beyond.

By eight the room was full, but there was no sign of our mother. Alice kept calling, but there was no answer in the cabin. Nicky and I tried to look concerned and shocked but, of course, what was happening was what we'd expected. Our mother was hiding out at home, taking drugs, making piles, working on the phones.

At eight-thirty, I went to call. I let the phone ring ten times, then hung up. Then twenty. Then thirty. Finally the fifth try—after probably fifty rings—she picked up.

"Luce," she said. "Things got out of control here. But at least the phone's working again. I'm on the extension and can hear you perfectly," she yelled.

"I told you to call it off," I screamed.

"Be a good kid and explain."

"What? What should I explain?"

"Well I do have a sensitive stomach. You know that. Tell them . . . tell them I had a bad reaction to something I ate. And I just couldn't stop throwing up or making diarrhea. Tell them I called the first chance I had."

"I'll never forgive you," I said.

"Don't be a brat," she said.

As I left the office, Alice was walking in.

"She's been in an accident," I said. "She's okay and the car's okay, but she's too upset to carry on tonight. She asked if you'd ever forgive her."

Something in my delivery must not have been convincing, some sorrow or anger or weariness coming through. For the kindly Alice just stared ahead, as if to consider, *Would* she forgive her old friend, who was, come to think of it, acting pretty strange these days?

"Is she really okay?" Alice finally said, and I knew she knew I was lying.

I shrugged, feeling my throat ache from holding back tears.

Alice pulled me to her, but I managed to get away.

The rest of the night, kids took turns being disc jockeys, and adults and children alike took turns offering Nicky and me sympathy—they were sure Tippy would be up and about from the accident in no time. Nothing got her down. Not Tippy.

Sally and Lance's daughter, Liz, was my best Pohogo friend. Putting her arms around me in that super-warm, slightly ostentatious Pohogo style I'd come to love, she said, "Mummy was in a car accident when the studio axed Daddy. She was so upset she didn't see the gate in front of her. It's such a cruel world we live in. People of principle get punished instead of rewarded."

To be kind, I guess, and because he fancied himself a bit of a troubadour and liked to sing impromptu songs in your face, Duane composed a little song for us: "*The dancer dances even in sleep, the dancer's dance requires no leap. / She comes to us, dazzling with light, the dancer still, though still in the night.*"

But it was so solemn and Gaelic and gloomy—and Duane kept smiling at me with a dreamy beatific look that said, I'm a wonderful person and give you my song in your need—that I covered my face, afraid I'd start crying or vomiting. And I think I would have, had I not been stabbed by the joyous spiteful thought of Duane getting thrown out of Hollywood, where he probably wrote the wrong tunes for every scene.

"Very nice, Duane," Nick said. "We'll sing it to Mom to speed her recovery."

And Duane shook our hands, holding them long and hard.

That night as we walked home through the dark roads, Nicky started talking again about running away. We couldn't, I said. There was our mother. And there was Rosie. They needed us. Besides, I said, we were still kids and needed to be home. Even back then, my logic seemed ridiculous, and Nicky and I, imagining the wreckage awaiting us, laughed loud furious laughs as we walked through the night.

"One day, I mean. One day, it's going to happen," Nicky said. "You'll see. . . ."

To get to the cabin, we had to pass the lake. It was past midnight and the beach was deserted. We walked down to the water and lay down on the shore. And studying the sky like hobos, we sang Huck and Jim's refrain, "Till I'm Free, Till I'm free." Till we fell asleep.

In the morning, when we tiptoed into the cabin, our mother was sleeping, evidently unaware that we hadn't come home the night before.

"What's up?" she said.

"Go back to sleep," we barked.

And then we got the broom and swept up the wires and pliers and clippers and tape and bells. Then began to pack to leave the lake.

105

11

Lucky Kids

Even in the worst times those years, Nicky and I sang: Italian partisan songs and love songs that our father had learned in the war; Yiddish songs that he or my mother had learned in childhood; folk songs from my mother's schools and camps; and show songs: 1930's tin pan alley songs; later on our own songs—early rock and all of those beloved Pohogo numbers. Unless things were really miserable, our parents, bequeathing to us not only their songs but a love of singing, would often sing along with us. My mother sounded like a bullfrog and joined in mostly for comic relief and one-line refrains, but our father had a beautiful tremulous baritone and, as he sang, he'd close his eyes like a crooner or a cantor, proud of the depth of his voice and sentiments.

If he'd been well behaved for a while and we were inclined toward him, we were touched by this; but if it was only a short time after a rampage or disappearance, we'd feel nothing but revulsion and close our own eyes in mocking disgust as he went on and on. No matter our present feelings towards him, if he sang opera, we'd gag and refuse to join in, our silence intended to tell him that we would never forgive the dreary afternoons he inflicted on us down at Liberty's, with the Puccini playing and our hearts yearning for a movie, fresh air, and his return home. But after an intense rendition of "Una Furtiva Lacrima," or "Un Bel Di," he took our silence for awed reverence, often treating us to an encore. When our father was on one of these opera jags, only an aggressive counter move on our part with some highly class-conscious song could change the program, with "Union Maid" and "Joe Hill" among our most effective selections.

But the fall after our final Pohogo summer, only Nicky and I sang, in a music group of our own that we started up.

We'd started singing duets together back in the old days with Ellie and Jerry, and many evenings, over the years, as our parents fought in the living room, we'd hide out in one of our bedrooms, learning new songs, putting together arrangements, trying out harmonies, all in all countering their sounds with our own.

But now, we sang every night. Every night after we finished our homework, we'd get together for a two-kid hootenanny. Armed with Nick's guitar and piles of *Sing Outs*—the monthly folk music magazine—we'd practice different arrangements of our favorite songs, our voices blending in what we thought heavenly thirds and fifths.

It was Tanta Ida's idea for us to "go professional." One morning after a particularly vicious night in our apartment, when Nicky and I had to stop our homework and our music a half dozen times to pull our parents apart and the cops came a record three times, Tanta Ida was standing in her doorway as we went off to school. Beckoning us to her, she whispered, "Such sounds." Expecting more understanding and indulgence from our kind neighbor, we stood before her door, shocked and hurt. I think I said, "I'm sorry." And Nicky said something like, "It's a bad period."

But she was smiling widely. "Such sounds," she said again. "Such sweetness. Have you ever thought of sharing your gift with the world at large?"

And again we could hardly speak as she gave us little pecks on the cheek, big hunks of babka to eat on the way to school, and her promise that if we were "inclined to go professional," the sisterhood would be only too happy to hire us for their biweekly executive committee and tri-monthly general membership meetings.

From then on, our nightly music meetings took on a new rigor. Now we no longer wandered into each other's room after homework, asking, "Want to sing?" but marched in, saying, "Ready for rehearsal?" And as we practiced for our first gig, as our voices reached and scratched and broke and reached again, we knew without saying that we were rehearsing not only for the sisterhood's meetings, but for a life beyond the one we knew.

Our first official act was to give ourselves a name, and blending Lucy with Nicky, we came up with Lucky—the Lucky Kids. Tanta Ida put out some publicity, but it only said the Lucky Kids and not our names, so we were able to face our debut unafraid of any neighborhood friends coming to see us—not to mention our parents, whom we neglected to tell about the start of our life without them.

Our first night we did a program of Yiddish songs, some of which we'd learned from our parents, some from Pohogo, and some from *Sing Out*. We did one song about the hardship of life on the desert escaping Pharoah; one about a tailor father who weeps nightly because by the time he comes home from the sweatshop his son is sleeping and the tailor is too tired to even lift his only child, whose bright smiling eyes he can only see in dreams; one about love reaching across the sea to America, a sad ballad that bewails the fact that the beloved is "There, there over the water," and finally ends in a call: "Help me God, God in heaven. By me, it's not good." And with this line-up of tragic songs, the sisterhood ladies began their quarterly meeting in a flood of tears, and the Lucky Kids were launched.

In time, with Tanta Ida's help and a growing reputation for our sad songs, we got gigs in synagogues and community centers and Jewish clubs all over the Bronx and Westchester—sometimes the very same places sponsoring our mother's dance classes during the day, though by now she was working less and less, calling in more and more with a flu or the occasional car accident. In the beginning, following our mother's route pained us, not just because of the memory of how magnificent and magical she'd been not that long before, but because of our fear that some officious cultural director would detect our identity and yell at us for our mother's no-shows.

But after a while, it actually felt satisfying to be covering the same territory—like we were living in a wonderful dream, in which you get to correct the miserable details of some earlier horror. And if from time to time, lingering doubts and shames and terrors pursued us, our audience, I think, sensed none of this. Though we sang sad songs, to them we were simply the Lucky Kids, two winner kids from the North Bronx.

At the end of our gigs, which amounted to fifteen minutes of song before a meeting, the ladies lunged at us and, as if we were glutted with love but too good-natured to deny them, we allowed their kisses and "knips." As for our program, we quickly exhausted our small supply of tragic Yiddish songs and had to expand our repertoire. Still, sorrow was our penchant. I had a particular passion for morose songs about parental love and now and then I'd get Nicky to include "Danny Boy," or "Scarlet Ribbons," or some other song about great personal sacrifice for one's children. When I ran out of good-parent love songs, I'd include Broadway show romantic love songs, recasting them in my mind as parent to child. Nicky's passion was the blues, which he discovered the Snack Fair year when he started studying guitar. By the time Lucky Kids was a year old, Nick had perfected the aching voice and many of the guitar riffs, not to mention the facial grimaces of an old Delta blues man.

Nicky didn't like my favorite songs and I didn't like his. Imagining first my mother's or my father's face, I'd sing some Rodgers and Hammerstein's love song, my voice straining for both poignancy and joy, and Nicky would accompany me with rough tough chords that expressed what bullshit he thought I was singing. Then, when Nick would do something like "Saint James' Infirmary" or "A Motherless Child," embarrassed by the painful, bodily hurt of his blues, I'd come in for the chorus, betraying his ache with my cheerful falsetto. And though we overtly disliked the other's outlook expressed in the other's music, our respective excesses, I suspect, were mutually therapeutic. My conventionality probably lent my brother some hope, however corny, and Nicky's bleak misery kept me connected to painful realities I had to sort out. The earnest ladies, many of them having lost family in the war, were conversant in misery and pain, and as Nicky and I, each in our own way, pulled out our fears and longings at the front of the room, we won only oohs and ahs even for the weirdest arrangements. As long as we looked pained— which we were—and our program ended with the anthem from the Warsaw Ghetto—which it always did—we were a hit.

Although the local synagogue, where we performed most regularly, was only three blocks from our house, and though after a while our parents knew we were performing here and other places, we managed for over a year to escape having either one of them in the audience. Which was truly fortunate, for what was Lucky Kids but an attempt on our part to find substitute parents, a small sea of them smiling reassuringly as we cried in their faces. And what were our parents those days, but staunch defenders of their virtues as parents, all the more fierce and rhetorical as their abilities in this area declined. They'd be furious, we thought, if they knew we were out scouting for their replacements.

Then one night our luck changed. Surveying the faces at a biweekly Mosholu Sisterhood executive meeting, which we routinely opened, we saw our mother seated in the last row, lead-eyed and loaded, licking her lips. Terrified, we got through the minimum number of songs we could get away with and then, waving away the hugs and the soda and cookies, we raced from the *shul* knowing she would follow us out to the street.

"You two sneaky fucks," she shouted to us as she emerged from the building. "No one back there knows what sneaky little fucks I have for kids. And for what it's worth I offer you my artistic opinion: I find your whole act disgusting and maudlin."

"No one asked you," Nicky called without turning around to her.

"Oh, don't I know. You two sneaks don't need your parents now. For artistic judgment . . . or anything in life."

"Right," I said. I was thirteen and, though naturally timid, eager to practice sarcasm. "Sure. We don't need parents."

"I could teach you a thing or two about artistic projection . . . from a dancer's perspective. You know what I think about your hands? I think your hands look like dead fish. I think you don't know how to use your hands when you sing."

"I'm playing the guitar when I sing," Nicky screamed, still walking quickly, still not turning around.

"I mean when you're not playing," she screamed. "If you weren't so ashamed of your mother who paid for all your fucking lessons in the first place, you could use your hands and look good instead of . . . really bad. I hate to be the one to tell you, but you're really, really bad."

"Take that back, witch," Nicky screamed.

"I can take it back, but it will still be the truth. You're not good. Face it. I'm your mother and I'm telling you."

"You're my mother?" Nicky said. "You're a witch. A bitch. Whatever . . . but not my mother!"

"Have it your way. But you're still a ridiculous, pretentious fool, flapping your hands and looking really . . . shitty. *That*, I'm not taking back. The fact of your looking really shitty. And, if truth be told, sounding worse. Frankly, you embarrassed me. . . ."

It was late and the stores were closed and there was only us and a couple of drunks and our mother on the dark avenue. So there was no one to see Nicky turn and charge her. Or to hear me scream, "Nicky, stop," as he lifted her, then held her high in the air. He looked like King Kong serving Faye Ray to the night sky. Around and around, he turned, breathing deeply, from exhaustion and confusion, a dazed victor with a prize he hadn't a clue what to do with.

"Just put her down, Nick," I screamed.

"Yeah, put me down, you piece of shit," she shouted down at him.

My brother laid her down on the sidewalk in front of the bakery. His eyes on a model birthday cake, avoiding my eyes, he said, "Hey, you take care, Lucy." And then he ran off.

"Help me up, Lucy," she said. "He's a piece of shit, let him go."

"Nicky," I called, thinking to run after him to bring him back. But he was just a dark shadow I could scarcely make out in the dark sky, then a dark speck against the black railroad trestle, moving towards the park.

"Big man. Big man run into woods. Make war dance along river. You know what? He makes me want to puke," my mother said, pulling her skirt down but not standing up. "You're basically nice, but he's basically a piece of shit. For a while there, I liked him. When he was young."

"He's good," I said, meaning it, though I could feel some anger begin to flutter in me. How could he have left me alone with her? How was I going to get her home? I was used to him running off into the night, but he'd never left me alone with her. On the street.

"Get up," I pleaded.

"For you, I will."

But she just sat there.

"I didn't mind *your* singing, Luce. It was sweet," she said.

"Thanks, Ma. Now just get up."

"Even his wasn't *so* bad. Though I do have real feelings about your hands. Yours and his."

"We'll work on them," I said, so she'd listen to me and go home. "Get up now, Ma."

"You could have included me. For the hands and other movements. And in general," she said, making a sad clown face and starting to cry.

"Please, get up, Ma," I screamed.

"When I'm goddamn ready. You can't control everything, Miss Little-Officious-Bitch. Miss Got-it-All-Under-Control. Miss Kick-a-Mother-Out-of-Everything. Miss Lucky-Lucky-Lucky Lucky-Lucky."

That night, with the promise I never kept, of course, of allowing her to coach me in hand movements the next time we rehearsed and to all around being nicer, I managed to get my mother home, where, waving her hands like a Balinese dancer to show me the range of graceful movements I had been blind to, she passed out. Our father was gone for a few weeks and so I waited up alone for the runaway Nick.

"Nicky," I called from my bed when I heard him coming in

113

some time just before dawn. "Where'd you go?"

"The park," he said, standing at my door.

"What'd you do?"

"Walked around. Thought."

"She's asleep," I said.

"I saw. But you know what, Lucy? I don't care. I don't care if she sleeps in the street. Dies in the gutter."

"You care," I said.

He shook his head. "No I don't. It's hopeless. They're both hopeless. I was thinking tonight, I got my whole life ahead of me. I'm letting them waste my life."

Nicky was sitting now at the foot of my bed. And studying his profile, I saw he'd assumed his defiant nickel Indian look.

What about *me*? I was thinking. Do *I* have a whole life ahead of me? But I was afraid to ask. What if he said, no?

"It felt good walking along the river."

I nodded. You shouldn't have left me, I thought. You should have helped me get her home. Then we both could have walked along the river.

"She was a real pain in the ass to get home," I laughed, registering the fact that Nick's hair was wet and his face glistening. From the spray of the falls, I imagined, as he'd sat on the riverbank, thinking.

"You should have left her there. Really, you should have come with me."

"Really," I said, my voice dipping in sarcasm, then rising in relief. "Really?"

That night, through the wall, I heard Nicky playing the guitar and singing a song he'd never sung before. About flying from gallows, disappearing from coffins, escaping in the night, faster than a bullet. "The travelin' man, the travelin' man," he crooned. "I'm the travelin' man and this be my travelin' man blues."

On the last chorus, I called out a harmony, but then the next thing I heard were my brother's tired snores.

12

Advice on Life and Love

Those days, even our closest family friends had no idea of the turmoil in our house. They knew my parents fought, that my mother's impishness exasperated my father, that my father's exasperation wounded my mother. At parties, at picnics, which we'd still attend when our father was at home and our parents on a break from violence and drugs, family friends would be treated to the Tippy and Ralphie show—a sanitized version of the real stuff—in which our parents seemed quite adorable and no more troubled than Lucy and Dezi or, to the darker-minded, a charming poor man's Zelda and Scott. When things at home were calm enough for company, the doors of our house flung open and friends rushed in, eager to be part of the "colorful," "amazing Lehmans." Hearing their epithets, I'd always think of one of those Romanian or Bulgarian families on the Ed Sullivan Show, the "amazing" something or others, throwing each other around in the air.

By the time I was twelve and Nick was fifteen, when we started our singing group, we were living double lives: escaping our parents through such enterprises as Lucky Kids; burrowing back, during the periods of relative peace, eager to show the world and ourselves that we were indeed an amazing family. Toward this end, we became key players in the family act. In the next few years, Nicky came to be revered by family friends for his unwavering politics, his multiple

115

arrests at civil rights and peace demonstrations, his masterful guitar and deep voice, his dark hair and dark, dark eyes.

More and more, Nicky submerged himself in the blues. But when guests came, he'd surface to grant them their every musical request—Spanish Civil War songs, union songs, miners' songs—and they would cheer and hoot for their young Pete Seeger. And our parents, whose shouts and fights most other evenings would drown out poor Nick's playing, would smile proudly with that weary but it-was-all-worth-it look of prodigies' parents.

The friends soon looked to Nicky as a political analyst as well. Though my brother still roamed Bronx Park most afternoons with his local quasi-delinquent friends, as he moved up in his teens, he'd spend evenings running around the city going to meetings and demonstrations, with his nights split playing the blues and reading political theory. Glutted on song, our guests would say, "Nicky, what about Albania?" Or, "How are we doing with building class consciousness in the student peace movement, Nick?" Or, "Will socialism come here through democratic process, given our democratic traditions? Can we escape the excesses inevitable for the poor Soviets?" And Nicky would slowly explain the state of Albania, class awareness, democracy and socialism, the future of humankind, as he saw it, using his tools of dialectical materialism, rising to some height of righteousness and vision, which would again get them cheering and clapping.

When guests came I might sing a song or two with my brother and offer a modest observation about history, but Nick was getting so good and so flamboyant at both political rhetoric and guitar that shyly I moved more and more to the side. Here, I had my own busy, if somewhat subdued, act. For, if Nick was the singing gypsy, I was the gypsy fortuneteller.

At that time the *New York Post* ran a daily advice column written by a sensible psychologist named Elsie Kranzblue. At night Nicky read Lenin and Marx, and I read Kranzblue for tips about living with people, hoping for hints about what was going on with the people I lived with. Ever since my mother started deteriorating, the year my father went to Liberty, I'd read this column—"Advice on Life and Love"—looking for a letter from someone who was too sad to eat, or whose father hit or left or both, and later on, someone whose mother took goof balls. And though most of the letters involved jealous lovers or overly concerned parents, I continued to scour the column daily, finding much solace and wisdom in the litany of questions and responses: "Do people change?" Rarely, Elsie maintained. "What's the best way to get others to change even if just a little?" Elsie claimed positive modeling. Do unto others. "Why do people who you know love you act like they hate you?" Elsie said insecurity was at the root of most hostility, and recommended reassuring others always of the love you had within you. "Was ignoring people who were offending you a good strategy?" Yes and no, Elsie said. Surely it gave one a sense of power. But one must be sure that one could tolerate the apartness that might follow.

I loved it. And every day as my mother turned to me more and more to predict the course of our lives—Would everything be okay? Would the panics abate, the swallowing improve, our father return quickly this time, the fighting stop finally?—I'd read Elsie Kranzblue, less for particular answers than for the suggestion that there were human solutions, even if they were eluding me at present.

To my mother's relentless queries, I'd developed some answers of my own, largely Dr. Kranzblue spin-offs. These included: Change takes time. Look inside yourself. Trust yourself. Give yourself credit. Don't stoop to a lower level. Be forthright but not aggressive. Know when to keep quiet.

"You're brilliant," my desperate mother would say. "I *don't* think well enough of myself. I *am* smart. But that doesn't mean I have to show off. I can act dignified. I can give my relationship with others and your father time. I can breathe deeply and be myself."

But then, in time, when none of my advice yielded any improvement at home, I began to doubt the whole process. Still, I had a reputation, built from my conversations with my mother, and bragged about to her friends. "Ask Lucy, she's a genius with human relations," my mother would say. And her women friends, coming into our house, would say, "Luce, give me a couple of minutes later. I need to run some things by you when we're done singing."

Generally, they went like this: Someone had a husband, who, she was sure, loved her but he talked a lot about his secretary. Should she confront or hold back? I'd say, Be forthright, but not aggressive. "You're right, Lucy-o, I'm going to tell it to him straight. Nice but straight."

After a while, feeling that Dr. Elsie's advice had failed me with my own problems and that my derivative advice, therefore, couldn't possibly help anyone but might actually cause disaster, I'd say less and less. I'd limit my comments to the most non-committal: "Look into yourself," or "Seek professional advice." But it didn't matter. Whatever I said was enough and greeted with energetic head bobs and intense stares. "Your mom's right," Lucy, they'd say. "You *are* a genius in the interpersonal department."

Did Mom tell you that it's all come to shit here? I wanted to say. That when no one's here she roams around like a wild goat? He . . . a wild cat? After a while, my feeling of fraudulence and impotence became overwhelming, and when people came over, I'd take to my room, and when they'd follow me there, I'd give them a line or two so that they'd leave, or I'd leave, doing laundry in the basement, or running to the Grand Union for something we needed, or walking over to the Botanical Gardens where I'd sit in the hothouse breathing in the scent of orchids.

One day, escaping to the Conservatory, I ran into our old friend Miss DiFrancesco. Since that spring years before, I hadn't seen her, hiding myself, ashamed, I guess, of the obvious need that had prompted her generosity.

Miss DiFrancesco came up to me and, taking my hand in hers, said, "Lucy, is that you?"

She said she'd thought about me and Nick a lot. How were things?

"Oh, fine," I said.

"Oh, really?" she said. "You look sad, Lucy."

Feeling a stab of pain, I quickly switched into automatic Dr. Elsie pilot. "Life's full of challenges," I said. "The trick, I guess, is to face them honestly. . . . People needed to look into themselves." And bla bla bla.

I remember looking down as I spoke, her lifting my face. I remember it was hard to look at her, at her beautiful eyes staring at me hard with unabashed, unshielded pity. "Lucy, come see me, anytime. We can talk. I think you need to talk."

"I got to go," I said. I had to get away from her and her eyes. Suddenly the greenhouse seemed intolerably hot, and quickly I stood up to leave, feeling if I sat there for another second I'd dissolve.

When I got home, Shirley, my mother's most needy and foolish friend, whom I had tried to escape in the Gardens, was waiting for me in my room.

"Lucy, I'm so glad you came back," she said. "I felt we were at the edge of something before. 'Look into myself,' you said. Which part? I'm half child, half adult, I know that in my heart. Everyone tells me that. Should I trust the child part or the adult?"

I shrugged and threw myself on my bed.

"Lucy gets moody now and then," my mother said wandering in. "I think it's because of her period," she stage whispered.

You asshole, I wanted to scream. I don't get my period yet! You know that! I was thirteen and likely to get it any day. But I lived in dread of this, thinking if I got my period, even more adult burdens would be dumped on me. You got your period, Lucy. Take over for real now, my parents would order. Get a job. Drive the car. I could feel Shirley's eyes on me still, waiting for me to answer: child or adult, which part to trust, deep down inside? I said nothing, but writhed a little, like I had cramps, and closed my eyes, like I was sleeping.

In addition to family friends, work friends came to visit and praise our happy home. My mother, the days she still managed to work, would sometimes bring Artie the Accompanist home for dinner, or another family-less pianist, or a young dancer studying in New York, eager for a taste of family life. My father, still suffering at the hands of one "snot boss" after the next, would sometimes find another "working man" who shared his intense opinions, or at least had an indulgent enough disposition to listen to his rants around our kitchen table. In these good times, we never mentioned the bad times, but just felt grateful for what could pass, to uninitiated eyes and even our own, as family fun.

Often the work guests stayed beyond dinner. "What a great family! I've never seen a family as special as this one," they'd say. And our parents would beam, proud that with all of their individual and combined "eccentricities," they were still pretty terrific.

One day, in the middle of a month's reprieve, in a sweet pill-less, rant-less lull, our father brought home a new friend, Toughy Blumberg, a carpenter who'd been building an extension on the grocery where our father was shrink-wrapping cheese. Toughy's real name was Harold and his nickname was an ironic one for this gentle man with thick glasses and a lisp. Still, Toughy, in his own quiet mild way, had shown the proper contempt for the boss's son and had laughed quietly but appreciatively when my father threatened to shrink-wrap his head, making my father feel less lonely in the mini-mart and the world generally. In gratitude, we all cooked Toughy, a lonely bachelor, a lasagna dinner. After dinner my father began asking Toughy about carpentry, and Toughy took from his bag a hammer and a small saw and began showing my father how he did things. And since it was such fun for us all—watching Toughy's favorite swing, his favorite cut, his favorite rip—and since Toughy's landlord was a pain in the ass—a real "phony-pious, slum-lord type," our father said, who conned Toughy into doing jobs for him free but wouldn't let Toughy do any other carpentry work in his little apartment in the two-family house—our father invited Toughy to stay. Our parents were equally enthusiastic about overnight guests, each hoping, I think, that their presence would inhibit the other's excesses. Though until Toughy, it didn't work. Usually our company left just minutes before an outburst, even the dumbest visitor sensing some change in atmosphere, some barometric plunge, which suggested it was time to take off.

To say our father was a completely different man after Toughy's two-week stay would be no exaggeration. Just as his spiel about boss oppressors and his need to shun them on moral grounds conveyed wisdom about his own killer instincts, so his rhetoric about working man's hands reflected some inkling about himself and his deep need to be kept physically busy.

Now every night in our living room, our father and Toughy hammered and sawed and ripped and planed. Their first project was a simple pine bench, which Nicky and I sanded. Their second project was a pine table. And then a set of pine stools. Our mother was the official tester, sitting on or at each piece with Chaplinesque earnestness and smiles. Eyes closed, she'd let her bottom roam the seat, her hands the table tops—for fit and smoothness—and then satisfied, she'd nod and clap. Nicky and I were the official finishers, allowed to darken each piece with a different stain in Toughy's stain kit.

Was it the smell of stain, reminding her of her father, that did it? Or the force with which our father slammed the wood or bit on the long nails he stored in his mouth as he worked, reminding her of all the beatings and biting? Or maybe it was nothing so specific, just her inner call to drugs, which by now worked with its own addict's rhythms and rules. At any rate, midway through Toughy's stay, she took to her room.

When Toughy finally left, all hell broke loose. But the amazing part was not her, but him. She emerged from her room in rather typical drugged-up condition, saying she hadn't moved us to the new apartment to escape the horrible old stained walls, only to be surrounded by more ugly stain. And then she picked up a hammer and began to examine the furniture to see how she could best destroy it.

Her druggy nastiness hit the mark—the furniture *was* pretty crude and awful, particularly our muddy stains. But we'd all worked so hard on it, that it hurt. And as she went on—"I'm tired of this wood shit, fake wood, real wood. Keep your wood. And keep your faggy little carpenter, who makes you feel like a real man, you prickless wonder"—we looked to our father, wondering where he would plant his blow. But he just smiled with the same sad adoration he had the day he came home from Liberty. And he said, "I'm sorry, Tip."

For one brief moment, Nicky and I looked at each other, trying to gather meaning from the other's eyes: Sorry for what? What did *he* do? She's the mean one now. But the next moment, he was patting her head, and, of course, we understood. Sorry for everything. The long bloody reign of terror.

"Hands off the merchandise," she shouted. "You crazy creep. Now, everyone, get rid of this shit. Now that we got rid of Mr. Bang Bang. . . . Talk about bores."

Her room, as we followed her to calm her, we saw, had a couple of stools standing on their heads, each with one leg gone. "I'm doing my part. Now everyone pitch in on the tinker toys," she screamed.

Again, Nick and I locked eyes. She'd gone too far now. For *this* she would pay. But again, our father just stood there, smiling. It was only when she said again, "You make me sick, you little Mr. Builder. I remember you when you were a little Mr. Breaker. And don't you forget it, oh prickless one," that he got her in a half-nelson. But it was obviously half-hearted, and he just looked down at her grimacing face, confused, as if to say, Now what?

"Just kill me, big man," she said. "Just try. "

"I don't want to kill you," he said. "I love you."

"Oh, that's a good one. You hear that one, children? Your father loves Mommy!"

13

Another Jewish Carpenter

We were thirteen and sixteen now, and this change in our father was all we had hoped for since as long as we could remember. He didn't even have to try to be good, as he had from time to time, returning to the family contrite. Now his good behavior seemed to come naturally. For the month after Toughy came and went, our father became Toughy's partner, and the two of them did well building bookcases, kitchens, porches, basements, whatever wood could be made into, throughout the greater metropolitan area. At his most grandiose, those days, my father called himself "another Jewish carpenter" by which he meant, like Jesus, he was honest and humble and good and kind. True or not, our murderous father, after a full day of swinging and knocking, appeared at the door without the energy or will to fight, and for the first time looked on us all with something that felt like love.

How blessed we felt. We had the father we'd never had except for the brief Snack Fair period and, riding around with him in his pickup truck, we'd feel that same joy and possibility we'd felt in the old fishy station wagon. And though my father's name was just added on to Toughy's so that the business was officially and simply called "Harold and Ralph's Woodwork," with none of the resonance of Snack Fair, it felt like the same magic all over again. But this time, we told ourselves, it would last.

Now we became our father's children as we'd never really been.

He talked to us about wood, politics, the war, and we held his hand. Weekends, he let us help in the downtown shop, planing and lacquering. If our mother no longer took us to Bob's, it no longer mattered. Our father took us for big lunches at a diner near his shop on West 13th Street, where we ordered with the abandon we had with our mother years before, our formerly mean and stingy father now beaming by our side as we gobbled our goodies.

For the first time since the Snack Fair era, there was money. Not lots, but enough so our father was calmed into some generosity. In addition to food, we were indulged in clothing and, most important to our father, in "good" shoes. Good shoes were sensible shoes, which he claimed now meant the difference between a solid or silly life. Good shoes gave you a foundation in life and let you navigate steadily and without undue pain. Every three months, suspecting some pinching of our growing feet and the resulting undermining of our footing in life, he'd take us to the Florsheim on Fordham Road and get us each a new pair of brown oxfords. These were always immensely comfortable and they did allow us to feel set up in life for the first time. And though, from time to time, we wished for something more fashionable like our friends wore—unsupportive loafers or floppy desert boots—we were proud of the shoes our father bought us and the love and concern they signified.

Sometimes when we helped our father on a job, he'd let us ride in the back of the pick-up. Going to the jobs, which were mostly in Westchester, we'd sit, or stand, waving like soldiers. But on the way home, we'd lie down in the back, nestled in wood chips, singing into the night, watching the canopy of trees and sky, tingling with happiness and hope, as our father, singing to us through the open cab window, drove us safely back home.

Now our father was back from the war *for good*! And thinking this, I suddenly felt close to all he'd been through. I'd recall the night at VanDam's. How just *imagining* death, I had escaped into unconsciousness. But our father had witnessed destruction and deaths for years during the war. No wonder he'd disappeared, the man our mother had loved. He'd been wounded, as if a bullet had pierced his brain, I told myself. And I began to love him wildly, and he began to love us back, making up for lost time.

Home, our father would hurry us off to our rooms to spare us our mother. Those days, she'd mostly hide in her room, emerging to glare at us in jealous fury. It was as if our father's new kindness was a cruel joke at her expense, coming too late, exacting too much along the way. To her, I think, his new happiness meant only one thing: he had won and she had lost.

She hated us now as much as she hated him, her eyes seemed to say. As she padded from bedroom to bathroom to kitchen, guzzling her pill concoctions, she looked like a ghoul, scheming who she would *get* next. Over the years, when our parents didn't want us to know what they were saying, they'd speak Yiddish; now our mother started speaking to *us* in Yiddish, as if English wasn't strong enough to express her contempt. Our father would come in holding our hands and she'd say: *Gib a kook ve der tater.* Look at the father. Or, the *zeese maydle.* The sweet girl. *Der shayne brieder.* The nice brother. Twisting Nan's tender phrases into sarcastic barbs, she'd always end with *der freyleche meshpocha*, the happy family. As if putting a curse on all of us and our newfound joy.

Ostensibly as a gag, but secretly, perhaps, to reverse her spells, Nicky began talking to me in his own made-up Yiddish. Adding an *en* to the end of English words, he'd say, *Lifen willen stayen gooden. Lifen willen neveren turnen backen to shiten.* Life will stay good. Never turn back into shit.

Those days our father would guard our doors, shine our shoes, lay out our breakfasts. As she'd pass by, he'd look at her with pity. And when she'd shout her witchy Yiddish, he'd look at her with awe and admiration, sometimes even envy, like someone who's given up drinking but still can crave the old rush.

"You children may not remember, but I used to be very angry and negative. But I've learned to control it. . . ."

And our mother would say, "*Der kluge man.*" Wise man. Or maybe wise guy.

Sheen isen nutsen. She is nuts, Nicky would say. Buten nowen ween haven himen. But now we have him. Foren nowen and everen. For now and ever.

Inen theen footen ween knowen theen hearten. In the foot we know the heart, I said, meaning that he was wonderful, this man who bent down to feel our toes weekly. That you could tell from the way he poked your foot that he was really sorry for the old days and wanted to make up for it in the days and years to come. People can really change. Let bygones be bygones, I'd think, drawing on Dr. Elsie, whom I rarely consulted anymore, so certain did I feel of my new father's new love and the positive direction of what Nicky termed *theen brighten newen eraen withen himen.* The bright new era with him.

After about a year of the new nobility, our father started saying he needed a couple of days' rest, and we'd say we understood. Being a wonderful father was draining, we told ourselves. And he wasn't used to it.

He was demoralized, he'd say, and we'd nod. And grateful that our new father wasn't angry, just discouraged, we'd help him pack a bag, and send him off to Toughy's for a night or two, hoping he'd come back good as new.

Sometimes he'd come back with stories of wonderful new sauces in Italian restaurants he'd been to with Toughy. And we'd be excited when he'd offer to make them for us, like he'd brought us special gifts from a trip. But he never got home early enough to buy the right ingredients. So it never got better than scallion or lettuce pesto. Tuna fish "clam" sauce. Mayonaise Alfredo. Still, Nicky and I would praise anything he concocted and poured on noodles. But sauces reminded us of Liberty. She'd picked up some new recipes and won him back, we worried. Whenever we called him at Toughy's he wasn't there. Liberty was claiming him again, we fretted, as we ate our father's food.

One night, returning after a few days away, he called Nicky and me into the kitchen for a family meeting.

"There's something I want you kids to know," he said, looking down, tossing a bowl of the phony Alfredo.

"Liberty?" I whispered.

He shook his head.

"Whew…that's a relief…I was scared," I laughed.

But he wouldn't laugh. "Her name is Mona," he said. "You'll like her. She's a good human being."

"So was Mommy," I said.

"Really, you kids will like Moan," he said.

Nicky looked like he was going to vomit. He said, "I doubt it. I never knew anyone named Mona who wasn't boring. And 'Moan' is the ugliest nickname I ever heard."

He glared at us, then at the bowl of noodles, like he was going to flip it over to emphasize how selfish we were being. "I don't have to take this," he said. But quietly, his heart clearly not in the furious lunatic act. Quietly he stood and walked to the door.

"I'll come back for my things, kids. I'm not angry . . . I'm just clear about what I need in life."

My mother was banging around in her room.

"Don't leave," I called.

"I'll visit," he said. "You'll visit with us. Mona likes kids."

"Don't," I shouted again.

"Your mother's sick. I can't help her and I'm only wasting my life here."

I looked to Nick. That's what *he* said the night he left me with *her* in front of the bakery, my mother lying out on the street. But for all his big-shot talk, my brother was sitting beside me still, biting his fist. What about us, Daddy? I wanted to say. What about *me*?

But I didn't have the nerve to ask the question. Or hear the answer: You're on your own.

"Don't," I screamed again. "Daddy, don't."

I looked down at my shoes. Who would polish my shoes? Who would ever buy me new ones?

"My toe hurts," I screamed. "You can't go."

But when I looked up he was gone.

"*Vu es der zeese tate*r?" our mother asked stumbling into the kitchen. Where's the sweet father?

"He left . . . for good," I cried.

"Oh, no," she said, breaking into English for the first time in weeks.

And then she cried some real tears. After which she started digging in the closet for some electrical wire because she thought our TV reception could be significantly improved and thought she knew where to splice to make it really happen.

Nicky and I went downstairs and sat on a bench on the upper Parkway by the soldier's monument. My brother was smoking cigarettes now and then, rolling his own with Bull Durham. We passed one back and forth, breathing in deeply, like our father did.

For months we tried to get him back, telling him that Mona, a perfectly nice catalogue librarian at NYU who gave us discarded books and lectures on the Dewey decimal system, was a cheapskate and a dunce. But it didn't work as it had with Liberty. He had to live his own life, he said.

"One day I hope my children will understand me," he'd say.

"I don't understand, " Nicky would say when we were alone. "We were getting so close."

"He seemed to really like us," I'd say.

"You know what they are?" Nicky would say. By now he'd stopped his pig-Yiddish and was talking straight. And I'd lean toward him to catch his insights, always forgetting that he was as stumped as I was. "He's a scumbag... and she's a douche bag," he'd say.

I'd shrug, not sure of the difference.

"Scumbag and douche bag," he'd repeat, like he'd just discovered some new vocabulary that suddenly made sense of the whole spinning world.

14

The Blues

By Bronx kid standards, we'd managed to make a fair amount of money over the two years of Lucky Kids' modest success—enough to supply us with decent clothes, after-school snacks, books, records. Nicky had saved five hundred dollars, which he used to buy a top-of-the-line Martin guitar. Before that he'd played a cheap Stella, which he upgraded to a Sears. His Martin Classic, the guitar of guitarists, was so beautiful and valuable to him that he slept with it every night. By now, Nicky was old enough to have a girlfriend and handsome enough to receive a handful of flirtatious calls daily. But I think, given the tumult of our lives, he was more comfortable stroking the curves of his golden guitar.

All in all, now that he had his wondrous new guitar, he seemed totally self-sufficient. He'd talk to it, sing to it. So what did he need with anyone—especially his little sister, who always had to tag along.

We were out in the park, walking down Spider Hill, when he said he thought Lucky Kids should split. "We can still sing at home together," he said. "It's just that . . . well, the blues is so important to me. Try to understand. It's something I feel inside me. It's aching to get out."

I started aching. Hadn't I sung along with him through all those dreary songs? Hard-hearted this and that. He was a hard-hearted bastard, I thought, and I picked up some dirt and threw it in his face.

Then I watched him lift his hand to slap me.

Go on, big man, I wanted to shout, my mother's words filling my mouth with such bitterness that I started to spit, and cry.

Nicky dropped his hand and buried his face in it.

When he looked up, he said he was sorry. He didn't really want to end the act. It was just a thought he was trying out.

"Really?" I said.

"Really," he said, pulling me toward him for a rare hug.

Still, I knew our singing days together were numbered, which I knew meant more than singing, of course. For years my brother and I had been, if not inseparable, then indispensable to each other for understanding and solace. And now Nick was dispensing with me, or would soon, I was sure.

Nicky started to walk north up the river to the old Lorillard Snuff Mill where he and his neighborhood friends hung out in the afternoons. Nicky now attended Music and Art High School and was friendly with a bunch of boys and girls whom I knew little about but who, in the brief glimpses I got, certainly looked pensive and smart with their black turtlenecks, sepia pens and volumes of Dylan Thomas. But after school, my brother returned to his "roots," as he liked to put it. Which meant rain or snow he hung out in the park with his neighborhood buddies, drinking Thunderbird wine, singing horrible drunken a capella rock and roll arrangements, drawing dirty pictures, and slapping each other's asses with canned camaraderie. Because I was Nick's sister, I was given a measure of respect, but this was shown by largely ignoring me, except perhaps for an occasional offer of candy or chips.

That day, as much as I hated the Snuff Mill scene, as Nicky walked north and I turned south to the Conservatory, I wanted to call, Take me with you.

And Nicky sensing my desolation, I guess, turned and said, "Hey, Luce, you want to come?" though I knew he hated me hanging around when he was being cool.

"Na, that's okay. I got a lot of homework," I said, waving again and walking on.

For a few minutes I sat in the larger greenhouse, thinking about the first time my father left.

"Daddy," I called, knowing this time he'd really left for good. Would Nicky be leaving for good too? "Nicky," I called, aching for him so hard that my arms began to hurt.

It was fall. Outside the sky was beginning to darken. I stood up to disperse my miserable mood. I'd go home. Make supper, do homework. Then Nick would come home. It would be okay. Together we'd face our mother. But my projection of the evening immediately ahead of me only deepened my sadness, and I imagined my life one long endless night with my mother shouting her viciousness, my brother off singing the blues, me alone in the kitchen making miserable casseroles that I alone would eat. Reaching the gate, I turned around and started running to the museum building.

Miss DiFrancesco was sitting at her desk.

"Oh, there you are," she said, as if she'd been waiting for me single-mindedly since we last met, a year or so before, that time in the orchid room when she held my face in her hands.

I started to speak, but I couldn't. My chest was heaving and my throat tightening. I felt my old awful Miss Mousy shaking start up.

"I'm so sorry, Miss DiFrancesco," I said.

"For what? I asked you to come," she said. "When you needed to talk. And here you are."

It was all so simple with her. She just opened her mouth and spoke plain truth. Nothing fancy, nothing showy. But I wasn't used to it, and the candor and honesty made me feel naked and exposed. I felt my trembling take off, my whole body begin to twitch.

"I should look inside myself," I said. "I probably have the keys to my own happiness. . . ," I tried, searching desperately for some Dr. Elsie wisdom to spring me from her stripping gaze.

"Sit down," she said, patting the chair beside her.

I stopped talking and let her talk.

I could work here every afternoon and on weekends and holidays. She needed someone to help in the office and also in her little lab upstairs. She was still working on plant nutrition and was starting on a new cabbage project and needed another pair of hands. Nick could work here too, though at his age he was probably busy with other things. And I nodded. She looked at me hard and said she could find me, or us, a place to live if it came to that. *Had* it come to that? she asked, and I shook my head no. But *had* it? I didn't really know.

She told me about her family. There'd been seven kids at home and her father drank. "Three became drunks, one a priest, two nuns, and me. A something or other."

An angel, I thought. "The nicest lady in the world," I blubbered.

"You'll make some money and you'll do some good."

"I want to do good," I blurted out. "That's really all I've ever wanted to do. I only threw dirt at Nick because he hurt my feelings. I know I was wrong though."

It was all the talk about priests and nuns, I guess, that got me to feeling confessional, and her sweet perfect gaze on my red hot face. I started thinking about where it would lead, my work with Miss DiFrancesco. I'd help with her planting, her cataloguing, her anything. Maybe I'd ask her to adopt me one day, or she'd volunteer. And I'd stay here forever in the high domed building, sitting beside her. Or maybe she'd introduce me to her sisters, the *sisters*, and I'd become a nun. And live in a quiet stone convent with my own quiet room. Then I wouldn't be a burden to anyone.

"Do you have to be Christian to be a nun?" I said.

"Some people of other faiths have converted and joined different orders."

"Even Jewish?" I said.

"Some were Jews," she said. "But you don't need to be a nun to get away from home, Lucy. Believe me. I know."

And then I remembered Teeny's story about how Miss DiFrancesco had decided not to be a sister in order to study plants.

"But later on if I still feel a calling?" I said.

"Do you feel a calling?" she laughed.

I shrugged. Did dreams of a still room, soft voices, an early peaceful bedtime amount to a calling?

"You need a rest, not a calling, Lucy," she said.

When I got home that night, Nicky was all charged up. On his way to the Snuff Mill, he'd stopped at the stone terrace above French Charlie's and found an old man on the bench playing the guitar.

"And guess who he was?"

"Old Man Time," I said, trying to sound snappy and jolly so our afternoon rift would be forgotten; feeling fairly snappy, in fact, after my talk with Miss DiFrancesco.

"Wise guy," he laughed. "Reverend Freddie Johnson."

"Who's he?"

"Who's *he*?' Why just the greatest living blues guitarist in the world. And he lives off of Allerton in the projects. And he said I could visit and listen to him play."

I nodded, trying to look enthusiastic, though I felt disheartened. I had wanted to tell Nick about Miss DiFrancesco. How I was going to help her water and catalogue. How she said he could help too. But suddenly it didn't sound like much.

"I'm going to go tomorrow. You can come if you want."

I said I'd see. I had to check my calendar. And I could see Nick tucking in his teeth, trying not to laugh.

Miss DiFrancesco said I could begin anytime I wanted, so I called her and told her Monday. The next day was Wednesday and when I got home from school, Nicky was waiting downstairs. And we walked across the park to Reverend Freddie's.

I loved this long trek to the end of the park—for our Nan lived on Allerton Avenue—and our walks there past Twin Lakes, past French Charlie's and through the woods were usually rewarded with her sturgeon and pumpernickel. As we walked across the park, I started feeling my stomach growl.

"Do you think he has anything to eat?" I said.

"He's famous. He's not going to feed us," Nick snapped. "He'll just give us tips on the blues. If we're lucky."

"Lucky Kids," I laughed, waiting to see if Nicky laughed back, a sign to me that he was still with me.

"Damn straight, Jack," he said, bluesy and cool.

The project looked like a jail with its square design and bars on all the windows, uniformed guards and guard dogs walking the grounds.

"Maybe I'll wait downstairs," I said.

"He's the greatest," Nicky said. "You'll be missing a chance of a lifetime."

When we got to Reverend Freddie's apartment, we rang the bell and a dog started barking.

"Fussy," Nick said. "His seeing eye."

"He's blind?" I screamed, scared.

"Yes, but not deaf, so shut up!"

"Who's that?" a man's throaty voice asked through the door.

"Nick, from yesterday, in the park, Reverend Freddie," my brother said.

"Does he know I'm coming too?" I asked.

"He won't care," Nick said. "He's great."

The door opened and Reverend Freddie wearing a brown suit, a plaid shirt, a polka-dotted tie, and a black Stetson hat stood there beside a big German shepherd, who sniffed our feet.

"Welcome," he said.

Nick said, "I brought my little sister, Lucy, Reverend Fred. She admires you as I do."

Reverend Fred extended his hand and I shook it. It felt like leather—harder than leather, a rough, dense stone.

"I was jus' playin' some solitaire," the Reverend said. "So you kids be comin' at a good time. I wouldn't mind playing some guitar for a break."

"How many hours do you play guitar, Reverend Fred?"

"One hour in the morning. One at night."

"What time?"

"Upon rising in the morning, first thing. So you be fresh. And at night just before you say your prayers. You try that an' you be in good shape."

"I'll try it, Reverend," Nick said.

"And then in the afternoon if you feel moved and fresh. Never when you're weary. Even though the blues be a tired man's music, don't mean you want to be tired for your daily practice. You want that fresh feeling."

And then Reverend Freddie was handing Nicky a guitar. And picking up one himself.

For a while they went back and forth, the Reverend showing Nick chords and riffs, Nicky trying them out. Even I could hear and see how special the Reverend's guitar playing was. His left hand seemed to spread twice as far as a normal hand so his chords were varied and fast changing. Even I, with my developing resentment against the blues, which threatened to take my brother from me, could hear and see his splendor.

Nicky said finally, "Say, I can't get those chords, Reverend Fred."

And Reverend Fred said, "That's because you don't have my lucky paw. I broke that paw when I was just a boy and they set it bad, and that's how come I got to have my wide, wide spread. The Lord moves in mysterious ways. He took my eyes, but he gave me my blessed paw. Amen."

"You'll just have to practice for those chords, Nick," I said. I could hear my voice cracking in fear for Nick was eyeing his own left hand, thinking, I knew, Could I break my paw too? Get it set wrong? Get a blessed chord spread like the Reverend?

"It happen to me in a fight for a woman before I went to Jesus. Don't you never fight for no woman, Nick. Again for me it turned out lucky. I got many friends got poisoned and died."

"Robert Johnson," Nicky said naming his number one favorite blues guitarist. "Blind Lemon Jefferson," naming his number two.

"And others," Reverend Fred said, shaking his head, "So you be-ware a woman whose heart you broken."

"I will, Reverend," my chaste brother said, hugging the Reverend's guitar tight.

135

And though I was not a woman but a fourteen-year-old girl, I looked at my brother and thought, You're breaking my heart. For I can tell you'll leave me soon. Daddy broke my heart.

Just then, the Reverend began to play, not just chords and riffs, but a song. At first, I couldn't make out the words, but it was, clearly, the most beautiful song I had ever heard, lulling and repetitious, then suddenly spiraling into a high wail. Reverend Freddie's hands flew over the strings, like fluttering birds. "*Oh, Lord, Oh, Lord, do you hear me, Lord, the one I love? / I asked you once, I asked you twice, I'm sitting right here till I see your light. / Oh Lord, Oh, Lord, do you hear me, my Lord?*"

I looked through the barred windows, out to the night sky. I heard Reverend Fred's throaty cries, my brother's soft echoes, "*My Lord, my Lord.*" And my whole body ached. I wasn't ready yet, but one day it would happen. My brother and I would part. But I wasn't ready yet and I ached like a baby. Across the project's green, I could make out the roof of Nan's building, and I felt suddenly so hungry I thought I would cry.

"Nicky," I said, "I'm hungry. Are you hungry?"

"Me and the Reverend, we're still playing. Hush now," he said.

But I wanted them to stop. It was making me crazy. I never felt sadder. And the only way I could stop myself from crying was to imagine Miss DiFrancesco's face and to see myself watering her plants, and then in the convent along with her sisters, lying in my own bed, with them all just down the hall with their dark, kind eyes.

When we got home, my mother was on a rampage. More and more, with our father gone for good, she sounded like him. A shrill transvestite him with furious rants and slaps, delivered in an old pink fleece robe—her costume of choice for a binge, pilled and gray from years of wear, splotched brown here and there from coffee and repotting.

Her latest complaint was that we stayed out late—which we did, there being nothing to come home to. But to convince herself that she was not a lowlife addict but an upstanding parent, my mother would hold tight to conventional standards of decency that she'd never cared about before and bludgeon us with them. Decent children who respected their mother called by five p.m. if they were to be delayed for dinner. Tonight, this was her theme. And Nicky made the mistake of asking, "What dinner?" And she picked up a book and hit him on the hand.

"I play my guitar with that hand," he said, lifting it to hit her, then placing it in his belt to stop himself.

"You raise a hand to a mother? You'll see what you do with that hand again, Big Mr. Guitar Man," she said.

And she raced off to his room. She looked funny—like Dennis the Menace on roller skates, with a fierce devilish look on her face—so we laughed, following her into the room.

Having just come from Reverend Freddie's, I looked around the room quickly at the pictures of blues heroes hanging on the wall, sighting near the window a framed *Sing Out* photo of the young Reverend with his black glasses and black hat. Our mother was just jumping around the room shrieking—like a monkey—so we laughed again. But then, she suddenly got purposeful and running to the bed, she found the Martin resting against the pillow. Holding it by the neck she screamed, "You will never beat me again. You will never lay a hand on me again. Never ever ever. . . ." And then she lifted the beautiful golden guitar high and threw it to the floor.

Its neck broke, its side cracked.

"Oh God, Oh God," my brother began to moan.

I cried, "Oh, God. Oh, Jesus."

"You deserved that and more, you brat," she said. "You're violent like your father. And you won't ever do that again. No more beatings. Ever ever. . . ."

Nicky was in the closet—I couldn't see what he was doing. And for a terrible moment, I thought he had a baseball bat, or a pistol, or a rifle in there. "Don't, Nicky," I screamed. And then I saw it was an old knapsack he was playing with, shoving in some shoes, some pants, running across the room to his bureau for socks, underpants.

"Let's go, Lucy," he said. "It's time. . . . It's time to go."

I could hardly hear him—his voice was low and weak. But I nodded and said, "Okay."

"Do as you like, you dope," she said to me. "You dopey copy-cat."

Then I went into my room and found my own old Pohogo knapsack and filled it with some clothes, went to the bathroom for our toothbrushes. And then we both walked to the front door. Nicky had his Martin in his arms, like a parent clutching a dead child.

I took one last look at my mother. She was dirty, she was crazy. I closed my eyes to see her glistening hair, to feel her strong back beneath me as I rode her in the park. And then I closed the door quickly before I changed my mind.

Outside, I started walking towards the subway. We were going downtown to our father, to Mona's apartment on West 10th Street, I assumed. But Nicky, whispering still, said, "Come, Lucy. Not *that* way, Lucy. We're going *this* way."

Arm in arm, we walked across Mosholu Park up to the upper Parkway, past Frankie Frisch baseball field, down Spider Hill. At the bottom of the hill, I looked south to see if any lights were on in the museum—maybe Miss DiFrancesco was still there. But I couldn't make out the building in the black October night.

Autumn, those years, smelled constantly of leaves burning—a cozy smoky smell that always made me think not of outdoor fires but of indoor warmth—afghans and hot chocolate before a hearth. Now, walking north besides my brother, into the black woods, I had to shake my head to dispel the thought of homey comforts.

"Where are we going?" I said.

But Nick couldn't, or wouldn't, talk.

To the north was Nan, whom we could rely on for whatever she had.

"I don't want to go to Nan's," I said. For Nan's wasn't Nan's, of course. It was a room in someone else's small apartment. And I knew her "Mrs." might not want us trekking in in the middle of the night and, even if she didn't mind, I didn't want to burden Nan. When we'd come to her when our mother had slipped too low, gone too far, she always sighed with such defeat and shame that we'd feel guilty for having brought more troubles to her sad old life.

Nicky nodded, still not talking.

"Where *are* we going, Nicky?"

But again he said nothing, just walked fast, squeezing my arm.

Above us was the terrace, which we would have to climb up to get to the streets where both Nan and the Reverend lived.

"Not Reverend Freddie?" I screamed. "I won't sleep in that jail. I'm afraid of that dog." I thought: Nicky will lay his Martin at the old man's feet. And all night they will sing the blues together, the broken guitar blues, the broken heart blues. They will ignore me. By morning, I will have killed myself.

"I'll kill myself," I said.

"No you won't," he said, "assuming we went to Reverend Freddie's, which we're not. Not that it's such a bad idea. . . . Maybe he can give me tips on fixing. . . ." But he couldn't finish his sentence.

For years, we'd escaped the neighborhood along the little path that hugged the Bronx River. Riding our bikes, before long we'd be in Yonkers, then Eastchester, then Scarsdale. That our little Bronx River—from which our modest borough took its name—could make it to such fancy neighborhoods always amazed us. And the sameness of the river, the constancy of its character, from the Bronx into Westchester, touched us—its narrowness, which made crossing easy; its small curves, which made suspense possible but tolerable; its little stone bridges which appeared every mile or so, assuring you that you were making progress but still in familiar territory. Now, silently, we walked through the leafless trees and bushes and slid down the embankment, wet with dead leaves. And finding the path, we walked north, still not sure where we were going, but knowing we needed to be here, following the river, far away from home.

15

Traveling on the River

Even in the cold dark we could see it shimmer, remember springs and summers when we swam here, floating under the falls, whose splash we could hear ahead of us now, luring us on. I could tell Nicky was still unable to talk but I could sense, by some nighttime radar, that the river was pressing its song and rhythms on him. I heard his breathing grow steady, and then he began to hum. Snippets of river songs we'd been raised on. Paul Robeson's "The Four Rivers" and "Old Man River." Big songs about big rivers. "Shenandoah." "Banks of the Ohio." Mississippi levee songs. "Deep River." "The Water is Wide." I hummed along with him, taking turns holding the shattered guitar, feeling one minute scared and hopeless, the next brave and determined, as we left geometry tests and Spanish quizzes, our father who forgot us, our mother whom we wanted to forget, following our own little river, which was in many places no more than a creek, to some new place and new life.

By midnight we were too tired to go on and, under a stone footbridge at the northern edge of Yonkers, we stopped, nestling into the stone arch beneath.

"I'm tired," I called. *Tired, ired, ired*, my echo rang.

"Me too," Nicky said. *Oo, oo, oo.*

And lying there, listening to the spooky sounds, I thought how next week would be Halloween. "Next week is Halloween," I said.

141

"God damn it," Nicky shouted. "We're not going back. Besides we're much too old for that stuff."

"I know," I said, not feeling old at all, but as scared as a five year old in the cold wet tunnel. "I was just thinking."

"Don't think," Nicky said. "Just sleep."

"Okay," I said. But I knew I couldn't, tired as I felt.

"It's just that we never ran away before . . . so I'm thinking a lot." I was thinking about Miss DiFrancesco, my new job, having no money coming in. I was thinking about how we'd eat, where we'd live, what it would feel like to have no parents to care for you even a little bit, no parents to care for either.

"We've run away before," Nick said. "I mean more or less. I mean we've rehearsed this many times. We knew it would happen. Eventually. This should come as no surprise to you, Lucy."

But I could tell by the high pitch of his voice that he was feeling surprised, shocked—and maybe even a little scared like me—that we had actually done it. Taken off in the night.

"It was inevitable, given the coalescence of conditions. . . ."

He sounded like he was making a speech for our family friends, or his school's assembly, on the causes of some revolution.

"I know," I said, though I didn't know what he was talking about. "But are we *ever* going back?" I said.

"What do you think?"

I shrugged, but he couldn't see me in the dark.

"Answer me, Lucy. With the goddamn right answer, damn it."

"I guess not. I just wonder if she's okay. And Rosie."

"We couldn't take Rosie. If it was feasible, we would have. Anyway she's good with dogs," he laughed bitterly.

"I guess so," I said. "I bought a case of Alpo last week."

"Yeah. And I got that bag of dry chow. They can both munch on it. Now, please, Lucy. No more talk of home."

"But I'm lonely," I said.

"You got me," he said.

"Yeah, but you said you'd break up the Lucky Kids. And I thought, first the Lucky Kids, then what?"

142

"But I said I was just thinking out loud. Can't a person think something? Jesus, don't you understand there's a universe of difference between thought and action?"

"I guess so," I said.

For a while we said nothing.

Then Nicky said, "Give me your finger?"

"Why?" I said, giving him my hand.

"You'll see. We're going to settle this once and for all. Say, 'We're in this together.'"

"We're in this together," I said.

"Say, 'We're never going back.'"

"We're never going back."

"Say, 'Lucy and Nicky forever.' Say, 'Lucky Kids forever.'"

"Lucky Kids forever."

"That's it," Nicky said. "Except for the blood."

Before I could scream, he had his trusty hunting knife out—I could see it glistening against my finger. And he pierced my right pinky with its point, then his, and we touched our blood, holding our fingers together for a while. Then, to my astonishment, I felt very calm. Together we'd manage a new life. Somehow. Somewhere. I could feel my finger feeling that, then the rest of me, and then I could feel nothing as I fell off in a merciful sleep.

We rose to the sound of rushing water. I opened my eyes and before me a man was peeing steamy pee into the river.

He had his back to us, but he turned his head and smiled. "Good morning."

He had no teeth and scarcely an inch of his face was free of scabs. Was that the face of *our* future? I wondered, feeling a terrible dread grab hold of me again.

"Good morning," Nicky called heartily, jumping up himself to pee. I had to pee too but didn't know where I'd find a place to go. And that uncertainty suddenly seemed the essential fact of my new life. What would my new life add up to but a constant search for a bathroom. But then, watching Nick's powerful stream arc into the air and catch the early morning light like a mini-rainbow, I filled with hope and thought, How could everything *not* work out? And then looking away as my brother zipped up and, studying the man's scabs again, I didn't feel afraid anymore and touched the little scab on my pinky, silently repeating our oath.

"I'm Vern," the man said.

"Nick," Nicky said. "And my little sister, Lucy."

"What happened there?" Vern said, kneeling down beside the guitar.

"An accident," I said, for Nicky was looking down in mute pain.

"I used to play the ukulele."

My brother nodded half-heartedly, hoping, I could tell, that the conversation topic would move on from string instruments.

But Vern went on. "This baby is severely hurt," he said. "No doubt about it. Opposite of me. My ukulele stayed in topnotch condition. But my fingers went."

He held up his right hand. Two fingers were missing.

"Frost bite, which led to gangrene. First thing led to the second. I no longer play."

Nicky just nodded again.

"Your fingers look topnotch. It's just your instrument that's severely hurt. But you can save your pennies for a new one. That's a better situation than yours truly's because even if I made a million, where would I get new fingers?"

I thought Nicky was going to cry, for Vern's lost fingers, his own lost guitar. But he just looked down and nodded some more.

Then realizing, I guess, he'd made him sad, Vern jumped up and said, "Say, are you youngsters hungry?"

We nodded and he ran up the embankment to a tree and started pulling things from a hole at its base.

"Severely hurt," Nicky said. And again, "Severely hurt." And then he started patting the guitar with mud and leaves.

"Nicky," I shouted. "What are you doing?"

"Filling the holes. . . ."

The one on the side was the size of a hard ball and, though its neck was still connected, the guitar was gashed in the back, the opening the size of a baby's head.

Nick was patting the wood hard, applying the mud. "Maybe it will dry and hold for a while. It's sort of a poultice I made here, you see."

Squatting by the river, patting mud and leaves, muttering, he looked like an Indian medicine man. And I wanted to squat beside him and chant something with him and pat things down and make the guitar whole again. Our world whole.

But Vern was running down the hill so I just said, "Yeah, till you get it fixed."

His patting and mumbling done, Nicky held the Martin in his arms and played a chord, but the mud fell out, spilling all over him, and he just squatted there blinking back tears.

"You youngsters go for chocolate?" Vern said, setting a sack on the ground.

Nicky wiped his eyes. "We do," he said. "We really do."

Vern's sack, we saw, was an old shirt. But what wonders it held: bottles of Yoohoo and packages of Hostess cupcakes and Mallomars; a couple of Almond Joys.

"I favor food that requires no refrigeration," he said. "Even in colder weather. It's a habit of the road."

No wonder Vern's face was all messed up. That's not food, I wanted to say, but of course I didn't, not wanting to be rude and hurt his feelings or cause him to withdraw all the goodies, true food or not.

"Delicious," Nicky said, grabbing.

And I agreed, eating a row of Mallomars, which I washed down with a Yoohoo.

"So what brings you to this neck of the woods?" Vern asked.

Nicky laughed loudly, and I joined in. For it *was* a neck of the woods, the thin little strip of forest we were in, a slim slice of the wide woodlands the river commanded back in the Bronx.

"We just needed a change. You know how it gets," Nicky said.

"Oh, don't I? I'm always in need of a change. I'm here and there.

I've been on the road . . . let's see . . . going on ten years. And the longest I stay in one spot is not very long. Maybe a year or two."

"How long have you been here?" I said, gesturing around us. "In this neck of the woods," smiling inwardly for my daring on the road talk.

"A year. I'm under the bridge till winter. Then I go up the hill and there's this little hallway behind the drive-in bank that stays pretty warm if you got enough coats and stuff. They never lock it up, so it's all mine. It's not half bad. It's not all that small. Say, do you kids want to join me? I'm going up there, any night now. I like Bronxville. This is Bronxville, not Yonkers, by the way. There's the divide," he said, pointing to another bridge about a half mile down the river.

"Thanks, but we've got to be moving on," I said quickly, for I could see my brother's eyes dancing with curiosity about life in a hallway. The tunnel-man, hallway-man blues. "We're due at our grandmother's," I said.

"But maybe not till tomorrow," Nicky said. He was glaring at me. And I knew what he was thinking: Let's stay with Vern. Let's learn his hobo ways. For our hard-travelin' future.

"She's expecting us," I screamed.

"Where about is that?" Vern said.

"Way up north. . . ," I said. "You ever hear of . . . Lake Pohogo?" I said, pulling it from the air.

"Yes," Nicky said. "Lake Pohogo." And he was smiling his first big smile since yesterday. And I could see the idea taking hold, my little spontaneous lie becoming his big plan. "It's great up there. We got a little cabin. . . ." He cut himself short, not wanting to brag to Vern, I guess, who had only a hallway, or to set himself up too much, with his hopes. That the cabin would still be there for us. That Pohogo would be ours again.

Vern shook his head. "Well if you change your mind, I'll be here, or there," he said, pointing up to the top of the woods to a street. "Left, right, left. First Westchester Bank in the back. Cozy as can be. Can't say I can promise to come up north and check you out. This is about as far north as I ever go since what happened with my fingers occurred, which was close to the Canadian border."

"We'll be okay," Nicky said, standing up. "We're going to be okay."

"No doubt about it," Vern said. "And you can always come back."

I stood up. "Hate to eat and run," I said, "but she really is expecting us."

Vern stood and collected the remaining food. "Take care," he said. "I can tell you'll do all right. Look, you found me. How many little runaways get chocolate breakfasts their first day out. I'd say you just started out, given how nice and clean you both look. I'd say you're two winners. Two lucky kids," he said, waving. "And I wish you more luck even."

And without irony, still buoyant from the chocolate and night's sleep, we thanked Vern, returning his good wishes.

"And may the Lord Jesus Christ look over you so you have as much good fortune as I have had. Or more."

To Pohogo. All morning as we trekked, Nicky sang, "We are marching to Pohogo. . . . Sing with me, I'll sing with you."

And though I was happy, thrilled by our sudden plan of hiding in the little log cabin at the edge of the woods, all I could think was, Pee with me, I'll pee with you. And how much harder it was for girl bums, just in terms of peeing even. For since we'd left the Bronx, I hadn't found a place to go.

The woods were so narrow here along the river, and every time I thought I'd found a tree that might hide me, a car would pass on the parkway alongside us.

"Jesus Christ, Lucy," Nicky said over and over. "The cars will never see you again."

"Still," I said.

"Still what?"

"Something's wrong," I said now as we walked along.

"What?"

I shook my head. "I think I made in my pants. I mean I don't remember doing it. But it feels like it."

"Jesus, Lucy."

And then I could wait no longer. My need to pee and my dreadful curiosity made me stop under the next bridge we reached. And there, though I could hear a car above me, I squatted and peeked and saw my underpants, all red and bloody.

"Go away," I called to Nick.

"What's wrong now?"

"Just go away," I said. "Go up there." I pointed to the road above.

"Did you pee in your pants?" he said, walking up the embankment.

"Shut up," I said. "Worse than that."

"Shit?" he said.

"Worse," I said.

I took off my underpants and shoes and socks and though the air was cool and the water was cooler, I waded in the river in the dark under the bridge, washing away all the blood. And I cried, for I hadn't wanted to get my period. I was already fourteen and probably the only girl in my class who hadn't gotten it yet—a fact that pleased me—still holding to that childish logic which told me if I didn't get my period, I was still a child and no additional grown-up burdens could be placed on me. But now, feeling the blood oozing, I couldn't stop crying as I stood belly deep, my skirt at my waist, in the cold river.

When I finally walked out and changed my underpants, I had nothing to stuff in to catch the fresh blood. All I could see around me was mud and leaves, and for one awful moment the holes in the guitar flashed in my mind and I had to fight back a fresh wave of tears at the thought of stuffing myself with that "poultice," like the broken Martin. But then I dug into the knapsack for another pair of clean panties and put them between my legs. Then, burying the bloody pants under a pile of twigs, I stood up and looked up the steep embankment for Nick, wondering what was in store for me now that I was grown.

"What d'ya do?" Nicky screamed, coming up behind me. "Bury a baby?"

"Shut up," I said, thinking, Yeah, me, my childhood.

"You get *it*?" he said.

I nodded.

"Now you're a lady, I guess."

"Shut up," I shouted.

"Well, we better get going?" Nicky said. "Now that you got your woman's stuff squared away." He lifted his knapsack and guitar and started walking along the path.

"Nicky," I called. But what did I want? Could I ask him to slap my face for me? My mother always told me she would slap my face when I got my period—that that's what Jews did. To show the pains coming your way from a woman's life? To distract you from your aching insides? She would slap me, she said, lightly, even ironically, just for fun. A love pat. She didn't believe in the other garbage.

Mommy, I thought, feeling my insides cramping. "Mommy!" I called.

"Stop bellyaching," Nicky called. "She's *dead and gone*."

"She is not, you idiot." I hated when he let lyrics take over our life, which was bad enough on its own. "Not dead and gone. She's sick."

"Whatever," he said. "We really are *motherless children* now. Motherless and fatherless." He laughed his low, hurt laugh.

"Mommy," I called again, silently. I wanted her so. I wanted to hug her real hard. I wanted to hit her real hard. Slap *her* face hard, for the hard luck that was on me now that I was grown up, the hard luck she had unloosed on me. And then, imagining my hand on her face, I started crying again, imagining the touch of her soft skin.

The Bronx River disappears suddenly at North Castle—the halfway mark between the Bronx and Pohogo. But we hadn't known that, and by the time Nick and I reached the end of our river, at its source of unseen springs, it was six o'clock and we were tired and hungry with another day's walk to go. With the river gone, inspiring our trek, we suddenly felt depleted of the will to keep walking.

Had I not gotten my period, I wouldn't have been afraid to hitch at the traffic circle ahead—for we'd always hitched around Pohogo. But now that I had decided more terrible adult things were coming my way, I was terrified of the perverts awaiting us in the recesses of cars.

Nick said, "We'll only get in with ladies."

Then he said, "Forget it. Ma's a lady, sort of."

But we decided this was the best plan—a lady with a station wagon, a family sort.

The first woman who came off the circle stopped for us, in a Nash Rambler wagon.

"Where are you kids headed?" she said, as we climbed in the back.

I studied the seats, which went down and wished I could set them back and take a nap. "Pohogo," I said.

"I'm going to Mapogo. Just beyond Pohogo. I can drop you off right on Route 6. Or take you home," she said.

"Route 6," we said in unison, not knowing where that was.

"I'm assuming you're not running away from home. You look sweet. Really sweet," she said.

"Thanks," we said, falling off to sleep.

The next thing we knew she was calling, "Kids, we're here. Route 6."

I opened my eyes. Route 6? This was Main Street. In the town of Pohogo. Pohogo Colony was just down the road.

"I know where I am," I screamed in delight.

"I should hope so," she laughed. "You live here."

16

Little House

We were tired and cold. But as we walked the half mile or so to the Colony, we passed the road leading to the lake and, without speaking, we followed Lake Lane down to the water.

How beautiful it looked: the dark still lake, the bare trees, the branches a mauvy lace against the blue-gray sky and water. The last time we were here was summer and we fell asleep on the beach singing that Huckleberry and Jim song. Now we'd become Huck and Jim, I thought. Traveling the river, homeless. Huck's father was a drunk. Our mother an addict. But things could be worse. Jim was a slave.

"We're lucky," I said. "Things could be worse. Being a slave, for example. Or even a serf or indentured servant," I said, drawing on what I'd learned in social studies so far that year. "We really are lucky."

"Oh, yes, we are very lucky," Nicky said. "I know that. We have our whole lives before us. And nobody to pull us down. . . . No shackles on my feet," he crooned. "My heart as free as air. . . ."

And we turned to leave, to get to the cabin before dark, singing our old Pohogo song as the sky emptied of light.

Pohogo Colony was largely a summer community, and there were no lights on in any of the houses we passed. We peeked in our landlord's house that fronted the road, behind which our cabin perched. But the Shapiros, if that was who still lived there, had covered the furniture with sheets. No one was around.

"We could go in *here*?" Nicky said.

"It's not ours," I said, in my shrillest monitor voice.

"Neither is the cabin," he said.

"It's *sort of* ours," I said.

And my brother, from whom I expected a new round of argument, just nodded, saying, "Oh, it's absolutely ours . . . we spent our childhood there."

"Three summers," I corrected him.

But I knew what he meant: The closest to carefree we'd known.

We had planned on some drama—jimmying the window locks, me climbing on Nicky's shoulder to come in the high bathroom window. But the front door was unlocked, and we walked right in.

Inside everything was the same: the sun porch with its long high windows; the kitchenette on the living room wall, the little glass-fronted cabinets with gingham curtains, the potbelly stove; the bedroom beyond with its clunky maple beds and dressers and pine rockers.

I jumped on my old bed, feeling right at home.

"My bed," I cried, waiting for the dream to spoil. The bed to break. Bears to come in and chase us into the woods.

Nicky was in the kitchen opening the cabinets, and I ran in to see. There were cans of soup and boxes of spaghetti. Chocolate pudding mix and flour and beans. And silently we began taking things from the cupboard to make our supper.

"Now what?" I said a few minutes later, as we ate our spaghetti and ketchup.

"Supper, bed."

"And then what?"

"Sleep. Wake up. Morning."

"Will we go to school?"

Nicky shook his head. "It would be dangerous. We could be caught."

"How long can we last here?"

"We'll get jobs. Save up some money. By spring, when people start coming here, we'll be able to move on."

I nodded.

"Where?"

"God damn it, Lucy. What do you want me to do, draw you a road map?"

And I nodded again.

But in the morning when we woke, all my anxieties were gone. The cabin was still warm and toasty from the night's fire and an electric heater we'd found in the closet. We ate chocolate pudding, which gave us pep. We straightened up the cabin. We sang our old Pohogo songs. The sandhog song about getting out of the tunnel just in time, breaking into the air. And singing there with Nicky, I felt like I could breathe for the first time in a long time.

We had a little Lucky Kids money left, which we'd stashed in our knapsacks when we ran out of the apartment. Underneath the cabin were some bikes. After breakfast we walked them down to the gas station on Main Street and filled the tires with air, then went to the little convenience store near the Taconic entrance and bought some cereal and milk and hotdogs and ice cream to keep us going. I needed some Kotex but was too embarrassed to buy it, but when I got to the checkout, a big blue box of the stuff was waiting with our food.

"Thanks," I said to Nicky out on the road.

"Just this first time, I figured," he said.

In the middle of the day we took a hike to the reservoir. Nicky ran off to explore and, sitting alone up on a rock, looking down at the water, I started thinking how the water supplied the Bronx, and felt gripped with sadness all over again.

Nicky must have heard me crying for he came barreling down the rocks, saying, "Get up. We're going." And watching him swoop down, like an Indian bird dancer, I felt my spirits lift.

Back in the cabin, Nick made a fire again. How strong his back

153

looked, how able his long fingers. I felt strength seeping into me and, as he poked the fire, I made a list of suppers for a week. Then lunches for a week. Then breakfasts. And though the variety was not great and we alternated between a few basics, writing it down filled me with hope. I made signs. Lucy's Room. Nicky's Room. I made a chore chart. I made a calendar for the next few months with pictures of the lake changing from fall to winter. And, taping my work to the wall, I felt hopeful and determined. We had no school but I felt like an important monitor again, with all my charts for our happy future. And my brave brother at my side.

Supper that night was hotdogs and beans. Because we used to grill so much at Pohogo, we decided to cook outside even though the air was brisk and, walking out to the edge of the property, we found the old stone pit still standing.

Nicky had bought gauze and adhesive tape and wrapped up the guitar—enough to play, he claimed. And as he sat on a folding chair by the pit, I cooked our hotdogs and the can of beans, and studied the Martin. A true blues guitar, I thought, hearing the sound struggling around the wounds before it got out. Our life was different now but it would be all right. We were together and it would be all right. As I watched the flames, my heart crooned with a sad joy. And Nicky strummed, "*Trouble in mind, I'm blue, but I won't be blue always. / Cause the sun's gonna shine. In my back door some day.*"

We heard a rustling from the woods. Then a call. And then a tall man was coming towards us, lifting his cap in salute.

"Big Will," Nicky called.

And though we needed all the help we could get, I thought, Oh, no. He'd want to know our whole story, and I'd start to cry. He'd call our parents, and we'd have to go back, just when everything was seeming possible without them. Our cabin, our meals, our work. And he'd talk to Nicky and ignore me, win my brother from me as he had my father. And I'd be all alone.

"Young Nick," he said.

I waved, but tentatively in case Big Will wanted to pay me no mind. But he said, "And Lucy. Young Lucy. A young woman, I can see."

For a moment I thought my period had seeped through to my skirt and he could see it, which told him I was a young woman, and I just sat there frozen, afraid to look down at my lap or up at his eyes.

"I remember you youth well," he said, and I felt relieved, realizing it was just the rhetoric of a veteran speechmaker that had termed me young woman. "And what a nice surprise. I smelled those wieners and said to myself, Big Will, it must be especially brave folks out here in the cold."

"It's not that cold," Nick said, proud of the compliment.

"Well, what brings you here? That cabin's been empty for a while. One year there was another family renting. But I always thought, That shouldn't be. That's the Lehman cabin. Tell me, how are you doing? How are your parents?"

I could see Nicky studying the old man hard, assessing him. How much could he be told? Was there place in Big Will's certain, forward-marching world view for the likes of us and our parents? Suddenly Nicky threw his head back and began to laugh. "They died, Big Will. . . . Don't think I'm happy about it or anything on account of I'm laughing. But it was sort of a relief. They were both sick for a long time."

"Oh, shit," Will said. "Oh, what a damn shitty fate."

"We were prepared," Nicky said. "And when it finally happened, we felt, as I said, some relief, believe it or not."

By now Nicky had his laughter under control and was working on an earnest expression.

"I believe it. When my wife suffered with her cancer, I was glad when she went. Fifty-eight pounds. We were both happy when the end came. What did they have, your folks?"

Nicky looked at me to take over, as if suddenly it had become too hard for him to talk about the subject of their deaths.

You idiot, I thought. You lying idiot. But then it suddenly seemed right, our parents being really gone. It was easier this way, less hurtful, less messy.

Now Big Will was looking at me too.

155

"Gangrene," I said, Vern's story fresh in my mind.

"Imagine that. And it took them?"

"They were always so busy giving," Nicky said. "You know, their political work. They caught it. . . ." And here my brother's hand grabbed at the air, which was freezing up, giving him his next line. "They caught it in the cold giving out leaflets together. I mean frostbite. And then they just didn't take care of it, because, you know, they were too busy thinking of the world's problems and taking care of us. And anyway . . . one thing led to another. In the end it was a relief."

"Poor people. I was very fond of them. Very fiery and substantial. A bad way to go, though. Gangrene, you say?"

I nodded and because Big Will's face looked twisted in sorrow and puzzlement and more than a little doubt, I said, "Yes. Definitely gangrene. And then general infection."

He nodded. "Secondary infection . . . I see."

"Yeah. They were very infected in the end. They even stank," Nicky said. "It was awful."

"Jesus, you kids have been through it."

"We really have," Nicky said, breaking into big genuine sobs.

I put my arms around him and his miserable guitar. "It's okay," I said. "We got each other." And I started bawling too.

"And me," Big Will said. "Young Nick, don't fear. You got yourself a guardian. And you too, young woman. I'm better with boys, but I'm going to try my damnedest, for both of you youth."

And he lunged at us and covered our bodies with his. When I started squirming for air, he was sensitive and let me go. Which made me think that maybe he'd be a good guardian for me too. He complimented me on the franks and beans, which we gobbled up quickly to get out of the cold. And then Big Will walked us inside to see how we were set up and, assured that we had sheets and blankets and heat, he called out, "Good night then, young people," and we closed our eyes and were out.

The next morning Big Will came over early to "get us organized," and immediately I knew there would be trouble. For hadn't I

gotten us organized already? We didn't need his reading list and top-
ics for discussion. I'd included silent reading on my chore chart, and
Nicky and I talked fine to each other without Big Will telling us
what to talk about. Origin of the Family. Meaning of Wealth. The
Individual and the Nature of Choice. That's what he wrote under
Topics for the Future on the bottom of my calendar.

Who wanted to talk about all that? We had no family, no wealth,
little choice, it seemed. And seeing his useless topics announced in
his stiff print, which darted out into the middle of my lake pictures
like invading ships, I felt myself sink.

Nicky said, "Oh boy, now I get to deepen my theoretical understanding. I'm really weak on the idea of wealth and profit and family."

I wonder why? I thought sarcastically, slamming the door to the
bathroom, where I changed my napkin, studying the clots of my
blood, fascinated and terrified by the red and blue iridescence pour-
ing from me.

I reassured myself it would take time to get the books, which
Will said we'd read before each discussion session. But that first
morning of his guardianship, he took us to his house, a cluttered
little blue clapboard about five minutes' walk through the woods.
Here, to my dismay, were stacks and stacks of books, multiple copies
of all of our "essential readings," as he called what we were to study
with him in lieu of school work. We'd do some "home study" for a
while, till we got settled.

In a way it was cute, Will's narrow frame house like one of the
houses in town in *Little House on the Prairie*. But just thinking this, I
started feeling homesick and schoolsick, for we'd read the whole
Laura Ingalls Wilder series in fifth grade and were learning about
frontier America this year in ninth grade and I was in the middle of
a pretty impressive diorama of a quilting bee. And then the countless
spindly avocado plants in the parlor where we were to study with
Will were insubstantial and depressing, making me miss the
Botanics, all the orchids and the chrysanthemum installations for
October, and Miss DiFrancesco's cabbages, which I was supposed to

start caring for on Monday, two days from now. And I even began to miss my mother's philodendra and wandering Jews—when they were still robust in their old pots before she dug them up and tossed them around.

The first book, *The Origin of the Family, Private Property and the State*, was mercifully thin, I saw, when Big Will handed us each our copy—about a tenth of the size of *Forefathers of a Great Nation*, which I was reading in social studies. But the print was tiny and it had no pictures.

Nicky wanted to get to work on the book immediately.

"This is good," he said, thumbing the volume. "'Savagery,' 'Barbarism,' 'Civilization,' 'Group Marriage,'" he blushed.

"I don't think I'm going to like this book," I said. "I can hardly read the words. The print is so teeny."

"She's crazy," Nicky said, embarrassed as much, I think now, by the stuff in the book about brothers and fathers doing it with the wife before the husband, as by having an ignoramus for a sister.

"It's good to put things in historical perspective," Will said. "I know you're still youth and feeling your own tragic events deeply. But this, hopefully, will deepen your understanding of the march of mankind and lessen your personal pain."

I examined the book again. God knows I wanted to lessen my personal pain. But it covered so many millennia in so few pages, prehistory in a page, the Stone Age in two, that I felt dwarfed into insignificance. It seemed to root for mankind in general, but I couldn't grasp onto any people in there. Which was my fault, I was sure, my narrowness, my neediness, which made me look for personal pats everywhere. A realization that made me feel even sadder holding the grim book in my hands, filled with information and tips I'd never get to know.

Will said, "It's going to take time to read."

"I read *Jane Eyre* in three nights. I'm a fast reader. But I don't know if I can get through this," I said.

"Jesus Christ, Lucy," Nicky barked.

So I skimmed. But the sex parts were few and dry, and the rest of it hopelessly abstract for me. Someone named Morgan said this, then Engels that. A foreword by Lenin said everything Engels said was 100% right. A preface by someone else said Lenin was 100% right.

We were sitting in the front parlor and Big Will was stretched out on a mahogany Morris chair. He leaned toward me, where I sat beside Nicky on a love seat, and said, "Try to read this book with an open mind. It's for you, the young women of the world, especially. This book expresses the idea that the women are very important. Once upon a time, lineage ran from women. In those communal societies there was no private property. . . ."

"None?" Nicky said. "That's very interesting. I like that."

"Well, when people developed to being farmers as opposed to wandering gatherers, and they started accumulating things, then the family as we know it developed. With family identity and property coming down from the men what with the division of labor at that critical juncture in human history. But the older way is very instructive for mankind. For society as we know it is . . . far from ideal. . . . Far from ideal."

I tried my hardest to get into it. Besides first nights' rights, which was handled in a couple of sentences, I was interested in the section on savagery. Who were the savages and why were they the way they were? Maybe if I gave the book a chance, I'd gain insights about why people were cruel or reckless or wild. Our father, for example. And then our mother after him. But all the writer said was that savages ate vegetables and then, later on, fish including mussels and clams and crabs, and they developed the bow and arrow and were permitted to have sex with lots of people. There was nothing in here for me.

"I miss school," I said, laying my book down. The diorama, the little figures bending over their patches of cloth. The responsibilities and recognition of a seasoned monitor. The Botanics in the afternoon. Miss DiFrancesco. Even my mother? Maybe she'd calmed down by now. "I really miss school," I called.

But they ignored me. They were busy talking about patrilineage and the Iroquois.

159

"I miss geometry. It's real neat."

"Neat's a stupid word," Nicky said. "It's corny." And he went on talking with Big Will about class divisions in Athens, private property in the South Seas, the subjugation of women around the globe, which didn't have to be, Big Will said.

"Why?" I said, suddenly interested.

But they didn't hear me.

"Why doesn't it have to be?" I said.

When they continued to ignore me, I said again, "Why? How's it going to go away?"

Had my mother known how it could stop, couldn't she have done something, gotten away from our father before she got ruined too?

"Shut up, idiot, and read the book," Nicky said. "When we have a classless society, women will not have to be subjugated."

"I'm going home," I said.

"Be careful in the woods," Nick said.

"I mean *back home*," I shouted. "The Bronx."

"But you have no home there," Will said.

"Actually . . . she does," Nicky said. "Actually . . . we do, Big Will," he whispered. "It's just that it's . . . far from ideal . . . you see."

Yeah, it's savage, I wanted to scream. But *regular* savage, not this fancy kind in this fancy book. Regular savage, with kicking and screaming and breaking of property. Was I so homesick that I was missing even that? I studied the strange room, Big Will's strange face. I sniffed the air for a familiar scent, but all I could smell was cold country dust. I wiggled my pinky to give my brother one last chance to remember our blood oath, that we were in this together, forever and ever. Just the two of us. But he was looking across at Will, and I felt so lonely I began to cry.

And poor Big Will, the bewildered one now, sat in his chair with his book in his lap, looking up, trying to understand, calling, "Young woman, young woman, what seems to be the problem?"

In the end, we told Big Will our story. He patted our heads and told us he'd left home when he was fourteen. There were twelve children and not enough food and a stepfather who beat crybabies.

"Don't go, Lucy," he said.

"Yeah," Nicky said.

I knew if I said what I thought—You two will be happier without me, reading your books, making your speeches—they'd deny it, but so halfheartedly I'd start crying again, which I didn't want to do. I needed all my strength.

"I'm just going back to the cabin," I said.

"But you're not leaving," Will said.

"Yeah," Nicky said.

I waited till morning to tell them.

Big Will called our mother and said he had us. He said Nicky could stay with him, but that I wanted to come home.

Did I? When I heard her voice as he handed me the phone, I started crying in confusion.

"I miss you too," I said.

"I can't wait to see you either," I said.

"Don't cry, Ma," I said. "I'm coming home."

"Sure," I said. "Sure, everything will be okay."

Big Will drove me to the Peekskill Station in his old Chevy. Nicky offered to let me sit up front, but I let him, knowing how much he wanted to be beside his new friend and benefactor.

"Nice old car," Nicky said when we got in. "You ever work in the auto industry, Will?"

"Nope, just in steel. Eighteen years in the steel mill."

"Of course," Nick said, remembering some of the old man's stories from our old Pohogo days.

"Till they threw me out for organizing. . . . Then I worked just organizing, you know."

"I'm going to work in steel, Big Will. Then organize."

"I thought you were going to be a blues singer . . . a blues guitarist," I said. "Make up your mind!"

161

My spite surprised me. But every day he was moving further and further away from me for something new. Blues, steel, organizing. If he'd only listen to me, I'd organize things fine. If he'd only listen to me and not to Big Will. I saw my charts, remembered my hopes from just the day before. Our quiet time, and reading time, and talking together time.

"Blues man needs something to sing about," Nicky said. "I'm going to sing about steel . . . hammering steel. Organizing men. But music will just be my hobby. Changing the lot of men will be my life. You know that, Lucy."

So much for women and girls, that whole speech.

"Yeah, I know," I said, glad we'd reached the station.

Big Will waited in the car and Nicky walked me up to the track. I thought about how much had gone on in a week. The guitar gone. My home with Nicky gone. Nicky with Big Will now, marching towards some new life. Me all alone.

"Big battles fought at Peekskill," Nick said, studying the station sign.

I nodded, but tentatively so he'd stop talking, about battles, organizing. I knew he meant the Peekskill riots when locals tried to stop Paul Robeson from singing and the sides lined up and heads got broken. I was raised on the story as he was and proud that our Uncle Pinky had been there with a scar on his chin to prove it. But I didn't need a speech now. Just Nick's strong hand holding mine. And one soft word.

"I may not see you for a while," I said.

Nicky nodded.

"You sure you want to go?" he said.

I nodded. "It's good for you here. But. . . ." You don't need me now. You don't care about me now. But I couldn't bring myself to speak my thoughts. "But . . . you see . . . I miss school and stuff," I said.

"You're good in school, Missy," he was saying. "You stay good in school. You go to school. Don't just stay . . . home . . . you know."

Then he started crying and I felt so relieved that I laughed in his face before I clasped him hard and cried back in his arms.

"I won't," I said. "I'll get out and do lots of things. . . ."

Then the train pulled in.

"I can't wait till you're not subjugated, Missy," he said.

"Really?" I squealed, relieved again.

"Of course. That's one of the reasons I'm staying. I'm going to change this fucking world. For everyone. I got a fucking lot to do, little Missy."

"I know you do, Cocoa," I said, kissing his cheek, feeling his fuzz, trying not to cry. "You're a good Cocoa, Cocoa. You're going to be an okay Cocoa, Cocoa."

"Lucy," he cried as I turned to leave. "Lucy . . . and Nicky forever. Lucky Kids . . . forever," he cried, bawling like a baby.

"Forever," I cried back.

And then I let him go, and climbed up the step to the waiting train.

17

Just Lucy

I'd left Nicky the chore chart and calendar, and he'd promised, even though he was moving out of the cabin into Will's, to hang them on the wall.

"Otherwise, you'll just read those books all day," I'd said. "I know you like them but there are other things to do. It's a reminder," I said, handing him the rolled up papers, "of other things in life." I meant the things we did together. A reminder of them. Of me. I meant of course: Hang up this shit and think of me.

Now, in the train, I took out my spiral book from my knapsack to get my new life organized. For so many years, Nick had shared my life.

My new life, I wrote at the top of a page. And then I just sat there staring out the window, my face—singular, brotherless—staring back at me blankly.

People in Your New Life, I wrote, to get it going.

1. Dad (and Moan), I wrote.

Not too close—eighteen subway stops. Busy and on the selfish side. Thinking of my father and Mona, gripped by sorrow, I saw Liberty's fat face floating in my mind and I found myself missing her. For at least she'd tried to woo Nicky and me, however unsuccessfully, with her food and promise to be our mother, maybe meaning well and not knowing how it revolted us. But now I was fourteen and clumsy and chubby, so why should Mona bother kootchy-kooing me? I acknowledged she wasn't mean, just sensible. Sensibly she'd point to the pile of *discard* books she'd taken from her library, which I could take or leave as I wished. I could take or leave her as I wished. She didn't really care. I could discard her. It didn't matter to her.

To stop the sad croon starting up in my throat—for my lost father, who'd just turned nice and fatherly before he left—I quickly wrote, Positive Features.

I wrote: Sometimes her books are interesting. and sometimes they take me to restaurants (remember not to overeat at these in the future). Sometimes he remembers about shoes and is getting more flexible about style now that I'm a teen.

I didn't really want to put my mother on the list, because I didn't want to get more depressed than I was, but since I was trying to get things organized in my mind, I knew I had to.

2. Mom, I wrote.

Pills, mess, yelling.

Then for the positive, which I quickly turned to, I wrote: Good sense of humor, fun, understanding, good dancer and dance partner, beautiful.

She was two people, of course. For years she'd been two people. But now, seeing my list, I felt the realization like a slap in the face rousing me to consciousness. And I sat up tall, wondering which one would be waiting for me at the station.

Then to add some hope, I put more people on my list. Teeny. I'd call her when I got back. I put in Teeny's mother, who was the second Ida, the third Ida, and Nan, of course. And then I wrote:

Miss DiFranceso. Perfect. Not positive and negative, but perfect. The most perfect person I know. The most important person in my new life. The one who will make it a *new* life.

Then remembering that today was Sunday and tomorrow was Monday, when my new job would begin, I wrote, What I Will Learn in My New Job.

But I couldn't think of a particular thing. My heart was racing with joy at the thought of Miss DiFrancesco, her cacti and cabbages and mail. I guess I was thinking something like, You will learn that life can be perfect. I closed my eyes and saw the bright gleaming halls of the museum and her wide smile and almond eyes looking down on me like the Virgin Mary. And thinking of her, I must have fallen asleep, for the next thing I remember was the conductor calling out New York.

My eyes searched for her, and I hoped it would be the positive mother who had come to meet me at the station. I'd know right away from the way she walked down the platform, the way she held her jaw, how she called, if she called. If she were loaded, she'd try to hide that in public behind some demureness, walking super slowly, her jaw clenched shut and silent. If she were clean, she'd whistle like a coach, run to me, calling my name.

After a half an hour, I knew she wasn't coming and knew, of course, why. I didn't bother calling. I just took the shuttle to the D train, and the D train to our stop at the end of the line.

Two Hundred and Fourth Street, our shopping street, near where the subway lets out, was a typical neighborhood commercial street running four or so blocks, with a couple of bakeries—one Jewish, one German—a couple of delis—one Jewish, one German—a couple of bars—both Irish. At the end of the street, as you walked west, 204th Street crossed with another shopping street—with more bakeries, delis and bars. At the end of the street, as you walked east, though, there were no more streets and stores, but a trestle above the New York Central leading to Bronx Park. It was this trestle that Nicky had run across the night he dumped our mother on the street. And now I walked towards it, intending to turn before I reached it for the two block walk south and home. But across the trestle, in a red burst of maple and oak, was the grand dome of the museum, and I raced over the tracks, down the steps to French Charlie's, and then south through the meadow to the gate of the Gardens.

Miss DiFrancesco, Miss DiFrancesco, I thought, as I ran up the museum walk and the steps to her office. But the office was locked and dark.

The guard knew me. "Tomorrow," he said. "Monday."

I half wanted to ask if I could wait in the office till then. Or if I could have her home number. Maybe she'd let me stay with her sisters, the sisters. And I could bypass my old life altogether.

"Come back tomorrow."

"Yeah," I said. "I was just checking on the time she wanted me. Three-thirty, I guess, straight from school."

"Sounds good," he said.

Downstairs, the auditorium was showing a film on chrysanthemums in Japan. I sat in the back row watching the flowers open, then get picked and placed in perfect poised splendor. Then get bowed to by men and women in long floral robes. *"Shabui,"* the narrator said. "That simple modest grace. The chrysanthemum in the autumn conveys it to our Japanese friends as it lives. And as it dies," the narrator said, as the film showed the petals falling gracefully into eternity.

When the film was over, I walked up to the office again, knowing, of course, that Miss DiFrancesco wouldn't be there. But couldn't I just sit up there in the still hall outside her office? I felt desperate to live beside her, die beside her, if it came to that, in her still grace. But upstairs the corridor was dark and I couldn't even see my hand in front of me, so I tiptoed down the stairs, knowing I had to face *her* now.

Clearly, she'd been up all night. The apartment had the swampy smell of her drugs and her druggy efforts—the damp sweetness of her pill solutions and the soil from some manic repotting.

She was sitting at the kitchen table reading the *Police Gazette*. My mother had always read mysteries and Trollope and Shakespeare and Edith Wharton and Wordsworth, whose Lucy I was named for. Lately she'd taken to reading the *National Enquirer* or *Police Gazette* when she was high—a thrill for a thrill. When I opened the front door I saw her and she waved, real casual, and went back to her reading.

"I thought you were going to meet me," I said.

"I figured why reward a little coward. You ran away from your family responsibilities," she said. "And I don't like that. I don't like that and I don't respect that."

"I see," I said, walking past her.

"Don't walk past me," she said. "I don't like that either."

I walked into the kitchen and sat down at the table across from her. Her hands were filthy from the planting. Her face was streaked with dirt.

"You want a bath?"

"I'm not a baby," she said. "And you're not my mother. I run the show around here, young lady. Rule Number One. You obey your mother. Do you understand?"

"Yeah," I said.

"Yes," she said. "Say, 'yes' to your mother. Say 'yes, mother' to your mother."

"Yes, mother," I said.

"Say it like you mean it, not like a little brat."

"You're the brat, not me," I said.

And she stood up to slap me. But rising quickly, she got dizzy and fell to the floor. Which seemed to do her good, sloshing the chemicals in her brain around, making her less nasty.

"How's your brother, the major brat?" she called up to me.

"Ginger-peachy," I said.

"And that boring old fool?"

"Big Will's not so bad. He took us in. They'll be okay."

"He's a pedantic dud," she said. "I'd die if I had to hang around him. Tell me you didn't leave because it was so boring and you knew you'd die." She began to laugh, and wrinkled up her nose to invite me to laugh with her.

I laughed. "That wasn't it."

"What did they do? Gang up on you? Read Karl Marx and leave you out?"

"Engels," I said.

"I like Engels," she said. "He likes ladies," she laughed. "and I do like Marx sometimes . . . when I can understand him. But not for breakfast. That man eats them for breakfast and is humorless. Uh-oh."

"What's wrong?"

"Nicky. He'll be insufferable now. Talk about self-righteous. I'll never be able to tell him a thing now."

"You should tell him you're sorry about the guitar, you know." For suddenly I thought if she apologized, maybe he really would come back and I wouldn't be all alone with her.

"But I'm not. I'm not sorry one bit. He raised his hand to me and got what he deserved. And I don't just mean the loss of the guitar. I mean the loss of his mother. The love of his mother. I don't love a boy who hits his mother."

Her diction and syntax were getting weird—she was dentalizing and sounding sort of rabbinical in her repetitions—and I wondered if she would break into her nasty Yiddish next.

"He didn't hit you," I said to stop her drift.

"He was thinking about it real hard. I could tell."

I hope you die, I thought. It was a test, to see if she could really read thoughts. Could she tell what I thought? What I wished for? If she read my thoughts, she'd do something awful: bite my nose, slam my head like she'd slammed Nicky's guitar. But she just wiggled her nose to make me laugh.

Did I wish she'd die? A moment before, for a split second, she was cute. Her laugh, her nose. But she was also a monster. She was roaring something to me now. About Nicky. Then about her and me. With her head back against the floor, I could see into her wide mouth, down into her throat. And I backed away from her, hugging the wall, afraid she'd suck me up like a dragon.

Die, I thought again, watching her face for a response.

"We don't need him. We got each other," she said, turning her head from side to side on the linoleum. "I got you and you got me. You're my baby and I'm your mommy. And that's that," she said. "That's that. I say so." She wrinkled her nose again, so I'd laugh at her baby face, her baby talk. Maybe tickle her baby belly.

But I just stood there, and she passed out.

In the morning, she was still sleeping in her bed, where I'd carried her the night before. As I left for school, she opened one eye and said, "You look cute, Petunia. I like blue and green together. You know Mommy loves you very much. You're all I have. I bet you didn't know that."

On the way to school, I realized I didn't have a note from my mother for my days out. So I tore out a page from my spiral and wrote the note my mother had written for years, since I'd started staying home from school to take care of her: Lucy's tonsils gave us trouble again. But be assured she kept up with her studies. And I signed her name.

"Lucy, where were you?" Teeny asked me in the schoolyard.

I shrugged, meaning home, or not, and mind your own business.

"Oh my God, your mom told my mom you guys ran away. True or False?"

As high school loomed, Ida Klein was having the hyper Teeny coached on test-taking. And these days most everything in her barrage of constant questions was short-answer format. She thought it was cute.

"I'm here now," I said.

"And Nick? Oh my God, where's Nick? A—with friends? B—with family?"

I shook my head.

"Oh my God, I bet you miss him."

I nodded.

"Oh my God, it must be weird not to have Nicky around. My mom says that your mom says he's not coming back. Right or wrong?"

I nodded again.

I'd wanted to talk to Teeny, to catch up, hear about Ida, tell Teeny about my job in the Gardens and ask her to visit me in the office. She had gotten impossible lately, touching everything, dropping everything, asking a million stupid questions, but still she was an old friend, and the day before, as I rode the train, I'd thought that it might be nice to have her around. But as I replayed her words—not coming back, not coming back—I felt my throat lump up with tears. And I put my hands around my neck to stop it.

"Oh, no, not your tonsils again?"

I nodded again, turning to go inside.

"My mom says it's not really your tonsils. You just say that. Your mother just says that so you can stay home with her. I wish I had a tonsil problem. I'd watch television all day. Ignore my mother. Have fun. All of the above," she whinnied.

I said nothing, just kept walking.

"Oh God, I can't believe it's just you and your mom now," she called.

"Nicky's never coming back? Correct?" she called. "Oh my God, that's so awful. Doesn't that feel awful?"

But I pretended I couldn't hear, which I guess hurt her feelings. For she called, "What are you, some kind of dummy? Can't talk? Can't hear? I can't believe my mother likes you so much just because you like to mop our floor."

In geometry, my favorite subject, I couldn't concentrate and took out my spiral and saw my New Life Without Nick list. I ripped out Teeny's page. She really was a dope. Then I ripped out my mother's page. Then my father's page. I still had Nan and the two Idas', but just their names, not having filled in sheets for them. The only person I had left for whom I had a full entry was Miss DiFrancesco. I added qualities to her sheet. Beauty. Intelligence. Kindness. Charity.

At three I raced to her.

But she wasn't there.

The same guard was. "Called in sick," he said.

"I see," I said. "I guess I'll just come back tomorrow. Did she think she'd be better tomorrow?"

He shrugged.

Again, I wanted to ask for her number. But what would I say? Sorry to bother you, especially when you're sick, Miss DiFrancesco. But you see . . . there's no one left. I need you. I love you. You're my whole life now. *My new life.*

I sat in the auditorium and slept through a movie on the life cycle of pussy willows. And when I woke up, it was after five and they were closing up the Gardens.

Outside it was dark—I'd never been alone in the park before after dark. Nicky had always been with me if we were out late skating on Twin Lakes or swimming in the river or just walking around in the woods. But now I was down the path behind the Conservatory all alone. Where was I going? What was I doing? I felt like an animal sniffing for something. I remembered the smell at home last night, the chemicals and soil. I was seeking a new life now with new smells.

The river's scent was floating across the glen, perky and fresh. But filling my lungs with it, I remembered Nicky. How we'd walked here together just a few nights before. And quickly, to dispel my sorrow, I changed directions, charging into a copse of pine saplings on the near side of the nearer lake.

Children of smokers can smell tobacco in their dreams. Walking along the shore, sniffing for the defiant, urgent smell of evergreen, I caught tobacco with every clouded breath. Someone was smoking. It wasn't Camels—my mother's brand. Nor Luckies—my father's. It was deeper, darker—Bull Durham, I was sure. And turning, I called to him. "Nicky, Nicky."

He came towards me from some taller pines at the rise in the ground where the two lakes meet. Jeans, a jean jacket, leather combat boots. "Nicky," I called again.

"No," he said. "Eddie."

"Oh, hi, Eddie," I said, seeing my brother's old friend, his white face covered with freckles, like a pancake ready to be flipped. "I thought you were Nicky."

Eddie was one of the Snuff Mill toughies, or else, I think, I would have rushed into his arms and cried, "Please be *him* for now."

"Where's Nick?" he said. "Haven't seen him all week."

"Upstate," I said.

"For good, right? I thought he'd take off. I might take off too. It's

173

so fucking shitty around here. My father is such a scumbag. He has the fucking audacity to call me a delinquent. I say, bullshit. I say, bullshit to his face. He drinks a fifth of Four Roses every night and wallops my mother, and just because I sip a little Thunderbird from time to time and smoke my little stuff and hang around and stuff, I'm the fucking delinquent. I say, bullshit. You're the delinquent, delinquent father, delinquent husband. So then he hauls off. Where's Nicky? I'll check him out. We'll hang out together. Enough of this bullshit."

"Far away," I said, thinking, *I don't get to have him, you don't get to have him.* "With our uncle."

"The doctor in Connecticut uncle?"

"No. This one's . . . a politician. In New York. Upstate."

"Like a mayor?" he said.

"Sort of."

"Uh-oh. No mayor would want a lowlife like me hanging around his chambers. I guess Nicky's behaving himself. Putting on his smart-ass act. Good old Nick. I'll miss him."

I nodded.

Then we said nothing, just sat on a rock, side by side, looking at the lake. Eddie had ditched his skinny little cigarette. Now he took a pint of Thunderbird from his jacket and took a slug.

"How old are you now, Lucy?" he said.

"Fourteen."

"Jeez. I thought you were younger."

I shook my head. "No. Fourteen."

"Fourteen. Ha. You know, I could fill in a little, Lucy. You know, protect you and stuff from lowlifes. And wild animals," he laughed, waving to the woods.

"Thanks, Eddie," I said.

He took another slug, then suddenly put his arm around me.

"How's that feel?" he said.

I shrugged.

"That?" he said. He was breathing in my ear now, like my father used to to make me laugh. "How's that feel?" he said. "That feel good?"

"I don't know," I said. "It sort of tickles."

I sort of liked it. It was warm, tingly, fun. I wanted to tickle him back. Maybe behind the ears. Like I used to tickle my father. And Nick. When we rolled on the floor in his room or mine.

Then he put his tongue in my mouth and moved it around. And I opened my mouth to give him room to dig around, for it felt good, like nothing I'd ever felt before. This was my first time kissing with a boy, and it was different than what I'd expected, far from the "disgusting" ordeal that other girls had reported. I felt like I was getting something to eat, something that would fill me up, but that wouldn't get me fat.

Then he took his tongue out of my mouth

"How was that?"

I shrugged.

He took another slug of the wine. "Let's try again."

This time he had his tongue out before it got to me. It was big and wide with pimples on the side, and suddenly it did seem like an ordeal. I thought, You don't know this tongue. And even though it had just felt interesting inside me, it really didn't feel right having it in me again. It was just too strange, a stranger's strange, ugly tongue. I started feeling sad, and as empty as I'd felt full the moment before. I shook my head, no.

"Come on," he said.

I shook my head again.

"Come on," he said again. "I'm crazy about you, Lucille."

"Just Lucy. And you hardly know me. And I don't want to."

Then, like he was feeling me for a pack of cigarettes, he started patting my chest. "I know you from way back. Come on. Come on, *Just Lucy*," he said.

I shook my head. "Stop, I don't like that," I said. But he kept doing it, here and there, up and down.

"Hey," I said, standing up fast. "Remember who I am?"

I meant, I'm Nick's sister. A week ago you were handing me candy bars, trying to speak fancy in front of me. Now what are you doing?

175

"What are you doing?" I said. "What were you just doing?" I said. Maybe I was wrong. Maybe he wasn't doing anything. Maybe he was just trying to feel cozy, not feel me up.

"I was just doing this." He grabbed for me, getting the zipper of my parka.

"Stop it," I screamed.

"Why, baby?" he said, grabbing at my chest again. "Why should I stop? I was just doing this," he said. And then I heard *his* zipper.

He pulled me down on the rock again, pushing hard against me. I tried to scream but he stuffed himself inside my mouth. And, pressing my head like a door buzzer, he cried, "Here I am, baby." His stuff squirted in me. When he pulled out, I tried to scream again. But again I couldn't. Vomit was flying from me.

"Oh Jesus," he said. "Oh Jesus, I'm sorry. I didn't mean to make you nauseous. It's the goddamn Thunderbird. I become an animal. And you're right. You're Nicky's little sister and look what it made me do. I mean even with him gone, you're still his sister, right?"

Between my retching, I shook my head, yes. I was still his little sister. Even though he'd left me . . . alone in the woods . . . among beasts.

"You want me to go away, Lucy?" Eddie said.

I nodded.

"I'm afraid," he said. "I'm afraid someone worse will come along if *I* go."

I shook my head. Go.

"Na. It's the only honorable thing to do now. To walk you home. And honest, I won't touch you . . . one drop more."

I shook my head again. And started walking.

"Hey, you live the other way. You're all confused. Boy, I'm glad you got me to direct you, as fucked up as I am."

I didn't say anything. I just kept walking east into the park.

"Hey, Lucy, where you going?"

Where *was* I going? If I went the other way, I'd reach home, and the last person I wanted to see now was my mother. Then, afraid if I didn't answer, he'd do it again, I heard myself say, "My Grandma's house." *That's* where I'd go. Suddenly I longed to be with my Nan, comforted in her thin, pale arms.

"Little Red Riding Hood," he laughed. "And I'm the wolf, watch out." He started wagging his tongue. "Just kidding, Lucy. Really, *Just Lucy*, I'm just joking."

Seeing his tongue again, I started vomiting again.

"I'll just escort you, Luce. That's what Nicky calls you, right? Luce. That's why I surmised Lucille. I'll just escort you, Luce. Little Luce. Little Lulu. . . . And I'll be quiet. I promise."

And he made a gesture to lock his lips and throw away the key. "And you'll be quiet, right Lucy? Nobody will know?" He pulled at my jacket hood. "Right, nobody will know?"

The moon hung above the edge of the park and I charged towards it. I wanted to howl at it, cry to it what had just happened. But I heard him behind me, then smelled him all around—the tobacco and wine, the sweat and cum, sharp like pepperoni—and everything started spinning. Then I willed myself to notice nothing— smells and sounds and tastes—to forget everything but how to breathe and put one foot before the other. And with only that in mind, I ran through the woods towards the white wondrous light.

18

Grandma's House

Evening in Paris cologne, *Cashmere Bouquet* soap, worn leather, *Lifesaver Wintergreen*, old flannel—that's my grandma's smell and it flies at me as my grandma opens the door and I fly to her. All other smells are banished—all other sensations—here in my grandma's house.

My grandmother's house is not really hers. It belongs to her Mrs., but Nan's room is big and looks out on a Tudor courtyard with iron benches and a star-shaped pool and pots of mums and a wishing well. I focus on these details only as Nan leads me into her room and I drop onto her bed. Let me forget, I wish, as I look out the window to the little stone well, before I drop off in my grandma's arms in my grandma's narrow bed.

In the morning Nan tells me she's called my mother, and I don't have to go to school. "We'll celebrate, she says," to cheer me up. "The usual," she says, to make me laugh. In the night, I know, I've cried. I remember Nan bringing me hot milk—which she does only when I cry from bad dreams. But the milk gave me memories—of *his* warm white stuff.

"You threw up," Nan says now. "But I washed my *zeeskeit* in a bath and held her as she slept. And now she's all better. No more crazy dreams."

"Come," Nan, says, and I follow her down the hall.

When Nan's Mrs. is out of the house we can use the kitchen—
and since Faygie is off at work, we empty Nan's shelf on the table.

"Oh, boy," I cry, to make Nan happy. I study the treats lined up
on the bright oil-cloth. Sturgeon and cream cheese and a few specks
of caviar. Truffles and strawberries and halavah. Raised rich, Nan
tries to buy a "half of a quarter pound" of sturgeon weekly to sustain
her spirits even in the worst of times. Life is not so bad, the smoky
fish tells her. Or if it's bad, it still has some flavor. This morning as
I've slept, I see, she's shopped, supplementing her usual fare. As I bite
into a sturgeon and caviar and onion sandwich, which Nan has prepared, I hope that the flavors are strong enough to expel the memories in the park, his awful flavors and smells.

I should eat and be happy, Nan says. *Zeeskeit*, she calls me again.
Sweet one. Her brown eyes—now a dreamy blue from cataracts—
settle on me. Such adoration deserves only gratitude and joy. The
salty fish does not taste like him, I tell myself so I will not cry. It does
not feel like him—wet and slimy in my mouth—I tell myself so I
will smile for Nan and not throw up again

"Nicky?" she says, looking for a cozy, happy subject. "Where's
Nicky?"

Today, she means, unaware that we've run away. Were I to tell her
that Nicky's gone, she'd run to the subway station, race down to
Grand Central, grab the next railroad north, beg him to come back.
And then what? He was never coming back. So I tell her Nicky's
busy, playing with a band downtown after school.

"*Caballerochka*," she laughs. Russian for cowboy.

The band will be traveling, I tell her.

She giggles. "Such a talented boy. He makes that balalaika laugh
with joy."

And I try not to think of the guitar, its neck broken, its sides
gashed, bandaged in gauze. If I told Nan the truth about Tippy smash-
ing the guitar, she'd shake her head and her eyes would fill with
tears, and she'd say what she always said confronted with another

disappointment from her daughter: "She was a beautiful child. Did you ever see her pictures?" And then she'd show me photos to document the splendid material our mother was made of, which, of course, I knew too well. "Something went wrong," she would say. And she'd look down because she thinks it's her fault. Working those long days in the shop. Dumping Tippy in those schools. And I'd say what I always said: "No . . . it was nothing *you* did."

But that day, like Nan, I think every defeat is *my* fault. That Nicky won't come back, or my father, or my mother from her crazy druggy realm. It's my fault that Miss DiFrancesco doesn't want to see me, that my life has no promise. It's even my fault that Eddie did what he did. If I weren't a sniveling wimp, my brother could stand being with me. And I wouldn't have been in the woods alone, and what happened would never have happened.

Sturgeon. Chocolates. Now glasses of tea. With cubes of sugar and a bobbing lemon half, which Nan says brings her joy, like the bright sun dancing on the dark Odessa sea. I look away from the little table of treats. Was this what awaited me too, dots of diversion in a sea of hopelessness?

"Bed . . . bath . . . breakfast. Now for your box," Nan says, "And we'll see a happy girl."

Nan says, "your box," but it's *her* box, with all of her important possessions.

"It will cheer up my darling," she says. "You'll take what you want. Except my citizenship papers and union card. Those I need, my little bandit." *Bandít*, she says, accent on the last syllable. Russian for bandit.

But the Red Cross shoe box, my grandma's treasure trove, which has entranced me for years, today looks like a heap of junk. The gold chains, I see, are brass; the lapiz lazuli earrings, blue plastic. The pile of near-win Irish Sweepstake tickets, which I've stroked for good luck, now seem receipts of defeat. And the tiny tower of ancient letters from the sister killed in the war, which I've read for years, touched and awed, seem only a fool's babble. *I have hope for the future,*

181

I have hope for the future, again and again, in letter after letter—a fool's refrain.

Sensing my brutal judgment, perhaps, Nan digs to the bottom, bringing up a crystal choker. "For you, *Lucychka*, now that you're growing up," she says, holding it to my neck.

I will myself not to shake my head, no. Not to say what's on my lips: I don't want your grown-up jewelry, your grown-up life. . . . I've had a childhood of adulthood. And one week after I got my first period, a boy put his penis in the place where I eat and speak. . . . *I have no hope.*

"*He* gave me that crystal . . . your grandpa. . . . What's mine is yours."

Did I cry, "No," or did Nan read my mind?

"A bright future awaits you. Not like me. . . . You'll find nice boys. You'll find good work. You'll have a baby when you're ready . . . not before. . . ."

But before she can finish her thought, I've run from the room.

Over the toilet, Nan holds my brow as I heave. A baby, a baby! I think with each retch. Last night I'd vomited him out. But now I'm afraid some of his stuff stayed in me, traveling from my mouth to my stomach, and seeping through to make a baby!

"I don't want to have a baby," I cry.

"Of course not," Nan says. "Later on . . . when it's time."

And then, though it breaks my heart, I know I have to go home. I'm certain that I feel something growing inside me. And if I stay here, Nan will know. And if she knows, she'll die.

19

In Trouble

"I guess people think I'm an answering service," my mother says as I walk in the door.

"Miss DiFrancesco?" I ask, my voice rising with hope. If she called, maybe I could have hope. Maybe I'd vomit up the baby. Or maybe I'd find a book on Miss DiFrancesco's shelf on catching pregnancy early and dissolving it . . . with a botanical mixture.

"Miss DiFrancesco," she mimics. "No not Miss DiFrancesco, whoever that may be. But your piece of shit father. Twice. What a piece of shit. I heard his librarian in the background. She hangs around when he talks to make sure he's true to himself. She probably steals books for him: *Be the Real Man You Can Be: Destroying Your Family as Self Realization*. What a pair of duds."

Thinking still of Miss DiFrancesco, I smile, then laugh.

"I'm funny," she says. "Your old mama's still funny."

"You are," I say. "When you want to be."

"Don't start on one of your prissy tedious sermons. Spare me, Luce. 'If you were fulfilled in life, you wouldn't resort to . . . additional support,'" she says. "I mean, you're not exactly reliable. So why wouldn't I turn to . . . additional support. You disappear for days at a time and sometimes you're rude. Sometimes you're quite rude. Sometimes I find you quite quite rude."

"You do, do you?"

"Don't talk back," she says. "Rule Number Two," she says, picking up from last night's lesson. "Rule Number Two: You don't talk back to your mother. It's provocative."

I know how it will proceed. I provoke her to seek out additional support. She never says drugs, not even pills, not even medication any more. And it's only me now. I'm the whole reason she's in trouble. I walk from the room, laden with my own new troubles.

"Rule Number Three in my household: You don't walk out of the room when a mother talks."

But I keep walking into the living room where the phone is ringing, while she screams, "Do you hear me? Do you hear me? Do you hear me?" Until she tires and then wanders off to her bedroom.

It's my father. He says that he heard we had gone, but he's glad to hear we're back.

"Just me," I say.

"Well, Nicky's a strong one. He'll be all right. It's you I'm worried about."

How worried? I think.

"I know you're okay. But still I'm a parent and a parent worries."

How do you know I'm okay? I think. I feel nausea rock me again.

"You're a strong child. You've gone through a lot. But you've come out whole."

I haven't come out yet, I think, from the hopeless pit you tossed me in. And I'm still a child. With a child in me, maybe. But it will do me no good to whine or cry, so I say nothing.

"How about dinner, with Moan and me, sometime next week?"

Still I say nothing. Next week. I've run away, slept outside, been raped in the mouth—or whatever you call what happened. I think I feel something inside me, growing, destroying. And he's examining his calendar for a convenient slot next week.

"What night is good for you?" he says.

I see a whole week stretch before me with nothing but my mother's screaming accusations and my new dread. How dare he ask me, What night, as if I'm a child star with a hectic schedule! "Only

Monday, Tuesday, Wednesday, Thursday, Friday, Saturday, or Sunday," I say. "Except for those days, I'm real tied up."

"Ouch," he says. "You're angry. You sound angry."

Mona is teaching my father about feelings.

I say nothing, because if I speak more, I will start screaming. And these days my father doesn't like screaming.

"Talk," he says, and I can hear her in the background coaching him. Telling him to let me talk it out? Moan saying, Let her moan?

"We slept in a tunnel. How could you let that happen? And yesterday. . . ." But I can't say it.

He's hardly listening anyway. "I take some responsibility," he says. "But life is complex. You're my child and I love you, but what do you want from me?"

"Come home," I scream.

"You know I can't." Then he says, "We each have one life to live."

"Not me," I say, meaning, I don't have one, just your life, and Mom's life. The spillover from your lives. And Eddie's spill, growing inside me? Was that true? Could I really be "in trouble"?

I hear my mother in her room laughing over a story in her tabloid—a ninety-year-old lady has mated with Russian wolfhound and given birth to triplets. "Imagine, Luce," she calls.

"Of course, you do," he says. "You have your life. And it will be very special. I believe that with all my heart."

He likes the phrase. So he says it again. "With all my heart."

She's cackling now, rustling her papers for me to come and read beside her and cackle too.

"Come home, Daddy," I cry. He's an asshole now, a selfish pompous fool. But still, he's more or less sane. She's more or less nuts, and I'm all alone with her. If there is a baby inside, how will I take care of both of them? "Come home, Daddy, please," I cry again.

"I wish I could."

You can, you asshole, I want to shout. You fucking asshole. How the fuck am I going to manage unless you come home? I think. You can come back and scream and beat us all up again. For one long dark moment, it doesn't seem so bad. Our life back then—at least

185

we were all together, I think. "Daddy, please, just come back," I beg.

"That life is over, Missy," he says. "I regret my mistakes."

"Daddy," I say. "What am I supposed to do?" With my mother. With my baby.

"Do the best you can," he says, "And think about dinner. Get back to me about when is good for you." And then he's off, my father who sounds like a distant uncle.

"He's a putz, right?" my mother says, padding into the kitchen. "Remember when he was a nut? I think I actually liked him better nuts. More substantial. And far more original," she laughs, freshening her pill beaker with tap water. "Even if he did ruin our lives."

I say nothing.

"Hey, you're supposed to say: They're not ruined. It's just a bad period. Look into yourself. Be *bla bla*, not *bla bla*. You're supposed to say whatever a bullshitter says, my adorable bullshitter. And my only hope in a miserable life."

Her eyes are begging me to say, We'll be okay. But I can't say it. "Ma," I say, taking her hand.

"Have it your way, Lucy," she says, pulling her hand away. "Be cold. I'm tired. Very very tired."

I'm very tired too, but too worried to sleep. When she leaves the room, I peek in the old Bob's malted glass she's left on the kitchen table. It's a "down" glass not an "up" glass, I can tell from the gray color. I lift it for a slug—to put me out. Then another slug—to kill the baby.

I woke to my mother's face in my face, shouting,. "Luce, there's a woman on the phone for you. It's the third time she's called. I tried to get you up. But you were dead."

"Miss DiFrancesco?" I asked.

"Miss DiFrancesco, Miss DiFrancesco—is that all you can ever say? All I know is whoever it is thinks she's a lot better than me but is using a sweet phony voice to protect me from that brutal truth."

"Be quiet," I said.

"Rule Number Four: You don't talk fresh to your mother. You hide your vicious judgments about your mother behind a sweet daughter's sweet face."

"Fine," I said, padding to the phone in the living room.

She sounded like an angel. I could hardly hear her words. This afternoon, see you this afternoon. After school. After school.

Sitting down on the couch next to me, my mother said, "I feel a little better today. What do you say we take the day off. Play hooky. Do our nails. Set our hair. "

I shook my head, which hurt from the drugs the night before.

"I have to go to school," I said. "Then work at the museum."

"Aren't we the model citizen. I just thought you'd like a little fun. But I see we're getting very serious. And boring. Sorry for asking, Miss Dag Hammarskjold."

That afternoon, as I left school for the Gardens, terror seized me again. I tried to review what I knew about how babies happened. But all I could put together was a chaotic mound of all the dirty talk from all the years of dirty shouts in my house and on the street. "Prick," and "scumbag," and "tit" and "fuck." What had really happened? What happened with "dick" and "cum" and "mouth"? I thought. Could *that* do it? Walking down 204th in the chilly October air, I felt as scared as I had that October years before when I was sure my father was hiding at Mr. VanDam's. Why not? I thought as I had back then. Oh, baby, he'd cried. To make a baby. He did it in my mouth so I wouldn't know what he was up to!

Was I mad? Who could tell me the truth about what had happened in the woods? If I called my brother, he'd want to kill Eddie. So would my father. So would my mother. I saw them marching into the park—for a brief family reunion—stringing Eddie up on the weeping willow at the end of the second lake.

The nausea gripped me again. Was I pregnant or not? I had to know. In a few minutes I was to appear before Miss DiFrancesco to start my new life. But could I have a new life, or was there a life inside me, claiming mine? What was going on? And again, I felt back in time, when we thought our mother had taken poison. And a simple phone call had led me to the truth.

Bob's had a phone booth in the back and, waving hello to Bob, I rushed to it.

"Uncle Mort?" I said when he picked up. "This is Lucy. . . . Can I ask you a medical question?"

"Tippy?" he cried. "Not Tippy?" And for the moment I was touched that he still cared about my old mother, whom he hardly called anymore.

"No. Not anyone you know, Uncle Mort. . . . It's a girl I know . . . and she thinks she may be in trouble. . . . Some boy who's friends with her sister did it to her . . . in her mouth . . . even though she told him to get away. She says she thinks a few drops may have gone down to her stomach and traveled, you know. She's nauseous in the morning . . . and other times, so she's concerned. . . ."

Uncle Mort started laughing. "I'd be *nauseous* too. . . . But you can tell your friend that babies aren't made in mouths and stomachs. You can tell your friend that she's okay. Will you tell that to her from your Uncle Mort, honey? And tell your friend to tell that awful boy that your Uncle Mort will kill him if he ever does that to your friend or any other girl again. . . . And will you tell her mother that I love her and I'll be down soon to dance?"

Dance. I hung up the phone and, waving to Bob again, I ran to the street, skipping and twirling, dancing my way across the trestle and down the sweep of stone steps into the park. I didn't care that he'd seen through my story. He'd told me what I needed to go on. If I passed Eddie, I'd tell him I may not have a father or brother in my life, but I had an uncle, and he'd kill him if he ever touched me again, and I had my whole life before me! But the park was empty, and I galloped past the lakes, into the Gardens, down the wide walk, and up the marble steps.

20

An Experiment

Miss DiFrancesco was at her desk when I arrived, but she still had a horrible cold and her voice was different—thick and nasal—and it was hard for me to make out her old kindness.

"Here I am," I said, unabashed in my joy.

"*Dere* you are," she said. She sounded like a gangster, a lowlife. A little like my mother.

"I was in the country for a few days," I said, grasping at a subject to her liking. The country, nature, plants. "Nice vegetation around the lake." I wanted to perk her up, get her back to her old sweet-sounding self.

"*Dat's* great," she said. And then she smiled her beautiful smile, which brought her back to me. That indulgent, toothy smile which broke out of her austere face. "I was in bed. *Gold* virus. I'm afraid I'll get you sick. I know I said you should *gome* in *doday*. But maybe you should go home and *gome* back *domorrow*."

I must have looked alarmed, for she said quickly, "Oh, who *gares* about a little *gold*?"

I nodded.

"It's not so *derrible*. Even if you *gatch* my *gold*."

I nodded, beaming, thinking: I'd love to catch your cold, catch your every germ. I closed my eyes with joy, hearing the sweetness come through her foghorn of a voice.

"*Come* here," she said, "And shake my hand. You're my official assistant."

I raced across the room and took her hand. She smelled like Vicks and unwashed hair from days in bed. And I leaned in close to breathe in and catch anything of her I could.

File and file and file. That's all I wanted to do, as if every insertion in every folder might redress the mounds of clutter at home, the years of chaos and confusion my parents had strewn across my life. And for a few weeks, Miss DiFrancesco let me do what I wanted, alphabetizing, fine-tuning file systems, so there was a place for every letter, every word, so her office was in total order.

Then one afternoon she tapped my shoulder as I was bent over the files and said, "Come, Lucy. Let's start with the plants."

I nodded, yes, but I didn't feel ready. Still, of course, I followed my angel upstairs to the lab, a little room with wide windows and no-nonsense gray slate counters.

I was nervous, in this strange room, and as she showed me around, I knocked a vial over on the counter.

Miss DiFrancesco got some paper towels.

"Don't worry about the benches," she said, pointing to the counters, "They're indestructible. They can take anything."

"Benches?" I said. "Do you sit on them?"

Miss DiFrancesco laughed and then explained that the lab counters were called benches. And I laughed too.

But then I smelled the soil, which reminded me of our stealing for our mother's repotting, and I felt sodden with hopelessness and suddenly knew that all I would do for the rest of my life was knock things over. And feeling very sad and tired, I wanted to climb up on the counter, which maybe really was a little bit of a bench too and not just called that, and lie down and go to sleep like a park bum. What was I but a park bum? A junior bum, blowing the biggest handout I'd ever gotten.

But she pulled me from my misery, taking my hand and leading me over to a long line of sparkling glass boxes. "These are your plants. This is your little garden. They're in your hands," she said, smiling down at me with what looked like trust.

Was I trustable? Suddenly I worried that I wasn't and that her faith in me was a big mistake. I wanted to take care of easy things only—mail and folders and stamps. I was tired from the nights with my mother, the years with both my parents. The cooking and cleaning and hauling and worrying and wishing. These days even Rosie the dog seemed an immense burden. And when I'd walk her in the early morning and again late at night in the park, I'd rush her, saying, "Jeez, Rosie. I got a life to live too, you know. Get on with it." And then when her dark eyes pleaded up at me for a little more time out in the grass, I'd hate myself. My very own garden—who was I kidding?

"Come on, Lucy," Miss DiFrancesco said.

I peeked in the box. It was filled with tiny cabbages.

"Brussel sprouts," I squealed. They were my favorite vegetable. And then I felt scared again. Would I eat them up instead of caring for them? Feed myself instead of them?

"Not quite," she laughed. "Brussel sprouts grow off a common stem. And, of course, stay small. These are just fairly small cabbages. They're going to grow much larger. We're studying them to get more understanding of what some hormones have to offer in terms of cell nutrition."

I nodded. I was studying biology in school and knew a little about plant nutrition and photosynthesis and, of course, knew a fair amount about human nutrition from trying to feed my mother over the years.

"You'll be giving one box the regular diet. And one a hormone-rich diet. We'll be measuring growth and other markers."

"Like color?" I said.

She nodded. "Yes, because the darker the green, the greater the nutritional absorption."

I nodded. Encouraged and interested, I tried to think of what I thought made a good vegetable, besides color.

"And crispness?" I said.

She nodded. "And do you know why?"

"Because good nutrition would contribute to strong cell walls?"

"Exactly. And we don't really know what the hormones do. But it looks to be promising in enhancing absorption of nutrients. I'll go over the procedures with you tomorrow. How much of what for which box. Scientists call their procedures protocols. Bench, hormones, protocol," she smiled. "That's enough for today."

I nodded. But suddenly, seeing her smiling face, I wanted to go on. The little cabbage heads looked friendly too. They seemed to be looking up at me, as if to say, Hi, you're going to feed us, right?

"Right," I said aloud, convinced suddenly that I could do whatever Miss DiFrancesco needed me to do.

"Tired?" she said.

And I nodded, though I wasn't, but afraid to tell her I'd been talking to the cabbages.

Soon I began racing through the office work, to get to my cabbages. Miss DiFrancesco didn't mind at all. "I think you can file in your sleep," she said, which was close to the truth. And after a few more weeks, I switched my routine around, going to the plants first when I was full of energy and coming down to the office when I was tired.

The hormone-fed cabbages were bigger. They were greener. They were crisper. The cabbages with the regular nutrients were healthy looking, but not quite as dark in color and not as firm against my micrometer. But still they all looked robust. Smaller than average cabbages because of their breed, but robust for what they were.

At the end of each week, Miss DiFrancesco and I went over my lab notes. One Friday, Miss DiFrancesco said she wanted us to do a new experiment. A new hormone instead of the one we'd been using. And after that a mixture of the two, perhaps. What did I think?

I said. "How about looking at cabbages that don't get even the normal diet?"

What was I thinking of? My mother? Nicky and me—what our

childhood was like—missing so many of the things other kids got. Not food so much but other things. And not just us. I found myself thinking of the Snuff Mill kids—even Eddie. Fighting their pain with nicotine and Thunderbird. Turning into monsters.

"You mean just water?"

I nodded, not knowing what I meant. "Yeah," I said. "Just water. And light."

"And air," she laughed. "We can't suffocate them as we starve them."

"I don't mean starve. I just mean . . . less, I guess."

I was afraid she'd turn her beautiful eyes on me, understanding what I was hardly understanding yet, and I'd start crying. But she spared me, assuming her girl scout cheerful voice. "Let's try it," she said, and we began to plan it out.

In a few weeks, my special cabbages had begun sprouting along with the others we'd just planted. Would they be okay? I had to control the urge to give them extra water, extra sun, to ensure their future.

In a few weeks they were tiny cabbages, little knobs bursting out of the soil. Maybe a little smaller than the others—I couldn't tell.

A week later they were all above soil. Smaller. Paler. A little less firm. But they seemed fine.

One day, watering, studying them all, I noticed that some of them didn't look like cabbages any more. They had turned from green to white and their leaves had curled like petals.

My heart pounding, I raced down the stairs. "The cabbages," I said, bursting in on her.

"Yes?" she said.

"They've turned into flowers!" I said.

Miss DiFrancesco followed me upstairs. There was no question, as I looked again, that about a third of my special cabbages looked like roses.

"Vegetable roses?" I said. "What's going on?"

"They're lovely," Miss DiFrancesco said, holding my shoulder.

"Hey, is this a big discovery? A new breed?" I said.

She didn't say anything.

I put my hand in the box, to touch the biggest of my cabbages. Its petals, or leaves, or whatever it was that was gathering around its center, started falling.

"They're very fragile," she said. "They're very beautiful. But very fragile. We're going to have to feed them more."

"I don't want to," I said. "They're so beautiful. The others, they're so smug. So sturdy and smug. I like the flowers. . . . I like the flowers."

"So do I," she said. "But they need a little more than what they're getting."

I said nothing. I could feel her eyes on me.

"I'd like to meet your mother," she said.

Still I said nothing.

"I'm not sure you can go on this way. . . . In your box." She pointed to the cabbages, the glass boxes. "I think we may have to do something. . . . Make some adjustments."

"I love my mother." I said.

"I know," she said.

"She'll die without me," I said. "I'm all she has. I cook and clean. She has problems."

She nodded.

"She'll die without me," I said again. And I stared down at the cabbages in the rows of boxes, pale and dark, weak and strong, flower and vegetable, feeling her watching me. "She has a condition," I said, remembering her phrase from the old days.

"Maybe I can come with you after we finish up here."

Could she? What phase was my mother in? She'd just finished a binge, so she might be sleeping, or shaky from it all. Probably she wouldn't be ranting. Most likely she'd be sad. She might be sweet, even amusing, if she wasn't all jittery or nervously refueling for a follow-up binge.

But the house was a mess. That I was sure of. She'd been into the closets. Just that morning I'd tripped three times getting out of the

apartment. On shopping bags of fabric, on piles of linen she was going to dye with Ritt for an "ethnic" feel, on an old typewriter and
some typing books.

"Not today," I said.

"Let me come home with you and help you, Lucy."

"No," I shouted. "I'm not ready."

I meant I had to clean, of course, straighten up and clean.
Straighten her up too, clean her. Make sure she was presentable.

"I once told you to tell me if home was not okay anymore.
You've never come to me for that. But I have a feeling it's not all
right. And I want to see. I really want to help you."

I stood there saying nothing, feeling like a deer stunned into im-
mobility as her eyes trained on me.

"It's going to be all right. You're going to be all right.
Everything's going to be all right."

I just stood there, saying nothing, looking down, waiting for the
sound of her footsteps as she left the room.

Miss DiFrancesco pointed out the New York Central tracks she
traveled every day downtown. "An indulgence," she said, "but there
are no crowds and I can read."

I showed her Spider Hill, the baseball field. We chit-chatted, but
my heart was fluttering as I saw my apartment building come into
view as we climbed to the top of the hill. Run, I thought. Into the
park or the police station across the street. Report Eddie. Report a
lost dog. Anything but take her home.

Miss DiFrancesco, sensing my thoughts perhaps, took my arm,
and I was stuck. It was winter but she identified the trees in the strip
of park in front of my house, praising the abundance of magnolia
and dogwood as if I and not the Parks Department were responsible,
trying to cheer me on, I guess, as we crossed the Parkway.

Run, I thought again, as we reached the red brick building. But
she just held my arm tighter.

"Nice azaleas," she said, studying the courtyard's concrete pots.

You don't have to, I wanted to say, as she tried to give me points for our landlord's plantings, meager even in season, dried up ugly stumps now that it was winter.

"Attractive pots," she said.

Then we were inside the building.

"Nice sconces," she said, pointing to the flickering wall lights, once brass—now painted brown by an overzealous super.

I wanted to say, You don't have to say anything. You don't have to be here. Go away.

But knowing there was no escaping her, I just raced up the two flights, hearing her behind me. And then we were there.

The living room was filled with boxes of chocolate and perfumed soaps, and my heart sank. I heard her in the bedroom, clanging things. "Luce?" she called, "Is that you?"

"Yes," I said. "And someone else. Someone's with me."

"You're kidding," she said.

The piles from the night before were still out, of course. But there were new additions. Mounds of *Dance Magazine*—some issues untouched, some ripped up into articles and piled according to subject, it seemed. Mounds of dance costumes had been dragged from a closet and piled according to what principle of organization, I couldn't tell. Color, it seemed at first, for there was a blue heap and a black heap and a red heap. But then there were just mixed heaps, like deposits in a dump, which I studied, awkward, pained, wanting to disappear, as Miss DiFrancesco just stood there smiling.

She came out in a Russian gypsy costume, extending her hand.

"I'm Tippy Lehman," she said. "You've caught me in the middle of . . . a show. Lucy probably told you . . . I'm a dancer. I teach children dance and choreograph for local theatrical companies."

Three lessons in the last year, I thought. And a no-show at the last amateur musical production at the Gun Hill Y.

"I'm just getting ready for a production."

I'll say, I thought, thinking of the night of sorting that lay ahead of us when Miss DiFrancesco left, the night of sorting accompanied by loud condemnation for springing a stranger on her.

Miss DiFrancesco extended her hand. "I'm Teresa DiFrancesco. Lucy helps me out at the Botanical Gardens in the afternoon."

"Great girl," my mother shouted, smiling a big phony smile at me, her eyes glaring.

Miss DiFrancesco nodded. "I was just wondering, though, if there's something we could do to help her a little."

"How so?" my mother said, adjusting the floral kerchief on her head.

"I mean . . . I know things are hard for you here."

"Not really," my mother said. "We do fine here. Things are a little disorganized here, pre-production, you know. But we do fine."

My mother kept talking, about dance and movement, about the strains of production. About the state of arts generally in the city, country, and world.

"It boils down to the role of the artist in society. Where do you put us?"

In the garbage, I thought. I wanted to grab her and bury her head first in one of her junk mounds. Shut her up. But I said nothing. Miss DiFrancesco said nothing. She just watched as my mother spoke and strutted back and forth and smoked.

"I don't know about Lucy," my mother said at one point.

"What do you mean?"

"I wonder if she's artistic. Like me. She's very organized, you know. That doesn't usually go with artistic."

Miss DiFrancesco said, "She's fourteen years old. She's only fourteen years old. . . . God knows what she'll be, who she'll be. If she ever gets a chance." Her face was red—I'd never seen her face get red before. Red and blotchy and angry.

"*Pardonez moi*," my mother said.

"She's very young," Miss DiFrancesco said again. "Very young."

"I know how young she is," my mother shouted. "No one has to tell me how old or young my own kid is. Or look at me with little mean judgmental eyes. I can see what you think of me. But you can't see what I've been through. You go through what I've been through, and then come back and we'll talk. You can't even imagine what I've been through. . . . You don't have the imagination."

I wanted to walk out of the room, escape the rant that would, no doubt, be starting up again. About imagination. People with imagination, like her. Versus unimaginative duds like Miss DiFrancesco and her sidekick, me.

But my mother was running out of steam. And she just sat down on the floor and started sniffling. "He was terrible . . . the children's father. It was terrible. But you don't care about that."

Miss DiFrancesco's face was pink now, moving from anger back toward her usual calm. "I don't know anything about that. And it's not that I don't care, but there's Lucy to think about. Whatever happened was probably a long time ago, and there's *now* to consider."

"'There's now to consider,'" my mother mimicked. But then lost energy for this and said, "It seems like he left just this morning," breaking into sobs. "And I still feel very sad."

"Lucy," my mother cried, opening her arms for me to run to her, cry with her.

But I wouldn't. I felt bad abandoning her in public, but I couldn't bear the thought of her arms around me. Being stuck in her embrace.

"Lucy, tell her how hard it was."

"It was hard, Mom," I said. "But it's over."

"That's easy for you to say," she sing-sang. "Miss Have-Your-Whole-Life-Before-You."

"Mom, stop."

"What?" she whined. "Stop what, Miss Bossy-Bossy?"

"Stop talking like a baby."

"I feel like a baby, Lucy. A big baby. Tell Miss What's-her-name I wasn't always like this. Tell her I used to be really nice. And quite responsible. But still lots of fun. Which isn't always an easy balance to strike, fun and responsibility. You owe it to me to tell her that."

I nodded.

Miss DiFrancesco nodded.

My mother sat on the floor wiping her tears with the palm of her hands like Shirley Temple.

"We'll talk more," Miss DiFrancesco said, standing to leave.

My mother shrugged. Whatever.

"See you tomorrow, Lucy," Miss DiFrancesco said, at the door. "Goodbye, Mrs. Lehman," she called. "I came here as a friend."

"Sure," my mother said sarcastically. Then because she wanted to be remembered well, I guess, or because her drugs were taking off, or both, she screamed, "Sure thing. No hard feelings. Goodbye, dear."

I took my time walking back to the living room. I didn't want to hear her screams about my bringing Miss DiFrancesco home. But the uppers had obviously kicked in now and she was laughing. "Poor you. Such a humorless little goody-goody. God—you have to face that every day?"

I said nothing, just stared at the piles, the costumes all around.

She said, "I mean, she's not our type. Talk about righteous and humorless. I don't see you two together one bit. I'd flip out if I had to see that pale face daily. Honestly."

She was scratching her head to show me she wasn't just saying this but was really thinking hard, coming to a really reasoned judgment. And her gypsy red floral scarf began slipping down over her eyes, like a blindfold. Kill her now, shoot her now, I thought, feeling all the humiliation of the last hour shoot through my arms in vicious energy.

To get me to laugh, my mother stood up and started to do a mock flamenco dance. To get me to laugh and show her that I liked her far more than I liked Miss DiFrancesco the graceless, humorless dud.

I watched her stamp her feet and twist her hands around and around. But I couldn't laugh. She looked *off*, like a very pretty girl with fairly serious cerebral palsy.

"You're becoming a real creep. You know that?" she said, standing suddenly still. "You'll end up as big a creep as Miss What's-her-name."

"Why'd you have to put on the costume?" I said. "You look crazy."

"I'm sure she thought nothing of it. I explained how we were in production."

"Who's *we*? What production?"

"She got the idea. I'm an artist. Dancer, choreographer, and what–not."

"Whatever," I said.

"The Gun Hill Players is just dying for my assistance. All I have to do is pick up the phone and they'll scream with joy. She got the idea that things were hectic here because of my creativity. . . . I am creative, you know," she screamed. "Extremely."

Now she was lying down on the blue pile. I was exhausted and wanted to lie down too, but I settled for sitting beside her.

We had to talk. It really couldn't go on. Miss DiFrancesco's eyes on our bizarre lives had told me that.

"Ma. This can't go on."

"Don't 'Ma' me," she said. "You're not my friend. You brought that stiff in here. And all she wants is to look down on me and take you away."

She began to cry, a big baby bawl.

"She doesn't want to take me away."

Did she? Would she put me with the sisters? Would I leave my mother for the sisters? How long could I hold out here if things didn't change?

"Then what was she doing here?" she shouted.

"She just wants to make things better," I said.

"They can't be," she said. "Can't the dummy see that?"

"Why can't they be?"

She shrugged.

"Let's make them better," I said. "We can do it. I don't want to leave you."

"There you said it," And she began laughing a nasty rapid laugh, like machine gun fire. "*Et tu*, Lucy."

"That's not fair, Ma," I began to cry. "I try and try. It does no good. *You* have to try too."

"Yeah, yeah, yeah," she said. "And more yeah. All I know is that wasn't very nice what you said about me not being a dancer any more."

"I didn't say anything."

"You didn't have to. I can tell your opinions from those contemptuous little nostrils of yours. You flare them out like, One more sniff of that witch mother and I'll die. You got to wake up early in the morning if you want me not to know what you're thinking in that stupid head of yours. Especially if it concerns me."

Die, I thought. Let the kerchief slip down again, past the eyes to the neck and let it strangle you. I looked at her to study her eyes, to see if my thoughts were registering.

But the kerchief had slipped over her eyes again and not seeing must have given her the idea of sleep. For she buried her face in the mound of blue, rolled over, and was out.

21

In My Arms

It was hopeless. Miss DiFrancesco's visit hadn't helped make things better, but only made me see that everything here was hopeless.

On the table behind the couch were all my mother's cups and beakers in a disorderly row. I lifted the big malted glass—a binge's supply of seconal. A gulp and I'd be out. And a bunch of gulps?

For a few minutes I stood there studying the glass in my hands, her paw marks on the filmy residue. I could never just walk away. Maybe the only solution was for me to drink the whole glass to float away, and die. I lifted the glass to my lips. I studied the world I'd leave behind. Her on the floor. Junk all around.

Through the small window panes, I studied the night sky, the bare branches against the purple dark. How beautiful the trees looked, as if they were dancing, naked and daring, in the clear freezing air. Did I really want to leave all this: the trees, the park, the beautiful gardens, the cabbages, and Miss DiFrancesco, who had wanted to make things better even though she couldn't? I opened the window to get a better look at the big world I might be leaving forever.

For the longest time I just stayed there, stretching my arms out, feeling the cold air blowing in my hair and down my neck, watching the trees in their silhouette against the sky. Come, Lucy, they seemed to call. And I thought of the cabbages, and how I'd thought they'd talked to me too. And how I'd talked back.

"But where?" I said to the trees, meaning to life or death.

I turned to see her again, my life here with her. Every inch of the floor was covered with mounds my mother had dumped—my mother the central dump in the middle of the room. Then the wind blew wildly again and my hair flew all around, making me feel like a twirling ballerina. Suddenly everything seemed very simple: I didn't want to die, but just to be able to move. All I wanted was a space cleared for me. Not very original, not very interesting, not very artistic—I heard my mother's judgment.

"Shut up," I said aloud. "All this is going."

And then I lunged and leapt and kicked, clearing all the clutter out of my way. I felt like an explorer cutting through the jungle.

"Maybe I'll be an explorer," I said, remembering that Miss DiFrancesco had said that I could be something.

Then, cleaning up some dying plants she'd tossed in a corner, I thought of the cabbages. "Or maybe I'll be a scientist," I called.

I filled bag after bag with garbage. "Or maybe a sanitation worker," I said, feeling my back muscles strain with pleasure.

For hours I cleaned, till I'd created some empty space in most of the rooms—stuffing garbage bag after garbage bag—and till I was too tired to go on. The mound where she lay sprawled, dopey and disheveled, seemed too much to attack, and she too heavy, in my tired condition, to lift and carry to bed. So I didn't move her that night, but just let her sleep.

"Sleep well, Ma," I called. "Tomorrow will be better. I can feel it. I just knew we couldn't go on like this. And I started making things better."

In the middle of the night, I thought I heard her calling my name, but told myself it was just a dream. Towards dawn I thought I heard her again. I told myself she was okay. I hoped she wouldn't be angry in the morning because I hadn't gotten up.

In the morning she was smiling, a bright gypsy smile, lying still on the blue heap, but she didn't look friendly, her smile more like a grimace.

I said, "Don't be angry at me for Miss DiFrancesco. Or for not coming to you in the night. I was so tired. I cleaned so much. Don't be angry at me for throwing things out. It really got to be too much. But now things are going to be better. I can tell."

"Mom," I called, for her face looked frozen and crazy now, like she had just finished a performance and was waiting anxiously for applause. "Talk to me, Mom," I said, wondering if something was wrong. "Talk to me, Mom," I shouted, for I was beginning to feel afraid.

And then because she wouldn't talk and her color was paler, her smile wider than usual, I lifted the scarf off her eyes to get a better look. Her eyes were locked into a stare. I tried to shout, but nothing came out of my mouth. And I bent down and lifted her in my arms.

She felt light, and carefully, pulling her into me like a treasure, I carried her to bed.

I stroked her hair against the pillow. I studied the smile that wasn't a smile anymore, her face that wasn't her face anymore but a crazy mask. "Mommy," I cried. "Mommy. Don't leave me. I didn't mean it, I didn't mean it. I didn't mean for you to die. I was just so . . . upset."

I said, "I'm sorry I didn't put you in bed last night. I'm sorry I let you lie on the floor. I'm sorry for not answering you when you called in the night. For all the ways I let you down. I'm sorry, Mommy. It's all my fault. But now won't you please come back?"

"Come back!" I screamed. "Come back!"

I don't know how long I sat with her, shouting at her, stroking her, shaking her. I only know that after a while, I began not to feel there any more. The light in the room seemed to change, brighten in some spots, darken in others, like the light in a movie. I felt like I was in a movie. Suddenly I put my finger on her eyes and closed them, like I'd seen loved ones do in movies. Then I studied her face and suddenly she looked peaceful, like Yul Brenner when he died in the movie of *The King and I*, I thought, and I laid my head on her chest like the King's children did.

Then I sat up tall and said, "Your mother is dead. But you can face it." And as if to convince myself, I slapped my face to get myself ready to face it. Like I'd seen them do in the movies to get someone to pull themselves together. Like my mother was going to do when I got my period, but didn't get to.

I said, "Ma. I'm sorry if I helped kill you. I don't know how I'll go on without you. But I'm going to try. I'm going to try." I said that a few times, standing, like a hero in the movies when the music starts swelling, pushing out my chest.

I lifted her again. I'd carry her down to the police station on the corner. I don't know where I got the idea, from a movie, or if I made it up. But it made so much sense to me. The cops would know what to do with the body. No one would have to come into the apartment and see the terrible mess, all the bags of garbage all over the place. Then I'd call Miss DiFrancesco. She'd know what to do. Then I began crying really hard, but then I told myself, "You must be courageous." And I slapped my face again hard. Then, like Rhett Butler, I lifted her again and started walking to the door to leave.

In the hallway she felt too heavy to manage. At the door, she slipped from my arms, and we both went down. I said, "It's okay, it's okay." And I stood up to lift her again. But before I could get a grab on her, the strangest thing happened.

She sat up.

"Hey, what's the big idea?" she said.

And then *I* passed out—from relief and dread.

22

The Ride

I wish I could say that the brush with death transformed her, that she came out of near-coma with one of those realizations people get when they know they're dying and sort out their lives in seconds, returning reformed. But when her whole life might have flashed before her eyes, my mother was too drugged to see it, and she came back, if anything, worse than before.

And she came back more reckless—as if seeing the worst, she'd decided it wasn't so bad. She could live or die. Did death look interesting to her from her brief glimpse that night? Like some shiny vast appliance she'd get to take apart again and again in an eternity of all-nighters? She certainly didn't seem afraid of it judging from her increased drug intake. But because *I* was so afraid—of finding her again in a heap on the floor—I trained myself to sleep lightly. And I slept in her bed most nights, so I could check on her and then roll back to sleep.

A few times, though, I found her in a deep deep sleep, beyond my calls and pokes. And hooking her on me, like a fireman, I got her down to the street, into a cruising cab, and over to the local emergency room to have her stomach pumped.

"You overreacted and embarrassed me in front of those doctors," she'd tell me the next day. "You just wanted to look like a hotshot, taking me to the hospital, Little Miss Officious. I had it under control, dope. I bet you hoped they'd lock me up for good, you cold, cold, cruel grocer-girl, you."

Grocer-girl. Her latest idea was that I resembled the most tedious members of my father's family—the grocers and knish makers—a truth that had somehow escaped her before but was now clear as day.

"That's why you're always trying to feed me, when it's love I need. Pure love. But your Lehman genes don't let you know about such things. Poor you. It's really not your fault. You never had a chance in the soul and compassion and imagination department."

It seems crazy now, but I'd plead with her when she railed against me. Beg her to be reasonable and take back her words. I wasn't a grocer-girl. I fed her because I loved her.

And more and more, she said I'd leave her, that my genes were disloyal and, poor me, it probably couldn't be helped.

"I'm loyal," I'd cry.

"Yeah, yeah," she'd say. "That's why you're going to leave like the rest of them."

"I'll never leave you," I'd say.

"Yeah, yeah."

"I promise," I'd say, feeling like I was choking.

"Big liar," she'd say.

How *would* I ever leave? When she was clean of drugs, I still loved her desperately. When she was high and awful, I couldn't imagine whom I could ever leave her with. And alone she wouldn't last a week. Nor would our neighbors. She'd burn down the house, or flood it, or shatter it with her crazy screams.

My father, predictably, wasn't any help. At first, when she almost died the first time, I thought, At least now he'll see how bad we need him. But he stayed his new cool self—avuncular at best, and full of that phony control he was working on so hard as he lived his new non-violent, reasonable life apart from us.

Sometimes out at a restaurant with him and the Moan, I'd practice on them the idea of a future life for me.

I'd wait till their conversation slowed and I'd say something like, "Let's talk about my college education."

And my father would say things like my future was up to me and he was sure I'd choose wisely. But sometimes—because he needed me to take care of my mother, I guess—he'd say maybe it would be best for me to go to college in the city. That is, if I decided to go to college. Only sometimes did he sound like his old self, saying things like—*He* hadn't gone to college. And he was smarter than most college graduates he talked to. Sometimes when he went on like this, I'd wish he'd get into one of his really crazy old rants. Maybe walk across the restaurant and beat up a college graduate or two, be my old father again. Come home. So I could go.

But he'd just stop, on a relatively dull note, and say, "Well, think about what I said."

Finally, it was my angel who saved me.

One day, shortly after she'd visited, Miss DiFrancesco said that maybe I should go away.

I said, "Are you thinking of your sisters, the sisters?"

"Absolutely not. My sisters are very limited people. I wouldn't wish them on too many people. Certainly not on you. Anyway, they both live in Detroit. I hardly ever see them. We're not close at all."

"Oh," I said, looking down, thinking how for years I had held onto the dream of living with the beautiful nuns in their peaceful convent, if worse came to worst, which, probably, it had. I'd put all my hopes in that dream, and now it was gone. I started to walk away.

"But there are fine boarding schools," she said. "You're a good student. You could probably get a scholarship with no trouble."

Boarding school. Scholarship. I saw my mother up on the wild horse she was named for. Then lying on the floor in a heap. All her hopes collapsed into nothing. I thought, I'll never get away. Sisters, school, it didn't matter. I was stuck taking care of her.

"Oh, thanks, but I can't," I said.

"Don't be so sure," Miss DiFrancesco said.

One day, just after my fifteenth birthday, Tanta Ida came to the museum. I was up in the lab, feeding the plants, and she popped her head in.

I felt an alarm go off inside me, but I quieted it with a quick tally of sensible reasons for her presence. She just wants you to pick up some *shmatas* on your way back home, I told myself. Or she wants to bring some of the *shul* ladies here for a tour. Or she was in the Gardens and she just dropped by to say hello.

But studying her face, her red, frightened eyes, I knew that none of these made any sense. It could be only one thing.

Then I started scheming again. Of course, it had to do with my mother. But maybe it was just a broken arm—once before she'd broken her arm crashing from the toilet, where she'd fallen asleep. Or maybe it was a small fire. She still smoked in bed and, though she had never started a full-fledged fire, her night table was tattooed with burns. I'd warned her.

"I warned her," I said aloud. "I'm going to really have to scare her," I said.

But then Tanta Ida started crying and calling my name—and I knew and I started to scream.

"When?" I said.

"This afternoon. In the bath. I saw the water coming out under the door. I took my key. It was like a lake. She looked very beautiful. Like a mermaid. Looking up at me through the water with those gorgeous eyes."

Miss DiFrancesco was in the next room, and she ran in.

"I'm so sorry, Lucy," she said.

I studied her face. Her eyes were tearing, but was she really sorry? Didn't she hate her?

"She *was* a dancer," I said. "She was a beautiful dancer. She was wonderful. She was a wonderful mother. You didn't know her then."

She nodded. "I'm so so sorry," she said again, pulling me close.

"She was really gorgeous," Ida said. "And had a very agreeable personality. But she became in time a very nervous person. I tried to give her attention, but she needed a lot."

Ida Klein, Teeny's mother, was in the apartment when Tanta Ida and I got there. She took my face in her hands and said, "You were a good daughter."

'Not good enough,' I thought, but I just said, "Thank you. You were a good neighbor."

They'd already taken my mother down to the morgue, and Ida Klein got busy trying to mop up the flood with our towels. I remembered how she'd taught me to mop and cook. How I'd hoped I could save my mother from a terrible fate with a cozy, clean house and soft, tasty foods. But she wouldn't let me.

The water was everywhere, swelling above the towels with new force, from the bathroom to the back hallway, from the back hallway into her bedroom, pushing everywhere like the crazy force of her will. Had *I* been more forceful—or more clever, more artistic, more imaginative, more compassionate, more selfless, more loving, more honest—would my mother have been different and with me now?

"What was I to do?" I said aloud, speaking to my mother, hurling myself on her littered bed. Before, when she'd almost died and I thought she had, I'd accepted it in my own childish way, making believe I was in a movie. But today it all was brutally real to me. The water. The mess all around. The futility. Of all my efforts before. All my efforts from now on.

She'd been writing, I saw. My looseleaf paper and collection of fountain pens were scattered all around. Had she left me a note? That she loved me and knew I'd tried my best? That she was just very very tired? Or was it just a mistake, another extravagant accident in her mad reckless life? Oops, sorry, Lucy. Try not to make a fuss.

I looked around the bed. Just piles of the usual "Lists" of the usual "Projects"—Rewiring Jobs. Repotting Plans. Office Skills for the Future. A "Document" Called "Desires Declaration" with her three favorite headings: Life, Liberty, and Pursuit Of Happiness. Under each her favorite phrase—"New leaf."

Tanta Ida gathered me in her arms.

"Did she leave a note?" I said.

211

"Just this, for what it's worth." Another looseleaf page, but this one all wet with the ink bled all over, making it unreadable. "It was floating near the sink."

"Probably just another list," I said, gesturing to the mound around me.

"Or maybe a note with her best wishes," she said. "Saying that you should live your own life. And be happy and go on. That it was too hard for her but you would do just fine."

"Really?" I said, for a second believing.

That night I slept at Nan's. But neither of us slept much. We just held each other tight, every few minutes breaking into a new round of sobs. In my arms, in the narrow bed, Nan seemed smaller than ever, like the hot tears had suddenly shrunk her. Finally towards dawn Nan fell off to sleep. "*Zeeskeit*," she called from her dream, to Tippy, I knew. "Chin up, *zeeskeit*," she called, lifting her sleeping hands and chin. Showing Tippy, in her dream, how to keep her head above water? "Mommy, Mommy," I called, muffling my cries in Nan's flannel gown.

Every couple of hours I'd try to call Nicky. There'd been no answer at Big Will's since the day before and, hearing the phone ring and ring each time I went into Faygie's kitchen to call him, I'd cry, Nicky, Nicky, then, Mommy, Mommy, again. Where are you? Sitting in the dark kitchen, I thought about how close we'd once been, the three of us, when she was still okay. Then about how close Nicky and I were when she was not. Then about how alone I was now, with everyone gone but poor old Nan.

In the morning I reached Nicky. He and Big Will had just driven back from an organizing conference in Albany.

I said, "She's dead."

He said, "She's been dead for a while."

Then it hit him. "God," he howled. "Oh God, oh Mommy. . . ."

He said he wouldn't come to the funeral, though, unless I needed him to. He really had her dead and buried and he wasn't sure he could go through it again. He'd come down and get Rosie from Ida Klein when things settled down.

Maybe he'd go to college in the fall. He'd been accepted at one across the river. Or maybe he'd work in auto and organize. Either way he'd be living with Will. He'd started writing a book—*Notes From a Rebel Son*. It was the story of Big Will's life in the struggle as interpreted by Nick. I could help, he said. "Come back to us, Lucy," he said.

I was aching so hard I thought I'd break. I was aching to be with Nick, but I knew I couldn't. He and Big Will would talk and talk and ignore me. Write their book and ignore me.

"Nicky," I cried. "Cocoa."

Where could I go? Would Miss DiFrancesco really find me a boarding school?

"Hey, I might be going to boarding school," I heard myself say, praying it would happen.

"Get yourself a good nickname like she did," he said.

"I already have one . . . Cocoa."

"Little Missy. . . ," he said.

Was I still a Little Missy? A little Miss Mousy? I really didn't know who I was any more. The night before, watching Nan treading water in her sleep, I'd wondered if it was only a matter of time before *I* went under too, destroying *my* life. Maybe it was all fated. But then I remembered what I often felt with Miss DiFrancesco, or sometimes alone in the greenhouse, or that night when I leaned out the window and talked to the trees That I had a life ahead of me. That it wasn't just scampering and quivering and dread ahead. That a whole non-Miss Mousy life lay before me.

"We'll visit . . . Cocoa," I said.

Nicky said, "I'll miss you. . . . Jesus, Missy, I'll miss you."

And then we hung up so we wouldn't start bawling again.

After breakfast, Nan said we had to go through the box. I didn't think I could bear even a glimpse of Aunt Rosie's letters, Jess's false tokens. The crystal necklace—I had to have it, she said. It couldn't sit

213

in an old lady's shoebox another day; it had to breathe near a young woman's heart! I can still feel Nan's fingers at the back of my neck as she fastened it to me, my muscles tensing against the long rope, the hopelessly knotted hands. "Oh, Look, Lucychka," I can still hear her cry, and see the crystals shimmering on my chest, beaming back the rays of sun streaming through the window. "Forever and ever," I cried. I'd wear my beads forever and ever. How glad I am now that Nan pressed them on me, and that I took them. Every day they remind me that those years weren't all drab and bad but, when you least expected, shining with promise.

To get through the funeral, I pretended I wasn't there in the chapel on Fordham Road with all our friends and family lunging at me, my father and Mona pushing in on me from either side, suddenly and showily protective like bodyguards when photographers are on the scene. I pretended my Grandma Bessie was not there crying in my face how my mother had destroyed her "beautiful son's" life. I pretended Grandpa Jess wasn't there, worn and white, like a piece of old wood whose every last speck of stain had been scraped away. When he said, "Sorry, I'm so sorry, so sorry," I pretended he wasn't talking to my mother smiling in her casket, but to the undertaker, who I pretended was an usher at the opera whose toes my grandpa had stepped on by mistake.

Across the street from the funeral parlor was Alexander's Department Store. I pretended I was over there, picking out new clothes for boarding school. I pretended Miss DiFrancesco had it all arranged. I pretended my mother had jumped from her coffin to walk across the street with me. I pretended we were riding the escalator, arm in arm. Then we're up in junior sportswear, and she's the way she used to be, pulling out skirts and sweaters for me to model, calling me "stunning," and "adorable," and "just terrific" in this or that. I pretended my father had stopped patting my back as if I had to burp and put his hand in his pocket giving me lots of money to buy new clothes for my new life.

Only at the cemetery, for an instant, seeing the gaping grave, did reality seize me. But then Ellie and Jerry, whom I hadn't seen for years, appeared, standing at my side, and I pretended we were at one of Bobo's weddings not my mother's funeral, and I started to sing and for a minute, before they lowered her down, we all sang together, like it was old times. Then missing Nicky so bad that I thought I would faint, I pretended it was Nicky who took my hand and gave me the shovel so I could toss dirt on her. And then that it was Nicky, not Teeny's brother Billy, who grabbed the belt of my car coat to lift me from the grave when I jumped in to kiss her one last time.

I'd made Nan stay home—she was too old and weak—and Tanta Ida and some women from the sisterhood would be looking after her. But as I turned to leave the grave, I surveyed the surprisingly large crowd gathered at the Queens cemetery and I pretended Nan was in the back of the crowd looking across at me, pointing to my crystal beads to give me hope. And then I spotted Miss DiFrancesco's angel face. And I walked through the crowd and took her hand, and led her back to the line of cars. I climbed inside her car and slammed the door shut. I cried for a few minutes, and then I straightened up and blew my nose.

Miss DiFrancesco said, "I have something to tell you. I know it's a funny time to tell you. But it just happened . . . and I can't hold it in!"

I studied her face for clues. She was smiling so it couldn't be that all my cabbages had died. Or that she no longer could have me help her. What could make her smile her bright smile on this dark awful day?

"You've been awarded a full scholarship to the Tom Paine School in Brattleboro, Vermont. . . ."

A school far away. My mother gone away. I felt dizzy trying to hold it all in my mind, and closed my eyes to stop the spinning.

"It was my first choice for you," Miss DiFrancesco said stroking my hair. "It's a very special place."

Special. I wasn't sure how much more special I could take in my life. All I wanted now was *simple*. Like the simple stuff on a rule chart in any kindergarten, I thought. No Shouting. No Pushing. No Biting. No Hitting.

"Special as in beautiful and peaceful," Miss DiFrancesco whispered.

And I said nothing, but leaned my head against her.

My father and Mona offered to drive me up to my new school, but I told them no. My father whispered he'd take me alone and we'd stop for some new shoes on the way but, my heart breaking, I shook my head.

Eddie, who'd been coming around to the museum full of shame and apologies, offered to take me too. Since that night in the park, he had given up drinking, and he and some of the other boys had built a car in the lot besides St. Xavier's. It was mostly old pieces, but it rode okay, he said. I shook Eddie's hand goodbye and thanked him, thinking how my life was something like the boys' hodge-podge car. Old pieces, but still able to get somewhere? God, how I hoped so!

Miss DiFrancesco said she really wanted to take me up and get me settled. But I told her no too. I was afraid if she came with me, when it was time to say goodbye I'd cling like a baby, jump back into the car, cry to be taken home. And I didn't have a home anymore.

On the Greyhound I imagined I was *her* on a bus to boarding school a lifetime ago. Then on a lawn in front of a big white school. Hey, where do you keep the horses? I ask the smiling strangers. And they show me to a yellow barn, where I climb on a big black horse and we gallop all day and into the night.

Then I closed my eyes and when my tears stopped, I tried to imagine *my* life. What lay ahead at the end of the ride.

About the Author

Nora Eisenberg is Professor of English at the City University of New York (La Guardia) and director of the University's Faculty Writing Program. She has written three books about the teaching of writing and has been published in *The Partisan Review, The Village Voice Literary Supplement, Tikkun, and Choice.* She lives in New York City with her family.